THE
GLORY
HOUND

A Garth Ryland Mystery

THE GLORY HOUND

JOHN R. RIGGS

DEMBNER BOOKS • New York

To Mitch, who taught me,
and
Marla, who fed me

Dembner Books
Published by Red Dembner Enterprises Corp.,
80 Eighth Avenue, New York, N.Y. 10011
Distributed by W. W. Norton & Company, Inc.,
500 Fifth Avenue, New York, N.Y. 10110

Library of Congress Cataloging-in-Publication Data

Riggs, John R., 1945–
The glory hound.

I. Title.
PS3568.I372G5   1987   813'.54   86-6246
ISBN 0-934878-78-1

Design by Antler & Baldwin, Inc.

1

Deputy Harold Clark broke the surface of Phillipee's Pond and started walking toward us. He wore a wet suit, mask, and flippers and carried something with both hands. He carried it stiffly, out away from his body as far as his arms would stretch, and walked gingerly, like a man with a cake in the oven.

Rupert Roberts and I stood on shore watching him. Droll and leathery and wise, Rupert was sheriff of Adams County, and the best law men I'd ever known. When it came to keeping the peace, he was without equal. He was also without malice and without prejudice. He hated all dogs, drunks, and volunteers equally.

In the six years I'd known him, we'd learned to read each other well—well enough to know when to speak and when to listen, and when to keep our distance and our thoughts to ourselves. This was one of those times for me to be seen and not heard. Rupert had asked me to come with him, but he really didn't want me along. He'd done it as a favor to Ruth, to get me out of the house and my mind on something else besides Diana, but already I could see he regretted it. On this particular day even his own company was too much for him.

1

I'm Garth Ryland, publisher and editor of the *Oakalla Reporter*, a small weekly newspaper in Oakalla, Wisconsin, and author of a growing syndicated column that I still don't have a title for. I came to Oakalla six years ago, following the death of my Grandmother Ryland, who left me her small farm, enough money to buy the *Reporter*, and an earthbound legacy that was both my blessing and my curse.

I was thirty-five then and in the process of reconstructing my life after a painful divorce. That day I stood by Phillipee's Pond, I was forty-one and in the process of adjusting my life to a painful separation. Some things never seem to change.

Deputy Harold Clark, Clarkie as we all called him, finally reached shore and showed us what he'd found. Rupert took one look at it and said, "Throw it back."

Clarkie looked to me for help. He didn't know if Rupert was kidding or not. Judging by the set in his jaw and the scowl on his face, Rupert wasn't kidding.

"Throw it back," Rupert repeated, then spit in the sand for emphasis. "That's the last thing I need right now."

"I'll take it," I said.

Clarkie looked at Rupert, saw him nod his head, and handed the skull to me. Then he turned and trudged back toward the water, like a schoolboy returning to his seat after a spanking. A couple minutes later he dived beneath the surface of the pond and continued the search.

He was looking for Frieda Whitlock, a high school senior who'd disappeared from Oakalla on her way home from school three days before, on Thursday afternoon. Commencement was the next night, Sunday. It was looking more and more like Frieda wasn't going to graduate with the rest of her class. Or get teary-eyed when they played "Halls of Ivy." Or get to flip her tassel at the end of the ceremony. Or get to open the presents her parents had bought her. It was looking more and more like Frieda Whitlock was dead.

I tucked the skull under my arm like a football player his helmet and stood there on the beach waiting for Clarkie to surface. "Tell me again what happened," I said to Rupert.

He spat at a cabbage moth that had come to the pond to drink, narrowly missing. It rose and lighted again a few feet away. "No one knows for sure what happened. Her boyfriend was supposed to pick her up at school. For some reason he didn't show up. She started walking home. She never made it."

"Where was she last seen?"

"Along Gas Line Road. At least I got a phone call to that effect."

"From whom?"

"She didn't say. She just said she saw Frieda walk by."

"What time?"

He spat again at the cabbage moth, missed again. "I forgot to ask." Or didn't want to tell me.

"Were Frieda's parents home?"

"No. Harvey was in the field planting beans, and her mother was at work."

"What time did her mother get home?"

"A little after five. When she got home, Frieda wasn't there."

I remembered that Frieda's mother, Dora Whitlock, worked as a secretary for the insurance company here in Oakalla. She was a pretty woman, pleasingly plump, with curly brown hair and large sad eyes—someone who would sing second alto in the church choir and never forget your birthday. Someone who would lavish gifts and favors on her only child to the point of spoiling her.

"What time does school let out?" I asked.

"Three-thirty."

"Time enough for Frieda to get home and leave again."

3

"I thought of that," he said. Then gave me a look that was meant to shut me up.

I studied him. This wasn't like Rupert. Though he usually gave grudgingly, he'd never shut me out before. "Is something eating at you?" I asked. "Something you're not telling me about Frieda? Is that why you're willing to turn me loose in another direction?"

"No comment" was his answer.

"Are you her long lost father?" I persisted.

"Leave it be, Garth. It's not important."

"Well, are you?"

"No."

"What then? What is Frieda Whitlock to you?"

He looked out across the pond. He didn't want to tell me, but he did. "I'm her godfather."

"I didn't know that."

"Not many in Oakalla do. Her dad and I put in a hitch in the army together. We got to know each other pretty well."

His hitch in the army included the landing at Normandy and the Battle of the Bulge. He didn't talk about it much to anyone. But once, over a bottle of good rye whiskey, he told me the whole story. I remembered his saying that in the Battle of the Bulge he was shooting mortars at nearly ninety degrees. And that having extra pairs of dry socks was the only thing that kept his feet from freezing.

"You saved Harvey's life once, didn't you?" I asked.

"Like he saved mine. In war you got a lot of chances to be a hero."

"Then Harvey's your age?"

"Close. I'm a few months older."

"He had Frieda kind of late in life, didn't he?"

"Late for him. Not for Dora. He's on his second go-around."

"That's right. I forgot. Is Frieda his first child?"

"First and only. He puts a lot of stock in her."

4

"Does she deserve it?"

He gave me a stony look. "I'll pretend I didn't hear that."

"Don't be so sensitive. I was just asking."

"Don't ask. It's not your case. It's mine." He reached over and tapped the skull to make his point. "That's your case—until further notice."

"Are you saying you don't want my help?"

"That's what I'm saying." The tone of his voice left no doubt.

"Fine with me." If he didn't want my help, I wouldn't force it on him. Help, like love, couldn't be forced on anyone. It usually just led to resentment.

"Any particular reason why you're checking here?" I asked.

"Just covering all the bases. Her mother said Frieda used to like to swim here when she was younger. I thought she might've given it one more go for old time's sake. Got a cramp and went under."

"If she did, we should have found her clothes," I said.

"I know that."

"Besides it never got above seventy on Thursday."

"I know that, too."

"So what were you hoping to find?"

He spat again. A little more arc and he would hit that moth. "Nothing. Except I've looked everywhere else around here. I thought I'd give it a try at least."

I rapped on the skull. "And you didn't come up empty."

He looked away across the surface of the pond. "Don't remind me."

"What do you want me to do with it?"

"Mount it on your wall. Set it on your mantel. Give it to Goodwill. I don't really care as long as you keep it out of my hair."

"You're serious, aren't you?"

"As I've ever been."

"Why?" I asked.

5

"What do you mean why? I've got a missing girl on my hands. I don't have time to find out who that skull belongs to. Even if I did, it'd probably take me until next year. Then I'd have to find out what happened to him. You'll know within a week. Or sooner. That's because, among other things, you don't have to go by the book. I do." He sounded envious, almost bitter.

"Is this by the book? You don't normally hand me a skull and tell me to run with it."

"I can deputize you if you like."

"You already did once, remember?"

"Then it's official."

I found a log in the sun, sat down, and waited for Clarkie to complete his search. Not much more than an acre, Phillipee's Pond was neither very large nor very deep, and with its gravel bed Clarkie should have a good view of the bottom. It wouldn't take him too long to go over it.

Denny Patton and I had first discovered Phillippee's Pond when we were ten and on one of our many exploring trips around Oakalla. What intrigued us most was the wake thrown by what we perceived as a monster bass, swimming back and forth just under the surface of the pond, the fish that would put our names in the record book. What also intrigued us was that Phillipee's Pond was forbidden territory, guarded by Myrtle Phillipee herself—God rest her thorny soul—who had been known to eat small boys for breakfast.

Without fail she'd come swooping down over the hill, her hoe gleaming in the sunlight, just as we'd make our first cast into the pond. Then we'd take off running, dragging lines, hooks, sinkers, and worms, while she chased us, yelling threats and damnation all the way to the edge of her property line.

We never did catch the bass, though I now suspected it was a carp. And she never did catch us. It was one of the games of childhood played by boys and cantankerous old

6

women. Win, lose, or draw, as was usually the case, the fun was in the chase.

I closed my eyes and let the sun have its way with me. It'd been dodging in and out of clouds all morning, but now seemed determined to stay out. I hoped it would. May, normally my favorite month, had been cool and wet and grey—not my idea of spring at all. I was counting on June to do better.

Clarkie emerged from the pond empty-handed. He looked lost standing there in his mask and flippers, like a refugee from Atlantis, who couldn't make up his mind whether to chance it out here in the open or sink back into the depths again. Rupert decided for him. He waved Clarkie to shore and at the same time started for his patrol car. Since he was my ride back to town, I followed him.

"Where do you go from here?" I asked when we were in the car.

"I don't know. Probably someplace I don't want to go."

"Which is?"

He shook his head. He wouldn't tell me.

"Just remember," I said. "I owe you. Don't be afraid to call in your debts."

"Not this time, Garth," he answered. "Not yet anyway."

"The offer's good anytime."

He started the engine and put the car in gear. "I'll remember that."

He let me off at Doc Airhart's and drove on. Doc Airhart lived in a two-story white house with a concrete porch and stone pillars across the street from the Methodist church.

Doc was eighty-one going on twenty, and though he'd retired six years ago, he hadn't slowed down any. He was a small intense man whose energy, like his smile, was infectious. He had thick white hair, a slight limp because one leg was shorter than the other, and about the merriest blue eyes I'd ever seen. I only knew one other whose eyes

7

could match his and hers were more grey than blue, more mischievous than merry.

I knocked on Doc's door, but he didn't answer. I went around back and found him weeding his roses. He looked content, like a man should at eighty-one, that there was nothing left to prove, and nothing more important than what he was doing right now. He looked up at me and smiled, then went back to weeding.

"What have you got there?" he asked.

"Part of somebody," I answered.

"Where did you find it?"

"Clarkie found it in Phillipee's Pond."

"What was Clarkie doing in Phillipee's Pond?"

"Looking for Frieda Whitlock. She's been missing since Thursday."

He rose slowly and brushed the dirt off his pants. "I heard."

"Where did you hear?"

"At the Marathon. You hear everything there." He took the skull from me and examined it. "I suppose you want to know all about it?"

I gave him a questioning look. Doc and I had sorted some old bones just a few months ago. It almost cost us our friendship. "If you're willing."

"I'm willing. How soon do you want to know?"

"Whenever you get around to it. I don't think there's any hurry."

He ran his fingers across the base of the skull, then held it up to the sunlight. "I thought there might be."

"Why's that?"

He pointed to show me. "See that crack there. It's not original equipment."

"You mean somebody might have put it there?"

"Somebody or something."

"Maybe he hit his head diving."

"Then he did a back flip off a diving board. Not likely in Phillipee's Pond."

"What are you telling me, Doc?"

8

"I'm not telling you anything. You're the one in the driver's seat. You can have your answer this afternoon, or a month from now, whenever you want."

"Make it this afternoon."

He looked resigned. "I thought so."

I walked to the Corner Bar and Grill, drank a Leinenkugels, and ate a roast beef sandwich and a piece of homemade rhubarb pie. The regular Saturday crowd was there, but not the regular Saturday noise. Most of the talk was quiet, reflective, and concerned about the missing Frieda Whitlock.

Frieda was bright and energetic, a cheerleader and an honor roll student. And this year's Homecoming Queen. She was a well-known and well-liked girl. That's what all the talk was about, why the collective face of the Corner Bar and Grill was hushed and drawn in disbelief. It was like looking up one night and discovering your favorite star had burned out.

"What do you think, Garth?" Sniffy Smith asked me.

Sniffy was a retired barber, who cut hair part-time on Fridays and loafed full-time at the Marathon Gas Station the rest of the week. He liked to talk sports and politics. So did I, in small doses, which I'd found was the way I liked Sniffy best.

"I don't know what to think, Sniffy," I said. "To be honest I haven't given it much thought."

"That doesn't sound like you. I thought you'd be hot on the trail by now."

"I've been busy getting the *Reporter* out," I said. "Besides, it's Sheriff Roberts' territory, not mine."

"Yeah, I saw him talking to Joe yesterday at the Marathon."

"Joe Turner?"

"Yeah. He was Frieda's boyfriend, if you didn't know."

I knew, but I didn't tell Sniffy. It made his day when he surprised me with something. "What was he talking to Joe about?"

"Where he went Thursday afternoon. At least that's my guess. Why he didn't pick up Frieda like he usually did."

"Where did he go?"

Sniffy leaned toward me confidentially and sniffed a couple times in my ear. The more excited he became about something, the more he sniffed. Once at the Marathon he hyperventilated and fell off his stool while reading a *Playboy*. After that we kept them out of his reach.

"He wouldn't say," Sniffy said.

"Why not?"

"You know Joe. He don't tell nobody his business. Must be the hillbilly in him."

"Do you have any idea where he went?"

"I saw him drive south. Then a few minutes later here he came back north again."

"What time was that?"

"Long about three-thirty, the time school lets out. I thought he was going to pick up Frieda."

"Did you see her in the car with him?"

He sniffed three loud sniffs, so loud he turned a couple heads. "Just what are you asking, Garth?"

"I just asked if you saw Frieda in the car with Joe."

He sniffed again, fanning my hair. "That's the same as accusing him of taking her!"

Several heads turned now, as the quiet deepened. I didn't like the direction we were heading. "I'm not accusing him of anything. I just wanted to know."

"No! To answer your question. I didn't see nobody in the car with him!" But something in Sniffy's face said he was lying. Either that or he wasn't telling me the whole truth. But I didn't press the issue. Too many people were listening. Besides, it was Rupert's case, not mine.

"Later, Sniffy. Sorry to spoil your day."

Sniffy hung his head. "It ain't my day that's been spoiled. Me and my big mouth."

10

2

Outside, I stood a moment before deciding where to go. It was too early to check back with Doc, and there was nothing to do at the *Reporter* that couldn't wait until Monday. I could always go fishing, but I wasn't in the mood.

I wished Diana were there. I missed her every day, but it was on days like this I missed her the most. Saturday had been our day, even before her husband Fran died. She saved it for me. I saved it for her. We never did much—at most a drive in the country, but being together with time and thoughts to spend on each other was all that really mattered.

My favorite Saturdays were those in winter when I'd sit at her breakfast table sipping coffee, the sun streaming in her bay window, while she painted a few feet away. I loved to watch her work. Her face joyous and childlike, dripping with concentration, it was then she was most fully alive, and there was no one more alive than she. At these times I didn't try to talk to her. I was content to just sit back and watch her, drink my coffee, and let the sun lap over me.

But when I needed to talk to her, she'd stop whatever she was doing and listen to me like no one else could. I

11

missed that. I missed her. It seemed pointless to hang on and impossible to let go. She felt the same way. That was the hell of it. We were two right people in the wrong time and place, one coming into port, the other putting out to sea. As a romantic, I wanted to believe that love would eventually conquer all. As a realist, I knew it probably wouldn't.

I stopped by home to pick up Jezebel, alias Jessie, Grandmother Ryland's brown Chevy sedan. Jessie was the one thing I wished Grandmother had taken with her, or at least had buried alongside her. Jessie ran at her own convenience, which wasn't very often, nor very well, and just enough to keep me from junking her. I'd tried on several occasions to kill her, but for lack of courage or commitment had failed. Likewise, on more than one occasion, she'd tried to return the favor. Lately I'd been having trouble starting her. Not today, though. That could only mean the worst was yet to come.

I drove north, then west to Grandmother's farm. I still owned the ground, but a neighbor farmed it for me and kept the grass mowed around the buildings. In return I gave him half the profits, such as they were. In my case they were just enough to pay the taxes and buy me a new pair of jeans every year.

I didn't rent the house. I didn't use it, except to store a few memories, but I wanted to know it was there if I needed it. That day I wandered through it, touching base with all of the things that used to be me. It helped to tell me who I was, where I'd been, and where I should be going. But it didn't tell me where Frieda Whitlock was or whose skull Clarkie found at the bottom of Phillipee's Pond, or if and when Diana was ever coming home to stay.

I climbed the gate and walked through the pasture down to the pond. Lush and green from all the rain, the long grass squeaked underfoot. Bobolinks and redwing blackbirds called from nearly every fence post along the way.

The pond rippled in the wind—blue when the sun

12

was out, black when it went under a cloud. I shaded my eyes and peered into the pond. Among the ripples I thought I saw some nesting bluegill and a yearling bass. Then a muskrat swam out of the cattails at the north end of the pond and dived for his hole. A coot followed him out of the cattails, dived also, and resurfaced again about halfway across the pond. Life at the pond went on.

I'd turned and started back up the lane toward the house when I saw Rupert's patrol car pass by on its way south. I waved, but he turned east at the next crossroads and appeared headed back toward Oakalla.

I had to wonder what he was doing way out here. There were no towns to the north for ten miles, and very few farms. All of the northern tip of Adams County was a classified forest known as Mitchell's Woods, the wildest tract of land around. Comprised of sinkholes, heavy timber, and thickets that blocked the sun, Mitchell's Woods enveloped several square miles, and if you went in there, you'd better take a compass, or you might not come out again. Twice in my memory, once within the last year, someone had died in there. One from an apparent heart attack, the other from a cause unknown.

Next to Fred Pierson, who lived at its edge and hunted it often, I knew Mitchell's Woods about as well as anyone. Starting at the south edge and working my way in, a little further each day, I'd explored it as a boy until I knew most of its secrets. Not all, though. There were things about Mitchell's Woods that no one knew, that no one would ever know.

Its name was one of them. No one knew its source. No one named Mitchell had ever owned the woods, no one named Mitchell had ever lived in this area, and no one in Oakalla named Mitchell had been prominent enough to have a woods named after him. The closest I'd come to an answer were the letters MITCH carved on the trunk of a dead beech. I'd found them thirty years ago, but they had been carved there long before that. And who Mitch was and what happened to him was something I'd never been able to learn.

13

The barn, though, puzzled me the most about Mitchell's Woods. Built right in the heart of the woods, with only the remnant of a road leading back to it, the barn was one of the most beautiful I'd even seen, even for Wisconsin, which farm in and farm out had the world's most beautiful barns.

From its multicolored stone foundation to the sweeping curve of its wide roof, the barn was surely a labor of love for whoever had built it. Why then had it been abandoned, like Frost's woodpile, left to time and nature?

It was always my first stop when I'd come to Mitchell's Woods to trout fish. I'd park Jessie there and walk to whatever stream I wanted to wade. The barn was my reference point, the one place in Mitchell's Woods I always knew how to get to, and my refuge in case I got caught in a storm. I felt safe inside its walls, that neither wind, rain, nor lightning would find me there. Nor would the coyotes, if I wanted to spend the night.

I used to camp by the streams I fished, usually in the open air, since I hated to put up a tent. But that was before the coyotes moved into Mitchell's Woods. There was something about their presence, even though I knew I had nothing to fear from them, that made me want a roof over my head and a wall on each side. It wasn't a rational fear, but more a knee-jerk reaction when I heard them go yip, yip, yip in the night and felt the hair on my head start to rise. Probably a carryover from the cave when the beasts of the woods were a little longer of tooth than they were now.

Then, too, there was the rumor of the Coy-Dog that ran at the head of the coyote pack. Large and blond and bold, he was said to have no fear of man, that those few who had seen him had turned tail and run, instead of the other way around.

I hadn't seen the Coy-Dog myself, didn't know if he in fact existed. But prudence was the better part of valor. As long as he stayed in his part of the woods, I'd stay in mine. And until the day we met in the middle, I'd sleep in the barn and hope for the best.

14

Watching an anvil-like cloud cover the sun and shadow all of Mitchell's Woods, I rubbed my arms to get the blood flowing again. It seemed I'd just glimpsed its heart—where questions lived without answers and ghost dogs roamed freely without fear of man. Or maybe it was the day itself, which, after a morning of sunshine, had grown sullen and foreboding.

I drove back to Oakalla and knocked on Doc Airhart's door. When he didn't answer, I walked around to the back of the house where I found him weeding again. He was now wearing a brown leather jacket and a brown corduroy cap. He took no notice of me as the weeds flew in all directions.

"Any luck?" I asked.

He stopped momentarily. "Some. What do you want to know?"

"How he died, for starters."

He continued weeding. "Like I told you earlier, someone beat his brains out."

"Those weren't your exact words."

"Then they should've been."

"He couldn't have accidentally hit his head and fallen in the pond?"

"No."

"Why not?"

He was tugging on a thistle that seemed determined to stay where it was. "It took one hell of a blow to crack his skull like that. . . ." Finally the thistle gave and Doc almost toppled over with it. He righted himself, glared momentarily at the thistle, then threw it away. "He'd have to have fallen out of a tree backward and landed on a rock. How likely is that?"

"Not very," I agreed. "What about his age?"

"I'd say he's somewhere in his forties. Perfect teeth, so there's no help there. He's been in the water close to twenty years. At least that's my guess."

"Based on what?"

"My eyes. That's what they tell me."

15

"I usually depend on my nose."

"Figures. We're on different ends of the same teeter-totter. Neither one of us would stand up in court, though."

I nodded. In the age of computer specialists, instinct didn't count for much. "Anything else you can tell me about him?"

He stopped weeding long enough to think. "Nope."

"Any idea who he is?"

"Nope. I figure that's your end of the bargain."

"I'll let you know what I find out."

"See that you do."

I started for Jessie. He called after me. "Do you want your skull back?"

"Not today."

"Good. Then I won't have to get up."

I got in Jessie and tried to start her. She wouldn't turn over. She just sat there clicking her selenoid. That was par for the course. What was unusual was that we weren't out in the sticks somewhere. At midnight. In a driving rain.

I looked in the glove compartment. There was my usual assortment of tools that I always carried—screwdriver, pliers, wrenches, and spark plug wrench. Clothes hanger, in case the muffler fell off, which it had on three occasions. And a roll of duct tape that was good for anything from patching upholstery to sealing hoses.

I left the tools there. I didn't feel like making the effort today. I turned the key again. Jessie buzzed, then started. I didn't wait for her to change her mind.

I drove home and put Jessie in the garage. Then I walked around to the front of her just to make sure. No, my eyes hadn't deceived me. There was something new here.

In trying to popularize the state, someone had come up with the logo, "Escape to Wisconsin," which had been stamped on a million license plates and sold to all those who wanted more tourists here. I wasn't one of them. Neither were a lot of other natives. So it was inevitable that some disgruntled soul would strike back with, "Escape Wisconsin." It was also inevitable that Ruth, my housekeeper, would someday read it and want to display it—especially on Jessie, whom Ruth was willing to send anywhere at any cost just to get her out of her life.

I went inside where Ruth was watching a baseball game. She is a big-boned Swede with grey-blond hair, an iron jaw and a will to match. We've been together six years, ever since I moved to Oakalla. She keeps me in line and I keep her in groceries. It seems to work out for both of us.

"Who's winning?" I asked.

"The Brewers, I think."

"I thought you didn't like baseball."

"I don't. I just ran out of things to do."

"I know the feeling." I rummaged through the mail, saw nothing from Diana. "Thanks for the license plate."

"What license plate?"

"The one on Jessie's front bumper."

"It's been on there a week."

"I hadn't noticed."

She sighed, got up, and turned off the television. She walked to the window and looked out. The cloud bank had thickened, rolling down from the north. I could see her breath on the window.

"It's been nine months," she said.

"I know that. But Saturday was *our* day."

She continued to stare out the window. "Sunday was ours, Karl's and mine. We worked all the rest of them."

"And don't you still miss him?"

"Of course I do. Every day. When some people walk into your life, they never walk out again."

"So I better get used to it, huh?"

"You'd better make your peace with it. You'll never get used to it." She started to the kitchen. "You find Frieda Whitlock?"

"No. But we did find something else."

She stopped at the kitchen door. "What's that?"

"A skull."

17

"In Phillipee's Pond?"

"Yes. I took it to Doc Airhart. He thinks it's been in there about twenty years."

"Any idea who it belongs to?"

"Doc says a man in his forties. Whoever he is, Doc thinks he was murdered."

"How did you end up with it?"

"Rupert dropped it in my lap. He's too busy looking for Frieda Whitlock to bother with it right now. If I'd left it up to him, he'd have thrown it back in the pond."

"That's not like him."

"Agreed."

"So what's going on?" she asked.

"I don't know. He told me he was Frieda's godfather. That might have something to do with it. But there's something else, something I can't put my finger on."

She nodded to herself, but didn't say anything.

"Do you know what it is?" I asked.

"I might have an idea. But it can wait. In the meantime I suggest you stay out of Rupert's way."

"I was planning to. In fact, he told me to."

She nodded to herself again and looked wise. "I thought so."

"What are you thinking? What the hell's going on?"

She didn't answer. Instead she walked into the kitchen and started banging around in the bottom drawer of the stove, looking through her pots and pans.

"Will you give me some help at least?" I hollered at her.

"In what?" she hollered back.

"In finding out whom that skull belongs to?"

"I'll think about it."

The phone rang. Before I could take two steps, Ruth answered it. The only other time she moved that fast was when we were headed for the same bathroom, or when the neighbor's dog started digging in her flower bed. She frowned, then held the receiver out for me. "No rest for the wicked," she said.

18

3

Fred Pierson was on the other end of the line. Fred lived at the western edge of Mitchell's Woods alone with his dogs. A carpenter by trade, but a hunter at heart, he was considered the best dog man in the Oakalla area. Coon dogs were his specialty; black-and-tan his favorite breed. I could count on seeing at least three hounds around his cabin at all times. More when he was training for somebody else.

Most of the people I knew, I understood—at least to the point that I knew what made them tick. Fred Pierson wasn't one of them. Deep and elusive, he was in some ways like Mitchell's Woods itself. He might let you into his mind, all the way.if you were patient, but never into his soul.

In January his wife Betty was crossing Mitchell's Woods in a snowstorm, when she got lost, fell into a sinkhole, and broke her neck. Then the coyotes found her. Or so went Fred's story.

But in the days that followed—at her funeral, when he stood at the back of Fair Haven Church dry-eyed and aloof, at Oakalla's Winter Festival, when he won the tree-climbing and log-splitting contests hands down—Fred seemed less a man in mourning than a man in shock, that the good and orderly universe he once knew no longer existed. He seemed to be running on pure adrenaline, throwing himself headlong into everything, finding pleasure in nothing.

But he wouldn't talk about it, even off the record. Neither would Rupert, who personally conducted the investigation into Betty Pierson's death and then put a lead lid on the case. It was as though something had happened in Mitchell's Woods that was beyond belief, even for a hardened woodsman like Fred Pierson and a hardened law man like Rupert. And their silence was to spare the rest of us its terror.

"Yes, Fred, what is it?" I asked.

"You seen Sheriff Roberts lately?"

"No. Should I have?"

"I called his house. His wife said to call you."

"Did you try the dispatcher?"

"She doesn't know where he is either. He hasn't called in all afternoon."

I thought a minute. "You might try Harvey Whitlock's. He might be out there."

"Thanks, Garth." He seemed in a hurry.

"Is it anything I can help you with?"

No answer. Then the line went dead.

I hung up and walked to the window. Outside, it looked more like November than June. Ruth came in carrying a beer, took a couple sips, and set it down.

"What's wrong?" she asked.

"I don't know. My nose smells trouble."

"What else is new?"

"I don't mean for me."

"Who then?"

"I said I don't know. Maybe Rupert."

She took another drink of her beer. "He's been at this game a long time. He can handle it."

But I wasn't listening. "Maybe I'll take a ride out there. You want to go along?"

"Where?"

"Fred Pierson's."

"Garth! Rupert said to stay out of it," she warned.

"I'm not in it. I just want to know what's going on."

"No. You just want to stick your nose in where it doesn't belong."

"Who says it doesn't belong? As a newspaperman, I have a right to know. So do my readers."

"Not everything. And not when it means stepping on your best friend's toes."

"I'm not stepping on his toes."

"What are you doing then?"

"Does this mean I can't borrow your Volkswagen?"

"What's wrong with your car?"

"What's right with my car? You know Jessie."

"Well enough not to loan you the Volkswagen. Maybe one of these days you'll get fed up enough to buy you something that runs."

"That's your final answer?"

"That's my final answer."

"I hope we don't both regret it."

"And I'm not coming after you!" she shouted, as I walked out the back door.

I got in Jessie and drove toward Fred Pierson's. I took my time and the long way around. If he was on his way, I didn't want to beat Rupert there.

It started to rain, fogging the windshield. I turned on the wipers, fan, and the defroster. All worked. I should make a note of that.

When I pulled into Fred's drive, Rupert was already there. So was the ambulance from the local hospital. Not a good sign.

I knocked twice on Fred's door. No one answered. The only thing I raised were his coon dogs, who started baying at me.

21

I left Jessie in the drive and went into Mitchell's Woods. It was dark and still in here, made darker by the rain. And the further I went, the darker it got.

Then I heard something that made my skin prickle. It was the yip-yip-yip of a coyote. Not one, but a pack roaming somewhere close. I looked at my watch. Not yet six. The party was starting early tonight.

I stopped to get my bearings and discovered I didn't know where I was. The rain was misty, foglike, and made every leaf look the same. Now I had to find Rupert and Fred. Otherwise, I might have to spend the night in here.

I'd taken only a few more steps when I saw the glare of a flashlight coming toward me. I stepped into an opening where I could be seen. Three figures approached, quietly and sullenly, like specters in the rain. Not one of the three seemed pleased to see me. I guessed I should have phoned ahead.

"Evening, Garth," Rupert said. "I thought you might be along."

"I thought you might need my help."

"Like I told you this morning, not this time."

Fred Pierson and the driver of the ambulance continued walking. Between them they carried a litter and something covered by a blanket. Rupert and I lagged behind.

"Frieda Whitlock?" I asked.

"Dead," he answered.

"Coyotes again?"

His head jerked around and he gave me a harsh look. "How did you know?"

"A lucky guess."

"You make a lot of them," he said.

"And I'm wrong a lot of the time, too. Tell me I'm wrong this time and I won't ask any more."

"Wrong about what?"

"It wasn't coyotes."

"It *was* coyotes. At least that's what my report will read."

"She was killed by coyotes? Come on, Rupert. You don't even believe that. How do you expect me to?"

He reached into his pocket and pulled out his tobacco pouch. He took a chew and offered me one. As usual, I refused it. I liked the taste of the tobacco. I just didn't know when to spit. And ended up swallowing the juice and getting sick.

"I didn't say she was killed by coyotes," he said.

"What are you saying?"

He shrugged and walked on. He didn't want to answer me.

"I'll find out one way or another," I said.

He stopped long enough to spit, then continued walking.

"Why now?" I asked. "Why clam up now after six years? What's going on out here anyway?"

He stopped, but wouldn't look at me. Instead he stared into the rain. "Maybe I'm tired of hearing your name around town more than I do my own. Maybe people are starting to wonder who the real sheriff of Adams County is."

"I don't believe that. Neither do you."

"Well, it's a possibility I'd wish you'd consider. I've got an election coming up this fall, maybe for my last term. I'd kind of like to win big, go out in style. Not astride your coattails, like I have been lately."

"Bullshit," I said.

He turned to glare at me. "What do you mean *bullshit*? Are you trying to tell me how to run my life? What I should want and what I shouldn't want?"

"I'm telling you that you're too good a cop not to use every source you can. What you want and what I want doesn't have a damn thing to do with it."

"Go to hell," he said and started walking. He didn't stop until we were at Fred Pierson's.

I looked around. The ambulance and driver were still

there, but I didn't see Fred Pierson. He'd conveniently disappeared for the moment.

I walked to the ambulance and looked inside. I couldn't see Frieda's face, only her blond hair, which shone with a dull lustre in the near dark, like a faint, fog-bound moon. The back door of the ambulance was still open. I reached in and touched her hair and said I was sorry.

Then I felt something that was neither leaf nor hair. I picked it up and held it up to the sky to look at it. It was a piece of straw.

"I'll take that," Rupert said.

I handed it to him.

"Now be on your way," he added.

"It's a free country," I said. "A free press."

"Don't bring us down to that, Garth," he answered quietly. "Just do as I ask."

I shrugged. I didn't know what to do. The friend in me said leave, that Rupert was near the edge and it wouldn't take much to push him over. The newspaper-man in me said stay.

"What do I tell my readers?" I asked.

"You can tell them to go to hell as far as I'm concerned."

"Can I quote you on that?"

"You can do whatever you like."

"And do I mention the coyotes?"

His face was solemn and grim. "I wouldn't."

"Somebody will."

"Probably."

"Half-truths are the worst truths of all. They bring out the worst in people, confirm all their half-held fears."

"Not in this case."

I studied him. He wasn't kidding. "That bad?"

He spat into the grass. "Worse."

We watched the ambulance pull out of the drive and start back toward town. Come back! I wanted to yell. And bring Frieda with you!

24

There was something I needed to tell her, had planned to tell her tomorrow night after commencement. Thanks, Frieda, for who you are and what you've done. For giving all of us in Oakalla a reason to look at ourselves with pride and smile. We'll miss you.

Rupert turned abruptly, got into his squad car, and began to follow the hearse. I watched him go until his taillights turned east and disappeared. Then I heard the yip-yip-yip of the coyote pack, moving away from me and deeper into the woods. I waited a few minutes, hoping Fred Pierson would return. When he didn't, I took a walk around his cabin.

I'd wondered why Fred's dogs had suddenly quieted down. They were gone, along with Fred. A shudder passed through me, as I looked at Mitchell's Woods. It seemed a strange and forbidding time to go hunting.

"Walter Lawrence" was the first thing Ruth said to me when I walked in the door.

"Who's Walter Lawrence?" I stood over the register hoping for heat. I didn't feel any.

"He might be the one you found in Phillipee's Pond."

"Tell me more."

She noticed me standing over the register. "You cold?"

"To my bones."

"Why don't you put a sweater on?"

"I'd just like to feel some heat. I thought maybe the furnace would kick on."

"It's off for the summer, remember? You shut it off in April."

"May first."

"When there was still frost on the ground."

"A light frost. It was gone by noon."

"It came back the next day."

"Only for a week."

She sighed, opened the kitchen closet, and handed

me her sheepherder sweater. "Here, put this on." I put it on while she turned the fire on under the coffee pot and rinsed out my cup. "What happened out there?" she asked.

"They found Frieda Whitlock in Mitchell's Woods. And Rupert and I had a run in."

"In that order?"

"Just about."

"Was Frieda dead?"

"I'm afraid so."

"What killed her?"

"I don't know. Rupert says it was coyotes."

"And you don't believe him?"

"When was the last time you heard of a coyote killing anyone? I don't even know if there's a case on record. Besides that, how did Frieda get to Mitchell's Woods? Did the coyotes drive into town and kidnap her?"

"Maybe Rupert has good reason for not telling you everything."

"He probably does. I just would like to know what it is."

"What hurts the most, the fact that he won't tell you, or being in the dark?"

"Being in the dark."

"You're sure?"

"As I can be. There's so much in life I don't know, will never know because it's beyond my grasp. But there are some things in life I can know. This is one of them. Rupert knows that. He also knows it drives me crazy not to know, that I won't stop until I do."

"Have you ever thought his pride might be at stake?"

"Yes, but why now? He's never shut me out before."

"I could hazard a guess. But I won't. That's something you and Rupert will have to work out yourselves."

"Why don't you hazard a guess. You do on everything else."

"Why don't you just let it lie?"

"Because something within me 'does not love a wall.'"

"Frost again?"

"Frost again."

"Didn't you ever read any other poets?"

"Some. But Frost stayed with me."

"Figures." She poured me a cup of coffee. I sat at the kitchen table to drink it. She poured herself a cup and sat across from me. "Do you want to hear about Walter Lawrence or not?"

"Why not? It's too wet to plow."

"I can forget the whole thing if you like."

I yawned. "Go ahead. I'm listening."

"Then act like it."

"I'm listening, Ruth. Believe me. My heart's just not in it. What happened twenty years ago to somebody I don't know just doesn't seem as important as what happened this week to somebody I do know. And liked. I mean she was in the *Reporter* every other week. Frieda Whitlock does this. Frieda Whitlock does that. Frieda Whitlock does everything. Now she does nothing. Silence. That's all we'll hear from Frieda Whitlock from now on. I can't accept that, not without trying to find out why. Too much life has been lost, too much promise. It asks too much of me. Besides, how do I know that Rupert didn't plant that skull this morning just to keep me out of his hair?"

"There's only one way to find out."

"Walter Lawrence?"

"We do keep coming back to that."

4

I sat at the breakfast table. It had cleared in the night, the sun was out, and the birds were singing like there was no tomorrow. In Frieda's case, they were right.

Ruth had filled me in on Walter Lawrence. He was forty-three when he disappeared from Oakalla seventeen years ago. A partner in the law firm Wilson and Lawrence, Wilson and Tyler now, he'd disappeared after withdrawing fifty thousand dollars from his personal account. He'd left behind a wife and three young boys. His wife, Maxine Lawrence, still lived in the east end of Oakalla and was one of the jolliest people I'd ever known. At least she always had a smile for me. His sons had grown up, gone to college, and moved away. In the seventeen years since his disappearance, no one had seen nor heard from Walter Lawrence. Or if they had, they weren't admitting it.

I reached for a cinnamon roll, then put it back. I was ready to get going. Maybe I wouldn't find out what happened to Walter Lawrence. Maybe I would. But I refused to sit here and feel sorry for myself.

"What was he driving?"

Ruth looked up from her Sunday paper. Still in her

28

robe and slippers, she hadn't gotten very far that morning. "Who's that?"

"Walter Lawrence."

"How am I supposed to know?"

"I just thought you might."

She turned the page, scanning the news as she went. "It was a maroon Bonneville hardtop."

"What year?"

"1968."

"Thank you."

She didn't answer. She'd found something that interested her.

Hattie Peeler lived in the last house east on Gas Line Road before you passed the city limits sign. Hers was a two-story white frame house with wide windows, black shutters, and a red brick chimney that always looked freshly scrubbed. The house was surrounded by just enough trees to give you the flavor of the woods without its isolation. Shady in summer, bright winter through spring, mellow in fall, it was one of my favorite places to visit all year round.

Hattie Peeler was a full-blooded Chippewa who'd lived in Oakalla almost as long as the town had been here. I knew she was somewhere over eighty, but just how far I didn't know.

I'd known her since I was a boy. Here was my stopping off place on my way out of town. Usually I left my bike parked in her yard and hoofed it the rest of the way to the woods. Once, when I slipped on an icy log and landed in the creek, I'd sat for two hours in front of her wood range drying out, while she sat beside me drinking rye and smoking a corncob pipe and telling me tales that made my toes curl.

She tolerated me then. She tolerated me now. That was about as much affection as Hattie Peeler showed— and I felt honored with that.

Hattie was outside hoeing her garden. Slight and brown and bareheaded, her silky white hair gleaming in the sun, she looked like a thistle gone to seed.

"Morning, Hattie," I said.

She looked up to acknowledge me and continued hoeing.

I didn't say anything more for a while. I stood beside her and watched her work. It had a hypnotic effect on me, like watching my father hone the edge of a knife until it made the cut he wanted. Like Hattie, he made it look so easy it seemed that anyone could do it. That was true grace, the ability to make hard work look effortless.

She stopped hoeing a moment, long enough to wipe the sweat from her brow. "You want something?" she asked.

"Yes and no."

She grunted and went back to work.

I waited until she stopped again. "What I meant was," I said, "I have a couple questions I'd like to ask you. I don't need anything in particular."

"It seems you need some answers," she said, as she resumed hoeing. Then she stopped and said, "Ask. Then be gone with you. I want this garden hoed before the next rain."

"First question. Do you remember when Walter Lawrence disappeared from Oakalla several years ago?"

"I remember."

"He drove a 1968 Bonneville hardtop. Maroon. Do you remember that?"

"I remember."

"Do you remember seeing it the day he disappeared?"

"I remember."

"Did he drive by here?"

"Yes."

"Did he drive back by here?"

"No."

30

"Did you ever see him again?"

"No. Any more questions?"

I shook my head. I couldn't think of any at the moment.

"Good." She began to hoe, moving down the row away from me.

Thinking she'd soon tire, I tried to wait her out. Some more questions had come to mind, like who was with Walter Lawrence or was he alone? But when she got to the end of the row, she set her hoe down and went inside. After fifteen minutes I decided I'd worn out my welcome.

I walked on out Gas Line Road. There was only one house between here and Phillipee's Pond—if you could call it a house. It was a log cabin built sometime during the early nineteenth century and was probably the oldest dwelling in Adams County. And it showed its age. Weathered as grey as a November sky, it had settled at one corner until it tilted to the east, skewing the roof and twisting timbers as it did. Cracks had appeared in the walls as the mortar had fallen out, replaced periodically by patches of fresh mortar that looked like they'd been applied with a cannon.

That was the house. The yard was an assortment of weeds, junk, and doghouses. At one time I'd counted as many as six coon hounds, sitting on top of their doghouses, baying at the local freight as it passed to the south. At least that's the way it used to be. Recent times had seen some improvement since old Buck Henry, its owner, died two years ago. He'd gone coon hunting in a drunken stupor, fallen into a ravine, and impaled himself on a tree stob. His grandson, Josh, had found him and carried him all the way to the house, but it was too late. He was dead on arrival at the hospital.

Good riddance was the general consensus around Oakalla. Known for his slovenly ways and violent temper, especially when he was drunk, which was often, Buck Henry inspired more fear than love.

31

His one great passion, the one he shared with his grandson, Josh, was coon hunting. When coons were in season, he'd sleep all day and hunt all night until the snow got too deep for the coons to run. When coons weren't in season, he'd count the days until they were.

He'd owned an assortment of dogs over the years and claimed every one was a world-beater. I didn't know. The one time I'd hunted with him the only thing that had been beaten was the dog—by Buck. But at least Buck didn't shoot him, which he probably would have if I hadn't been along.

I approached the cabin and stopped a few feet away. I was surprised at how clean the yard looked. The junk had been hauled away, and the grass had been mowed recently. The cabin, too, looked better than I ever remembered. All the shingles were on and no cracks showed in the mortar. It still leaned to the east, but it almost looked livable.

I wondered where all the dogs were. I counted only one house. A large brindled hound crawled out of it, stretched in the sun, and yawned at me. He had to be the largest hound I'd ever seen. I guessed he weighed close to a hundred pounds.

I studied him. He studied me. Then I noticed his eyes for the first time. They were a pale blue. I knew malamutes had blue eyes, and I'd seen Australian shepherds with one blue and one brown eye. It was a mark of the breed. But never a hound with two blue eyes before. It made him seem more perceptive, more aloof than I wanted a hound to be.

Josh Henry appeared from somewhere over the hill. I didn't hear him coming, but I saw his shadow fall across my feet. Josh was roughly six feet two and weighed over two hundred pounds. He had curly blond hair, bright eyes, and a smile I found hard to resist. An eternal optimist, he reminded me of the boy in the joke, the one who got a sack of horse manure for Christmas—then immediately went looking for the pony.

Even though he was in his early thirties, not that much younger than I, I sometimes felt like Josh Henry's cynical father. I often fought the urge to step on his toes to take the smile off his face. But I knew it wouldn't stay off for long—at least not long enough to do any good. Josh was a not-so-perfect innocent, someone who'd learned to roll with the punches, but had never learned how to throw them.

Josh's mother, Buck Henry's daughter, had abandoned Josh when he was a baby and gone to Chicago to seek her fortune. That was the last anyone had ever heard of her. Josh's father was unknown, or at least no one stepped forward to claim Josh, and Josh's grandmother was dead, so Buck raised Josh by himself. In the ways of the wild. By hunting, fishing, and trapping. And poaching whenever they could get away with it.

When he'd earned a football scholarship his senior year in high school, I thought Josh might break away and at least see what was on the other side of the mountain. But it hadn't happened. He came home that same fall without even completing one semester. I blamed Buck Henry, who didn't want Josh to go to college in the first place. Josh said he got homesick, that Buck had nothing to do with it. I imagined the truth was somewhere between.

Now I very much doubted Josh would ever break away. For all of Josh Henry's looks and natural charm and whatever ability he might have, he seemed more than satisfied to live here by himself and work eight to four as janitor at the high school and hunt whatever was in season.

"Hi, Coach, what's up?" he said.

He'd called me that ever since I taught him how to tackle twenty-four years ago. He was a scrawny towhead then, trying to tackle boys several years older than he in a sandlot football game. I was a high school senior, visiting my Grandmother Ryland on Thanksgiving break. I didn't teach him much—just to keep his head up, his body low, and to keep his legs driving on contact. But it seemed to help. By the end of the afternoon he was more than holding his own. He'd never forgotten. Neither had I.

"Morning, Josh. What happened to your dogs?"

"Sold some. Shot the rest."

"Why? You give up hunting?"

He smiled broadly, even more broadly than usual. "Heck no! I just started. I got me a real dog now!"

"Yeah, I saw him. He any good?"

"Is he any good? He won the PCA world hunt two years ago with record plus points. I'd say he's good!"

"*You* won the PCA world hunt?" For some reason I hadn't heard about it.

"I didn't say I did. I said *he* did. I bought him afterwards."

"I bet that set you back some."

"Enough. My live savings and more."

His life savings wouldn't have amounted to much. Josh spent money like the proverbial sailor on shore leave, mostly on things like shotguns and bass boats and four-wheel-drive pickups, none of which he kept for very long. The "more" I didn't know about. Maybe he was buying the dog on time.

"What kind of dog is he?"

"Plott."

"I don't think I've ever seen one before. Do they all have blue eyes?"

"Nope. He's the only one I know of. Would you like to take a look at him? Up close?" He seemed eager to introduce us, like he might his girlfriend.

"Some other time maybe. I've got a couple other places I'd like to go this morning." In truth, I didn't think I'd ever like to meet the Plott up close. Right now, while sitting there docilely in the sun minding his own business, he seemed to be picking my brain, looking for a weakness.

"What's your hurry? You just got here."

"I like to keep moving on a day like this. Otherwise, it might catch up with me."

He scratched the blond stubble on his chin and gave me a foolish smile. That went right over his head. "Well, I guess you know best."

"There is one thing, Josh. Do you remember a man named Walter Lawrence? He lived here in Oakalla about fifteen years or so ago."

"Sure, I remember him. He used to drive this road quite regular."

"Where to, do you remember that?"

"Phillipee's Pond. At least he turned in there."

"Was he turning around?"

"No. He'd usually stay about an hour or so, then drive out again."

"Was he fishing?"

"I don't know. I never bothered to look."

"Do you remember what he drove?"

"He used to drive a red Oldsmobile. Then I think he bought a red Pontiac."

"A Bonneville?"

He shook his head. "I don't know. It was a fancy new car. I used to think how much fun it would be if it was mine." He blushed. "You know, with the girls and all."

I smiled. I knew. At that age a car seemed the answer to all of my problems. Now it was the source of most of them.

"But you do remember it was red?" I asked.

"Sure. A real deep red. I liked that."

"Do you also remember that Walter Lawrence disappeared from Oakalla?"

"I do. I saw him that day, too."

"The same day he disappeared?"

"I think it was. I'm sure it was. I remember telling Grandpop about it because everyone in town was wondering what happened to him, and he said to keep my mouth shut and mind my own business, or he'd take a strap to me."

"Why did he say that?"

"You knew Grandpop. He didn't like to meddle in other people's busines, or vice versa. He said it just led to trouble. Trouble he could do without."

"Where was Walter Lawrence when you saw him?"

"Driving along this road, same as always."

I was two for two. Hattie Peeler had also seen him. "Did he turn into Phillipee's Pond?" I asked.

"Yep. Same as always."

"Did he come out again?"

"He came out and went back toward town. At least the car did. I figured it was him."

I was now one for two. Hattie hadn't seen him come back into town again. Then neither had Josh. He'd only seen the car. "You didn't happen to notice anyone with him, did you?"

"Sometimes."

"On the day he disappeared?"

"I can't say. I was too far away."

"Thanks, Josh."

He looked puzzled. "You walked all the way out here to ask me that?"

"Among other things."

"Can I give you a ride anywhere?"

"No thanks. I'm not going that far." I started down the drive toward Gas Line Road. I stopped and turned back. As long as I was here, I might as well ask, even if I was stepping on Rupert's toes. "You knew Frieda Whitlock was missing?"

"I heard at school."

"Did you happen to see her after school last Thursday?"

"No. I get off at four. The kids are usually gone by then."

36

"And you didn't see her on your way home from work?"

"No. But then I didn't come straight home. I stopped by the elevator to pick up some dog feed and shoot the shit a while."

"Thanks again, Josh."

"Sure, Coach. Have a nice walk."

I walked to Phillipee's Pond and sat down on a log in the sun. It was pleasant out here, like Baby Bear's porridge, neither too hot nor too cold. The dew was still on, the air fragrant with pond water and wildflowers, as a newly hatched swallowtail shook the cobwebs from its wings and took flight.

I remembered it was a day something like this when I saw Buck Henry for the first time. I'd come to the pond alone, thinking I'd be less visible that way. I was fishing the north end, about to congratulate myself on finally beating Old Lady Phillipee at her own game, when I saw the brush move and Buck Henry step out. Short, squat, and powerfully built, he looked like a bear on the prowl, and I couldn't have been more scared if it had been a bear. He looked at me and snorted. I didn't wait to see what he'd do next. I left everything behind and didn't stop running until I reached Oakalla. When I came back two days later, everything, including my sack lunch and a stringer of bluegill, was gone.

I lived in fear of Buck Henry from then on. Old Lady Phillipee was nothing compared to him. She was torn jeans and skinned knees. He was certain death.

I never did completely get over my fear of him. Even the night we hunted together four years ago, I made sure he always walked ahead of me. And when I finally got in Jessie and started home, I breathed a huge sigh of relief that Ruth swore she heard back in Oakalla. It was the same relief I felt when, seven years ago, I walked out of divorce court shaken and shirtless, but alive.

I glanced at Gas Line Road. Traffic was slow today,

even for a Sunday. I guessed the word about Frieda Whitlock hadn't spread yet.

Harvey Whitlock's was the next house up the road. I knew it well. It was where Old Lady Phillipee used to live. I decided I had time to pay Harvey a short visit.

I walked around the pond and up a hill. I was crossing the fence at the top of the hill, when I looked down and saw a baseball bat lying in the fence row. The bat had been there for a long time, long enough for it to weather and crack and become entwined in a blackberry bush.

I jumped down from the fence and examined it. I couldn't guess its age. It was a Henry Aaron, Louisville Slugger, about thirty-two inches long. Its handle was too thick for me and it was about two inches shorter than I liked my bats. It seemed the kind of bat a contact hitter would use, or a banker. Somebody who liked a sure thing—not a free-swinger like me.

I wondered how it got there? I'd seen Old Lady Phillipee carrying a lot of things, including shovels and pitchforks, but never a baseball bat. Maybe it belonged to Josh Henry, though I had my doubts. When spring and baseball season came, Josh would have been deep in the woods hunting for morels. Which left whom? Frieda Whitlock? Not likely. Frieda had done a lot of things, all of them well, but I never knew her to play baseball.

I left the bat where it was. It wasn't going anywhere, not with a blackberry bush wrapped around it. I crossed the fence, walked through a small woodlot, and crossed another fence into Harvey Whitlock's yard. His two-story white farmhouse had been recently painted. So, too, had his red barn. Twin blue steel silos stood beside his new white hog barn and indicated modest prosperity.

Harvey was a pig farmer—farrow to finish, as he was proud of saying—and a good one. His land and equipment were his, not the bank's, and he knew how to stretch a dollar about as well as anyone. Sometimes we'd drink a

38

beer at the Corner Bar and Grill, or spend an afternoon fishing Phillipee's pond. We weren't fast friends. But good enough friends for me to feel his loss.

I knocked on the front door. Harvey opened it and invited me inside. He didn't seem to mind that I was wearing jeans and a T-shirt.

I went through the entry way into the living room. The first thing I saw was an eight-by-ten of Frieda Whitlock on top of the color television. She had brown eyes, short blond hair, a pixie face, and the eager look of a bird on the threshold of flight. She seemed like someone who would appear eternally young, even as she approached and passed middle age.

In contrast, Harvey was a big earthy man. At least six feet four with broad features and hands the size of a catcher's mitt, he had ruddy cheeks and large blue eyes, which at the moment were red and watery and out of focus.

He stared at her photograph. "I'm sorry," he said, as much to her as to me.

"If it helps any, so am I."

"Do you mind if we go outside?" he asked. "I don't think I can stand it in here much longer."

"No. I don't mind at all."

We went outside where the day was brighter than ever, and death seemed a thousand miles away. Harvey walked across the yard and stopped at the fence overlooking his hog lot. I didn't know what was going through his mind, but I guessed he would have traded it all, including his own life, to have his daughter back again.

"You here on business?" he asked.

"No. Just as a friend."

"I wish you were here on business. I've got enough friends. I want to know who killed Frieda."

"Rupert's handling that end of it."

"I know he is. And he'll do a damn good job. But I'd like your help, too."

I started to tell him that Rupert didn't want my help, but thought better of it. "I'm working on something else at the moment."

He looked at me. I didn't like that look. "What could be more important than this?"

I wanted to give him something. I didn't want him to think I was a complete asshole. "I'm coming at it from another direction."

"What direction's that?" He wasn't convinced.

"Through the past. I find it usually repeats itself in the present." It sounded so good I almost believed it myself.

Harvey, however, didn't buy it. "What could the past possibly have to do with what happened to Frieda?"

"Not her past. Someone else's. Maybe her killer's."

"You mean his father beat him as a child?"

"Not exactly."

But Harvey wasn't listening. "If you want the truth, I don't believe that shit. It's just an excuse, a way to get around the truth. My father wore my ass out with a razor strap, and I've never raised my hand against another human being. Except in war, when I didn't have a choice."

"I'm sorry, Harvey. I have to go at it the best way I can."

"I'm sorry, too, Garth. I thought you were a friend."

"I am, Harvey. Believe it if you will."

With nothing more to say, I left.

Hattie Peeler wasn't back in her garden. With four rows left to hoe, I wondered why? I walked to her door and knocked. The storm door was open and I thought I heard her inside, but she didn't answer, not even after I called to her twice. I thought about going inside, but decided against it. Later I wished I had. It might have saved me a lot of grief.

40

5

At home Ruth put Sunday dinner on the table—fried chicken, mashed potatoes and gravy, fresh asparagus, and strawberry shortcake for dessert. On every other day of the week, we ate in the kitchen, but on Sunday we ate in the dining room. I ate slowly, savoring every bite. Ruth ate like a lumberjack who'd been lost for two weeks in the woods. Then she sat back and waited for me to finish. It should have made me nervous, but it didn't.

"Buck Henry," I said.

Ruth picked up a drumstick from the platter, eyed it hungrily, then put it back down again. Instead she broke off a piece of crust and ate that. "What about him?"

"Did he have any money to speak of?"

"Some say he did. Some say he didn't. Nobody ever got close enough to find out—not and lived to tell about it."

"What do you know that I don't?"

"Seriously, do you want me to answer that?"

"About Buck Henry?"

"Nothing. What do you know that I don't?"

"Josh Henry's got a new coon dog. He says it's a

41

world champion. I just wondered where he got the money to buy it?"

"Isn't he janitor at the high school?"

"Yes. But he spends his money about as fast as he makes it. I can't see him having much left over."

"Maybe he stole it."

"Josh? Why do you say that?" I'd forgotten that Ruth didn't like Josh Henry. Though he wasn't the only one in Oakalla she didn't like. Her list was at least two volumes long.

"It fits his style."

"Which is?"

"A wolf in sheep's clothing."

"According to whom?"

"According to me. I watched him play football for four straight years, remember? You only came to a game or two."

"He made all state, didn't he?"

"He made honorable mention all state. With the team he had around him, *I* could have made honorable mention that year. In fact, I think one of the cheerleaders did."

"What else have you got against him?"

"He was Buck Henry's grandson. As the twig is bent, so grows the tree."

"Meaning?"

She got up and began to clear the table. "You figure it out."

"I don't think Josh is like Buck, if that's what you're saying."

"No. Buck was tougher and shrewder, and pure at least, like hard coal. Josh is the slag left over from Buck's fire."

"I think you're being too hard on him."

"And I think you've got a soft spot in your head for him. You've been a part of him for so long you can't see him for what he really is." She started for the kitchen with an armload of dishes.

42

"You still didn't answer my question," I called after her.

She stopped at the kichen door. "Which is?"

"Where did Josh get the money to buy the dog?"

"I already gave you my best answer."

"Do you know what a good coon dog's worth?" Because I didn't.

"Dead or alive? Alive—nothing. Dead—I'd chip in five bucks for whoever shot it."

"I mean to somebody who wants one?"

"Like everything else, it probably depends on how bad he wants it. I'd say a hundred dollars tops."

"I think it's worth more than that. I heard Fred Pierson was once offered a new car for one of his."

"Did he take it?"

"No."

"Then that's where two fools met." She disappeared into the kitchen.

"What would be the reason anyway?" I thought out loud.

"Reason for what?" she hollered at me.

"For Buck Henry to kill Walter Lawrence?"

She was back at the kitchen door. "Who said he did?"

"It was just a thought I had. If that's Walter Lawrence we found in Phillipee's Pond, then he was treading on Buck Henry's territory. If Buck killed him for some reason and hid the money and Josh found it after Buck died, then he'd have the money he needed to buy that dog of his. At least I think he would."

"You think he paid fifty thousand dollars for a coon dog? Garth, you've been lonelier than I thought."

"Maybe not that much. Maybe he spent the rest on something else. But it would still explain where he got the money."

"It might explain a lot more," she said.

"Meaning?"

She shook her head. She wouldn't elaborate. "Some-

43

thing I heard. But if you want a motive, I can give you one. Rumor has it that it was Walter Lawrence who got Rita Henry, Buck's daughter, pregnant. Walter was married at the time. That was one reason why he never came forward."

"Do you know that for a fact?"

"It's not written in blood, if that's what you mean. But it comes from a good source."

"Then Buck Henry could have bided his time, shaken Walter Lawrence down for the fifty thousand dollars, then killed him and dumped him into Phillipee's Pond."

"If you want to believe that," she said.

"Don't you?"

"Do you?" She fired back.

"Knowing Buck, I think it's possible. You don't agree?" Something in her look said she didn't.

"I don't know if I do or don't. Why would Buck wait seventeen years to kill Walter Lawrence? Why not the first time he found out Rita was carrying Walter's child? Josh, in this case."

"As I said, maybe he was biding his time."

"I don't think so. Buck was a vicious man, true, but not spiteful. If he killed someone, it'd be more by accident than by design."

"What do you think then?"

"I think you ought to quit looking for easy answers and go on about your business like you usually do."

"You're probably right," I agreed. "But I still think I'll follow it up."

She smiled at me. "I'd be disappointed if you didn't."

I went outside, got in Jessie, and turned on the key. Rat-tat-tat went the selenoid; then she caught and turned over. "Escape Wisconsin." Not a bad idea.

I drove out to see Fred Pierson. He was sitting on the porch of his log house with a troubled look in his eyes. Small, dark, and wiry with energy to burn, he reminded me of the French voyagers who first explored the North and who spent their short perilous lives running its rivers and trading for its furs. He had the same zest, the same sure-footed strength to look life in the eye and not blink, letting trouble run off his back like rainwater. In one way I admired him, his ability to hold hurt at a distance, to never let it get close enough to count. In another way, it seemed supremely lonely in there.

"A penny for your thoughts," I said.

"They're not worth that much," he answered. Then he clapped his hands and stood, as if to break a spell. "So, what brings *you* out here? I seem to have had a lot of visitors lately, more than I usually get in a year." Or want, his eyes seemed to say.

"I'd like some information."

"On what?" I thought I saw his guard go up.

"Coon dogs."

He smiled, seemed relieved. "*That* I'll be glad to talk about."

"As opposed to what?" I asked.

But he didn't answer.

He came down from his porch, and we walked north along the gravel road that ran in front of his house. "So what do you want to know?" he asked.

"What's a good one worth for one thing?"

"Anywhere from a couple of thousand to you name your price."

"As much as fifty thousand dollars?"

"That should buy you a good one. Then again it might not. Dogs are funny. Temperamental, too. They're a lot like people. The smarter they are, the more quirks they have."

"Meaning what—in layman's terms?"

"You might have a fifty thousand dollar dog, but that doesn't mean he'll hunt for you. Not if he doesn't like you and not if you don't know how to handle him. You've got to be smarter than he is. Otherwise, he'll go out and hunt on his own and do what he damn well pleases and you

45

won't be any the wiser. You might catch a coon now and again, but you won't have fifty thousand dollars worth of fun doing it. And you'll end up selling the dog for less than you paid for it—if you don't shoot it first."

"I've seen that happen," I said. "With bird dogs."

"So have I," he answered. "I've even shot a couple myself."

I bit my tongue and kept my peace. It wasn't something I would do or I approved of doing. But almost every good dog trainer that I knew had shot at least one dog in frustration. Better than shooting his kids, I guessed. "But fifty thousand dollars is not out of the question?" I asked.

"That depends on you, the dog, and what you want to do with him. If you just want to go out and catch coons, that's one thing. You don't need a fifty thousand dollar dog. Not unless you've got more money than sense. But if you want to win a world hunt, that's a different story."

"Say you did win a world hunt, would you have a fifty thousand dollar dog then?"

He looked at me to see if I was kidding, saw that I wasn't, and forgave my ignorance. "Fifty thousand dollars wouldn't even touch a dog like that. Not unless it was a female."

"Why not?"

"Stud fees. At five hundred dollars a throw, three times a week, fifty-two weeks a year, you'd have that and more again at the end of the first year. Tax free a lot of it, since somebody's bound to pay you in cash. Say the dog lived three years at stud, you'd never have to work another day in you life. Not if you didn't want to. Which I wouldn't."

"What if there was something wrong with the dog, say he was off-color or something like that?" I was thinking about the Plott's blue eyes.

"It might knock him down some, but not much. We're talking about hunting dogs, not show dogs. You don't care

46

what your dog looks like as long as he'll go out and catch you a coon every night."

"What if one eye was purple and the other brown?"

"In the stud dog? You'd take the chance the purple wouldn't reproduce. And you wouldn't be broken-hearted if it did, as long as the dog hunted well."

"What if both eyes were purple?"

"You'd take the same chance. At least I would, if the dog was good enough."

"Champions beget champions?"

"Not always. But often enough . . . somewhere down the line."

We'd turned around and started walking back. I had a question aching to be asked, so I asked it. "Fred, did you ever hunt with Buck Henry?"

"A few times. Money hunts at the Coon Club. Sometimes we drew the same cast."

"What kind of a hunter was he?"

"Probably the best around, at least at calling his dog. He just never had a dog that amounted to much."

"Why? Because he beat them?"

He gave me a knowing look. "That was part of it. His dogs were always afraid to take a chance, afraid they'd be beaten if they made a mistake. So they didn't get many first strikes or first trees. But more than that, he tried to inbreed them, back to the one good dog he had. It never worked out. They seemed to get worse instead of better. And to be honest, Buck never did have the heart to shoot the lot and start over, the way he should have done."

"The way you would have done?" I had to ask.

He gave me a strange look. His brown eyes had darkened like a gathering storm. "Why not? A man's lucky to have one really good anything in his lifetime. Why not give yourself every possible chance at it?"

"At what?"

He smiled. He was back in never-never land, the home of all childhood dreams. *"The glory hound."*

47

I nodded. I thought I knew what he meant. Except mine was *the glory hole*, a small lake I'd find one day deep in the Ontario woods. One that held a world record pike that I would catch and release. Alone. With only God as my witness.

"Did you ever have a chance at him?"

His smile began to fade and harden. "A chance at what?"

"The glory hound."

His eyes fastened on Mitchell's Woods. It seemed at that moment he could see all the way into its heart. And what he saw angered him. "Once."

"What happened to him?"

"I got rid of him."

"Why?"

He didn't answer. I could soon tell he wasn't going to.

Rupert and the county coroner were waiting for us in Fred's drive. Rupert frowned when he saw me. I seemed to be making everyone's day.

Rupert walked a short distance away from his car. I went with him. "I thought we had an understanding," he said.

"We do. I'm working my side of the street."

"Which side is that?"

"The phantom skull side, the one you probably bought from a museum."

"Is that what you think?" he asked.

"I have my suspicions. Otherwise, what happened to the rest of the body?"

"I have it back at the City Building. Clarkie found it in the pond late last evening with an anchor close by. You're welcome to it any time you want it."

"You might have told me."

"I tried. You haven't been home much lately."

"My apology," I said.

"Accepted. Now what are you doing here?"

"Just as I said, working my side of the street. I didn't

48

ask Fred a thing about Frieda Whitlock. Or even coyotes for that matter."

"Just like you didn't ask Josh Henry?"

"It slipped out before I could catch myself."

He softened a little. "I know you're trying, Garth. Just try a little harder from now on."

"I'll see what I can do." I started toward Jessie. I stopped and turned back to Rupert. "Did Joe Turner ever say why he left the Marathon the way he did?"

"No. I just talked to him again about it a little while ago."

"Did you mention the trouble he might be in if he didn't tell you?"

Rupert was trying hard to be patient. But he was starting to lose the battle. "I did. He stuck by his story."

"Which is?"

"He got a phone call. He went to jump somebody's battery. And when he got there, nobody was there."

"Where was that?"

He shook his head. He knew, but he wouldn't tell me.

"What about Josh Henry? Was he at the elevator when he said he was?"

"He was. He was there until five, then went up to the Corner and played cards until after seven. Several people saw him both places."

I wasn't sure why, maybe because of what Ruth had said about Josh, but I breathed a sigh of releif. "Thanks, Rupert."

"Will that hold you for now?"

"I guess it'll have to."

I got in Jessie, finally got her started, and drove back to Oakalla. Fred Pierson had given me something to think about. If the Plott was a world champion, as Josh said it was, it was worth far more than he could ever pay for it. Even with the fifty thousand dollars I'd arbitrarily given him via Walter Lawrence and Buck Henry, he still came up

49

short. That could mean only one thing. He was lying about the Plott. It was at best a world champion freak.

I shouldn't have been surprised. In trying to impress me in the past, Josh had told me some real whoppers. Still I was disappointed. It seemed he should have outgrown that by now.

I stopped at the Marathon service station. Joe Turner, Frieda Whitlock's boyfriend, came running out to wait on me. I was surprised to see him here. If I had been in his shoes, I would have been buried in the woods somewhere, as far away from everyone as possible. But then maybe no one had told him about Frieda.

"Afternoon, Mr. Ryland," he said. "What's the problem?"

I'd tried on several occasions to get him to call me Garth, but he refused. Either he was from the old school of manners, or I looked older than I felt.

"I don't know," I said. "Sometimes she doesn't want to turn over."

He nodded but didn't answer.

I studied him. I'd always had my doubts about Joe Turner. He was likeable enough, and hard working, holding down a job here the past two years, ever since he'd graduated from high school, while attending the automotive school in Madison. And he knew more about cars than I did any one single thing, including newspapers, so that put him one step ahead of me.

But there was somthing about him—maybe his slight, almost frail build, large ears and small nose, along with the drawl he'd picked up in Tennessee as a boy, that reminded me of Dopey, the Seventh Dwarf. True, Dopey was a mute, but if he would have talked, he'd have sounded exactly like Joe Turner. And once you got past the differential and the carburetor, you'd have exhausted his vocabulary.

Then, too, there was the hangdog look that was never far from Joe's eyes. It wasn't a conscious plea for sympathy, or something he was even aware of, but more a look of blind and eternal penance. It made Joe seem too eager to please, too anxious to serve anyone and everyone, and too damn polite for his own good.

"In any case I want you to check the battery," I said.

"Sure. Just bring her inside."

He raised the overhead door, and I drove Jessie inside the garage. He rolled out a large apparatus that looked like a cross between a robot and an electric chair. "Is all this necessary?" I asked.

Again he didn't answer. I wasn't sure he'd even heard.

He hooked Jessie up to the machine and took several readings. At any moment I expected her to start up and run him into the wall. I was disappointed when she didn't.

"There's nothing wrong with the battery," he said. "But it could be in your starter. I can check it if you like."

"How long will that take?"

"A few minutes or so. It depends on how busy I get."

Not much time, but more time than I wanted to spend in here today. "Maybe tomorrow."

He looked disappointed. "Whatever you say."

I reached for my wallet. "What do I owe you?"

"Nothing. This one's on the house. I'll get you next time."

"You sure Danny will agree?" Danny was the owner of the station.

"If he doesn't, he can take it out of my next paycheck."

I got in Jessie. The hangdog look was now in Joe's eyes. It made me uncomfortable, as it always did, like I should stay and listen when I really felt like going.

"Was there something else?" I asked.

"I'll bet you're wondering what I'm doing here today?"

"It did cross my mind."

51

"You heard that Frieda is dead?"

"I heard." I also had the feeling I was going to hear more.

"I didn't know what else to do, so I came here. It was better than staying home thinking about it."

"Don't you have a friend you could talk to?"

"I had one. Frieda . . ." Then it hit him all at once that she *was* dead. His knees buckled and he sagged against Jessie for support. He tried to cry, but couldn't. He could only wheeze and gasp, a man choking on grief.

I got out of Jessie and put an arm around him. That seemed to steady him, as gradually he got his breath back. Then he twisted away from me and stood alone in the center of the station, slightly bowed, like a rain-bent reed. Or in Joe's case, a life-bent reed.

He began to mumble, his voice brittle with shame and anger. "Her dad never did like me. He was always trying to bust us up. He thought I wasn't good enough for her. And him a pig farmer . . . I figured if I didn't look at the pig shit on him, he shouldn't look at the grease on me. But it didn't work out that way. Now Frieda's dead and we're busted up for good. I hope the old sonofabitch is happy!"

I put my hand on his shoulder. It was slender and strong, like spring steel. "Don't be too hard on him. Don't be too hard on yourself. You'll probably both need each other before this is over."

But he didn't agree. "I don't need him. He don't need me. Frieda was all we had in common. It's all we'll ever have."

"You're wrong, Joe. You share the same pain. It's the most common denominator there is."

But he wasn't listening. "I loved her," he said to somebody, not to me. "I knew I'd never keep her, not once she went off to school, but I loved her with all my heart. That's God's truth."

I got in Jessie and drove out of the station. Whoever's truth it was, I believed him.

52

* * *

Maynard Wilson, Walter Lawrence's former law parner, lived in an addition near the west edge of the park. The addition was once a field and woods where I'd roamed as a boy. A straw stack had sat just about where Maynard Wilson's limestone house did now. Wild strawberries used to grow in his back yard. I shot my first and only crow not twenty feet from where his wife Karen was now sitting in her lounge chair.

I knew it was Karen Wilson, even at a distance. Just as I knew it was Karen Wilson behind the wheel of her green Volvo from a block away; just as I knew it was Karen Wilson who ran along Gas Line Road nearly every morning and brought me up out of my chair and to my office window. Tall and willowy, with a wide sensuous mouth and curly honey-blond hair, she was the stuff of which fantasies are made. Though up until now I'd never met her.

I approached her lawn chair. She lay stretched out in the sun, drinking what appeared to be a gin and tonic. She wore a brown terry robe over what I hoped was a bathing suit, sunglasses, and the pink glow of a mild sunburn on her long and very lovely legs.

As her husband, Maynard, she too was a lawyer, though her practice was not in Oakalla. I thought it was in Montivideo, a small college town about twenty miles southeast of Oakalla.

She saw me coming and took off her sunglasses. She had bright hazel eyes and the assured look of someone who knew exactly what she wanted out of life. I guessed she was in her early thirties, about twenty-five years younger than her husband.

"Do I know you?" she asked.

I tried not to stand in her light. "I'm Garth Ryland, owner of the *Oakalla Reporter.*"

"Of course! We take the *Reporter.* You look a lot younger than your picture."

53

"That's because it was taken several years ago. It's aged since then."

She gave me the warmest smile I'd ever seen. It would have melted the heart of a snowman. Then she was embarrassed. Maybe it was the way I was looking at her. "May I get you something? A drink perhaps?"

The gin and tonic looked good, but I usually didn't start on them until July. "No thanks. I'm looking for Maynard. Is he around?"

"No. He's playing golf with friends. He won't be back until late this evening. I can have him call you if you like."

"It can wait. If I have time, I'll stop by his office in the morning."

"Is it something I can help you with?" she asked.

"What's that?" I was looking into her eyes, feeling very lonely at the moment.

"Is it something I can help you with?" she repeated.

"Probably not. You weren't that old at the time."

"At what time?"

"When Walter Lawrence disappeared from Oakalla."

The sun went behind a cloud. I thought I saw her shudder. "I was seventeen. Old enough . . . to remember him." She crossed her arms and hugged herself for warmth. I wished I had a jacket to loan her. More, I wished I had a free arm of my own. "I used to sit with his boys." She looked up at me and smiled. "Do you mind if we go inside? It's getting cool out here."

"I don't mind. But I'm sure the sun will be back out in a minute."

She stood and straightened her robe. She suddenly seemed self-conscious, too aware that I was there. "That's okay, I'm out of the mood now."

"Would you rather I leave?"

She thought a moment, then returned to me with another smile. "No. I rather like your company."

"You looked uncomfortable a moment ago. I thought it was because of me."

"You're very perceptive" was all she said.

I followed her onto the patio, then inside a sliding glass door into a combination kitchen and family room. It was a homey room, not in any way pretentious, and included a television, a stone fireplace, and a set of overstuffed furniture that looked just a few years younger than mine. Its walls were plasterboard, painted white and decorated with a few framed watercolors. A heavy black table and chairs sat in the kitchen, and a bouquet of daffodils and crocuses sat in a white vase on top of the table.

"Where did these come from?" I asked.

"The table and chairs? From San Francisco. Maynard and I bought them on our honeymoon and had them shipped here. They're from Mexico, I believe."

"I meant the flowers. I didn't see any growing outside."

She walked over to smell them. They seemed to revive her spirits. "From Hattie Peeler."

"Do you know Hattie?" I was surprised at that. They didn't seem to revolve in the same circle.

"For years. We're old friends. I take it you know her, too?" The thought evidently pleased her.

"I've known Hattie since I was ten. Though I wouldn't call us friends."

"What would you call it?"

I had to think about it. "Kin. Short for kindred spirits. She tolerates me. I put up with her. But there's an unspoken bond between us."

Again she smiled, once too often it seemed to me. But I couldn't find fault with it. Its warmth seemed a natural reflection of her soul. "Funny, I feel the same way about Hattie. But I wouldn't call us kin. We're more like . . ." She searched for the right word. "Fellow travellers. We both like to go our own way."

"Which way is that?"

"The road not taken."

"Emily Dickenson?"

"Robert Frost," she corrected. Then she gave me a curious look. It said I'm on to you, Buster. "But you already knew that, didn't you?"

"Maybe I did."

This time her smile was forced, a hostess smile— polite with lots of teeth, but no warmth. "Are you sure you won't have a drink?"

I thought it over. Dangerous ground, but I'd been there before. I thought I could walk the fence if I had to, though falling off might not be so bad. "Bourbon and ginger ale, if you have it."

"We do."

She fixed it for me, then poured some amaretto in a cordial glass for her. I sat on a stool at the counter that separated the family room from the kitchen. She sat across the counter from me. "So, how did you get interested in Walter Lawrence?" she asked.

"It's a long story."

Her eyes were playful, yet probing. "Meaning what? That you're not going to tell me?"

I'd heard she was a good lawyer. Now I thought I knew why. She disarmed you with her smile, while her eyes probed you for weakness. I didn't mind. I'd played the game before. But I'd rather have not played it with her.

"Meaning that it won't serve any purpose . . . *Counselor*," I had to add.

Her eyes never wavered. I'd scored a direct hit, and it didn't even phase her. If I didn't know it before, I knew it now. This wasn't Mary Sunshine across the counter from me.

"Was that really necessary?" she asked.

"Probably not. But I couldn't help myself."

"You know whom you remind me of?"

"No. Whom?"

"Jon Williams. He was my boyfriend all through grade school. Then he moved away in sixth grade and it broke my heart. Like you, he was always fighting—for something, against something, sometimes for the sheer joy of it. But, except for staying in for recess, he never got in any real trouble. Maybe because he was so bold about it. He was too honest to be anything else."

"That's me. Honest Garth."

"I used the wrong word. Upright would be as better one. He was only as honest as he had to be. But he couldn't escape his fundamental decency, his passion for what was right. I suspect neither can you."

I looked across the counter at her. It seemed the space had shrunk between us. "Thanks for the drink. I think it's time for me to go."

"You haven't finished," she observed. "Don't worry. I've said all I'm going to on the subject."

I left the glass where it was and stood. "That's not the point."

"Then what is the point?" she asked calmly.

"When I know, I'll tell you."

"You don't like people to get too close, do you?"

"No. I don't."

"You mind telling me why?"

"I always return the favor. It hurts when I have to let go."

"Who says you have to let go?"

"Sometimes you don't have a choice."

She nodded as if she understood. I left before I could change my mind.

Out of the hardness of her heart, Jessie started on the third try. I drove home. I didn't realize I was humming to myself, but Ruth did. She raised her brows, frowned, and said nothing.

6

The next morning I beat Ruth downstairs and had the coffee perking before she even opened both eyes. She sat heavily on her chair and held out her cup while I poured.

"And dressed even" was her only comment.

It was another beautiful day, blue and bright and calm, the kind of day when all things seem possible. I walked to my newspaper office along Gas Line Road, whistling as I did.

I didn't hear her coming until she was about two strides behind me. Then Karen Wilson, dressed in baggy blue running shorts and a white T-shirt, ran alongside me and slowed her pace to match mine. She didn't appear to be winded. I wondered why. She was making my breath come fast enough.

"Fancy meeting you here," she said.

"Yes, what a coincidence. Do you come by here often?" As if I didn't know.

"Almost every day that I'm in town."

"How come I never saw you before?"

"Maybe you weren't looking before," she answered.

I remembered the first time I had seen her—at a distance out the window of my office. With her long legs and graceful stride, I assumed she was much younger, probably a member of the high school track team, and not someone I should be looking at that way. What a joy it was when I learned the truth.

"Maybe I wasn't," I said.

"Well, I guess I'd better be running along."

"Don't hurry on my account."

"You could always join me."

"I tried it once. I didn't like it."

"Don't you like to sweat?" There was something condescending in her tone. Runners tended to look at non-runners the way non-smokers looked at smokers— not unlike the way the pharisees looked at the gentiles.

"I like to breathe better. I can't seem to do both at the same time."

"That means you're out of shape."

"For what?" I asked.

"For living . . . for life."

"I've managed so far."

She smiled in spite of herself. "Yes, I'm sure you have." She took off, then dropped back a step so I could catch up. "You didn't steal my sock last night, did you?"

"What sock is that?"

She pointed to her right ankle. "The one that matches this one."

Her right ankle was covered with a yellow sweat sock. Her left ankle was covered with a green one. "Maybe the drier ate it."

"No. I left them both in my shoes Saturday morning. That was the last time I ran."

"Where were your shoes?"

"On the patio drying out."

"Maybe the neighbor's dog dragged it off."

"I thought of that. Thanks."

She started running again, this time quickly putting distance between us. She was grace in action, a pure pleasure to watch. I had the feeling she'd be the same in bed. I smiled and shook my head. It was better I didn't think about it.

I went to my office and spent the next couple hours staring out the window, thinking about it. I could tell it was going to be one of those days.

I walked uptown to where Maynard Wilson had his law office above the drugstore. He was busy at the moment with a client, but his secretary, Norma Rothenberger, told me to have a seat, which I did.

The waiting room reminded me of the barber shops of my youth. It was spare, yet cozy. It had a black and white tile floor, white plaster walls, walnut wainscoting, a cherry hall tree in one corner, and a brass spittoon in the other. The magazines were at least a year old, but the cigarette butts were as new as today. All in all, a familiar place, and one that wore well over time.

Occasionally Norma Rothenberger would look up, sneak a glance at me, and go on with her typing. Close to sixty, Norma was a thin nervous woman with short grey hair, a dour face, and the harried look of someone who was always on her lunch hour. Whatever she did, she did with a flurry that made it seem like the most important thing in the world.

Perhaps to her it was. Unmarried, she poured all of her energy into the things and people around her. Some considered her a saint. Others, like Ruth, a few rungs lower. I didn't know what to think of her. She reminded me of my Aunt Bessie, who also had never married. Taken in small doses she was fine. Any more than that, and her Aunt Bessieisms drove you straight up the wall and out the window looking for your own space.

Maynard Wilson's client came out of his office, and I went in. We shook hands and I sat down in an oak chair facing him across his desk. Tall and dark, he had thin black hair greying at the temples, a thin black mustache, a patrician face, and an erudite style. He reminded me of

60

David Niven, someone who could never play the fool, even if he tried.

I first met him at the Community Club when he was president, and I was the new kid in town, trying to do a story on Oakalla's civic affairs. He commanded the podium and ran the meeting in rapid-fire order. I left with the impression that one: Maynard Wilson was a very busy and important man. Two: He wanted everyone to know that.

In the six years I'd known him my impressions hadn't changed much. It seemed he always had a point to prove, whether a fine point of law or the best way to bake a turkey. He did know a lot about a lot of things, including human nature, and I would have liked to have tapped that knowledge. But I could never get close enough to him to even try.

Today was no exception. Already he seemed impatient with me, as he hurriedly leafed through some papers on his desk. "Am I keeping you from something?" I asked.

He didn't look up. "No. I need to file this brief tomorrow. I want to make sure it's in order."

"Then I'll try to be brief. No pun intended."

He looked up at me. He wasn't smiling. Nor was the look he gave me particularly friendly. When I thought about it, his handshake hadn't been friendly either, but stiff and hard, like an exclamation point. "What was that?"

"Nothing. I can see I'm wasting your time. If not, you're wasting mine."

"I didn't know yours was so valuable," he said.

"Only to me."

He held up his hand in a gesture of good will. "I'm sorry. I was rude. That's not like me."

"Maybe I bring out the worst in you."

"Maybe you do. Karen told me you stopped by last evening. She spoke of you in glowing terms. Outside of her father, I've never heard her speak so well of anyone. Most men bore her. Me included."

61

"That's not the impression she left with me."

He smiled. It wasn't a pleasant smile. "It's okay. Have your fling if you like. At this stage of her life Karen probably needs one. But be discreet, for God's sake. Or I'll kill you both."

"Maynard," I spoke slowly to make sure he understood, "I just met your wife yesterday. She didn't mention an affair. Neither did I. So give us both a little credit. I don't want to get shot over something I haven't even thought about." Or had thought about for that matter.

He thought it over and decided to back off. "Again my apology. I jumped to conclusions. Again that's not like me. Nor was the ninety-seven I shot yesterday afternoon."

The truth began to dawn. He'd had a bad round of golf, probably followed by a bad round at home. I knew from experience the combination was hard to beat—for ulcers, coronaries, and the common malaise. That's why I'd given up golf. And perhaps why I'd given up home. After so many bad rounds, you had to give up something.

"I shot a ninety-seven once. It was my best round."

He wasn't placated. "I usually shoot in the low eighties."

"We all have a bad round now and again."

He glared at me. "What's your business, please."

"Walter Lawrence is my business. How much money did he take with him when he disappeared?" If I knew the answer to that, it might answer some other things. "Was it fifty thousand or was it more than that?"

"I don't know."

"I thought you were his partner."

"I was. I still don't know. He took it from his personal account."

"Then who would probably know?"

"Probably Willard Coates, his accountant."

"Isn't Willard your accountant?"

"As a matter of fact, he is."

"Didn't you ever ask him?"

"I did. He wouldn't tell me. He won't tell you either. But you're welcome to try." He went back to reading his brief. Our business was over.

I let myself out of his office. I almost ran over Norma Rothenberger in the process. "Please wait a minute, Garth. I couldn't help but overhear."

"Overhear what?" I was prepared to deny anything and everything. Not that it would help any. In Oakalla gossip spread faster than prairie fire. And Norma was known to fan her share of the flames.

"That part about Walter Lawrence. Have you found him after all this time?"

"No."

"Harold says you have."

"Harold?"

"Harold Clark, my nephew. He says he found a skeleton in Phillipee's Pond. He says it could be Walter's." She seemed on the verge of tears.

"Clarkie talks too much. We don't know whose skeleton it is yet. We're still in the process of finding out."

"Then why the questions about Walter?"

"He's a possible candidate. I'm following every lead."

"And the money? Has it turned up, too?"

"No, it hasn't." I said. "But you don't by any chance know how much it was, do you?"

"No, I don't." She lowered her voice confidentially. "But I do know something else you might be interested in. This law office was in trouble until the day Walter died. Then it suddenly got well again. What does that sound like to you?"

"Are you saying that the money Walter took ended up in the company store?"

"I'm saying that's possible."

"Thanks, Norma. You've been a big help."

"Garth?" She stopped me at the door. "If it is Walter

that Harold found, you'll see that he gets a proper burial? You won't ship him off to some college somewhere?"

"I'm afraid that won't be up to me. His wife might have some say in the matter."

The news wasn't well received. Norma looked more worried than ever. "Of course. I'd forgotten."

I left feeling that I'd just seen the tip of the iceberg, that there was more to the Norma and Walter story than even I wanted to know.

Willard Coates lived in a small brown house in the south end of town near the railroad. He dealt in gold and silver and stamps and ginseng and anything else people were willing to sell or trade. His house was stuffed top to bottom with things he'd bought at flea markets, auctions, and yard sales, things he'd accumulated over the years that not even he knew the source of. I'd been in it several times to just talk and browse. It was almost as good as visiting a museum.

As usual, Willard was working on his books. He saw me through the screen door and waved me inside. He was sitting in a patch of sunlight with a pencil in his right hand and his left hand on his calculator. His desk was piled high with books and papers. Above it, taped to the yellow wallpaper, was a sign that read, "A clean desk is the sign of a sick mind." Judging by Willard's desk, his mind was in perfect order.

He laid his pencil down, leaned back in his chair, and looked at me. Willard wore gold wire-rim glasses, a green bow tie, a white shirt, black slacks, and green suspenders. I'd never seen him wear anything else.

"What's on your mind, Garth? Time is money, you know."

"I've heard that. For me, money is time, the only thing I've got worth spending."

"You bring your books to me, you'd have more. I can almost guarantee it."

"More time or more money?"

64

"Both."

"I don't doubt that, Willard. Maybe when I make my first million."

"We'll both be long dead and gone by then. You should give me a shot at it while it'll do some good."

"I'll think about it. How's that?"

"Like most things these days, not good enough. You can think about it all you want, talk yourself blue in the face, and even get people to agree with you, but until you act on it, you ain't done a damn thing. Just beat your gums and spun your wheels."

"I'll bring my books in to you two weeks from Friday. It'll take me that long to get them in order."

"Don't bother. That's what you're paying me for. Now if you're through, I'm busy."

I didn't know how to tell him that I hadn't even started. "Before I go, I need some information from you."

"If you're worried about my rates, they're posted on the door. Right above the no-smoking sign."

"It's about Walter Lawrence."

He'd picked up his pencil and gone back to work. "What about him?"

"How much money did he take with him when he disappeared?"

"Can't tell you."

"Why not?"

"Policy."

"Whose?"

"My own."

I respected that, so I asked. "Can you tell me this much . . ."

"No."

"You didn't let me finish."

He looked up at me. There was humor in his grey eyes. "No need," he said. "You were about to play twenty questions with me. I said no once. That's what I meant. You'll be time ahead if you take it and go."

I took him at his word and left.

I walked up Perrin Street, then east along Jackson Street. I met Rupert coming from the east in his patrol car. He pulled off the road and stopped. I walked around to his side of the car.

"How goes your investigation?" he asked.

"It goes. How about yours?"

He leaned out the window and spat on the pavement. "I hear you were talking to Joe Turner yesterday."

"I wasn't talking to him. He was talking to me. I just stopped by to see about Jessie."

"I just brought it up," he said. "I wasn't asking for an explanation."

"Then what did you want?"

He spat again. This time the whole wad came out and splattered on the highway. "Do you think Joe's guilty?"

"Of what?"

"Killing Frieda."

"I don't know. I haven't given it much thought."

"Harvey Whitlock does. He's said as much."

"To you?"

"To me and several other people. He's wondering out loud why Joe Turner is still running loose."

"What are Harvey's reasons?" I asked.

"Joe was intent on marrying Frieda and keeping her here in Oakalla. He'd half talked her into it until she got that scholarship last Wednesday. Then she started thinking about going on to school again."

"What scholarship?"

"It's the one the local D.A.R. gives to the outstanding senior girl. Moneywise, it's not too much, but there's a lot of prestige that goes with it."

"And obligation?"

"That too."

"So to keep from losing her, Joe killed her?"

"That's what Harvey says."

"What do you say?" I asked.

"I say there's more hurt than sense to that argument. On the other hand, Joe's story doesn't hold much water either."

"What exactly is his story?"

"The same as before. He was working at the Marathon. Somebody called him away to give them a jump. By the time he got back, school had let out and Frieda was missing."

"Did anybody see him take the call?"

"Sniffy Smith did. But you already knew that."

I asked him if Sniffy had also told Rupert that he saw Joe Turner go south before he went north.

Rupert looked surprised and more than a little put out. "When did he tell you that?"

"Saturday."

"And you didn't tell me?"

"You didn't ask."

Rupert shook his head in anger. "How in the hell is it that you can come up with all the right answers and I can't? And you're not even trying."

"I wouldn't say that."

"You *are* trying, after I told you not to?"

"No. But sometimes I'm in the right place at the right time with the right question. I'd rather ask them for you, but you won't let me. So I ask them for myself. I *have* to know, Rupert, even if I don't act on it."

"I guess there's no harm in that. Besides, I don't see how I can stop you, short of cutting out your tongue."

"You could always throw me in jail."

"You'd still have Ruth on the outside."

"Plus all her relatives." Ruth and her relatives had a communications network that was second to none.

He sighed heavily and sat staring through his windshield at the cloudless blue sky. "You're right."

"Stay in touch." I started to move on.

"Garth . . ." He stopped and thought about it. He

wanted to choose his words carefully. "Stay out of Mitchell's Woods."

"Why?"

"Just stay out of there."

"Why?" I repeated. "What's in there to fear?"

He shook his head. He wouldn't tell me.

"Rupert, I think it's time to level with me. We're not the only ones involved."

"Then tell your readers to stay out of Mitchell's Woods, too."

"You know what that would do."

"Yes, I know. We'd have an army of them in there before nightfall. Half of them shot before morning. I don't want that to happen anymore than you do."

"Then why won't you tell me what's going on?"

"Because I promised myself I wouldn't."

"Why not?"

"Call it an old man's pride if you want, knowing he can still cut the mustard after all these years. I don't want to have to depend on you, Garth. I have been lately."

"I don't mind."

"I do." He put his car in gear and started to drive away.

"The straw!" I yelled after him.

"What straw?" He stopped the car.

"The one I found in Frieda's hair. Did you find out where it came from?"

"Not yet. But I'm working on it."

I watched him drive away. I didn't like the feeling that crept into my guts and lodged there. It said that with or without my help, Rupert was headed for trouble.

7

Maxine Lawrence lived in the last house on the north side of the road along east Jackson Street. It was a white house with green shutters and a cedar shingle roof that looked new. Surrounding the house on two sides, the north and the east, was a corn field, though this year's corn wasn't up yet. To the south was Jackson Street and to the west Minnie Linklighter's. And to the southeast across Jackson Street was a rambling two-story house sadly in need of repairs.

I remembered the house well. One of my favorite trees, a European white birch, used to grow in its front yard. I thought I remembered Karen Wilson, too. She was tall and skinny and used to throw gravel at me as I rode by on my bike. It was either she or one of her sisters. As I recalled, there were five of them, stairsteps, each one meaner than the next. And poor. Or so it seemed to me at the time. Their dresses always looked threadbare, and about two sizes too short.

I saw the mailman stop, leave something in Maxine Lawrence's mailbox, and drive on. Before he got to the next house, Maxine Lawrence hurried out the door and went for the mailbox, like a fly to a picnic. She had the mail

69

in her hands and was headed back toward the house before I could catch up to her.

"Maxine?"

She whirled around to face me. As she did, she stuffed a letter inside her blouse. "Goodness! You gave me a start!"

Maxine Lawrence was a pretty woman. She had high cheekbones, a small full mouth, and a small turned-up nose that she wrinkled at me like Bugs Bunny. But she carried about thirty extra pounds that rounded her body and made her look more jolly than sensuous.

I smiled at her. I liked Maxine Lawrence, especially her energy, the way she charged into things and back out again, the way she'd just come down the steps. She reminded me of someone who'd never stopped believing in Santa Claus.

"I'm sorry," I said. "For a minute there I thought you were going to get away from me."

"No chance of that." Her smile came easily. "Here is about as far as I ever get." Or want to get, her eyes seemed to say.

"It's a pretty place," I said. "It looks like you've had some work done recently."

"Just a new roof and paint job. And that new satellite dish in the backyard if you're counting." She was sizing me up, trying to guess my mission. "So what's on you mind, Garth? Another marijuana survey?"

"Not today. But I do have a question for you."

"Only one? That shouldn't be too hard."

"How much money did your husband, Walter, have on him the day he disappeared?"

She didn't even have to think about it. "Fifty thousand dollars, plus pocket change, if you want to count that. Our life savings."

"I heard that's what it was."

"I guess you heard right." She clenched her fists, as her face reddened. It was the first time I'd ever seen her angry. "I've never forgiven him for that. Not for leaving me that way with three boys to raise. Me, who only knew how to keep house and sack groceries. And make babies. I guess I have to count that, too. It was hard, let me tell you. But I helped put the boys through school and they've done well since. I've got two engineers and one dentist in the family. No lawyers, though. Walter will be sorry about that."

She talked as if he were away on a business trip and might be home any minute now. "You don't sound bitter," I said. "At least not as bitter as I would have been."

"You can't grow sweet williams with bitter seed," she answered. "I figured since that's the way it was, that's the way it'd have to be. No sense going on about it, to the boys especially. They thought the world of Walter. No point in trying to change their minds."

"You sound like you might still care for him, too."

"I do . . . did . . . whatever. Walter wasn't a strong man, but a likable one. All his sins were those of the flesh. *Women*," she said more pointedly. "He couldn't stay away from them. Old ones, young ones, blue ones, green ones, they were all the same to Walter. He thought he had to have them all. Maybe if I'd been smarter, I could've figured out a way to stop it. But I wasn't. Finished high school. That's as far as I ever got. Married Walter two weeks later and that was that. Put him through school just like I did the boys. Me with no education and them with all of it, and I'm the one that paid the bills. But a bargain is a bargain, and since I loved Walter and wasn't looking to change horses in the middle of the stream, I stuck by him. Would today, if he'd come home. But he hasn't."

"Do you have any idea what happened to him?"

"I did at first. But it didn't pan out."

"What was that?"

"I thought he ran off with someone. I could see it coming from ten miles back. But it never happened."

71

"How do you know?"

"Easy. She's still here."

"Do you mind telling me who she is?"

"I don't mind. But she might. So I won't."

"Not even a hint?"

"From what I know of you, a hint might be too much."

"Thanks, Maxine. You've been a big help."

I started home, then turned to watch her go up the steps. Already the letter was out from under her blouse and in her hand. I would have given a lot to know what was in it.

At home Ruth was eating a sandwich and watching television.

"I didn't expect you for lunch," she said.

"I didn't come for lunch."

"So what's the occasion?"

"Maxine Lawrence."

"What about her?"

"What do you know about her?" I asked.

"Enough. What do you want to know about her?"

"She said she helped put her three sons through college on money she made as a grocery sacker. Is that true?"

"Not quite. She also cleaned houses in her spare time. And delivered newspapers. She also signed up to fight forest fires and wrestle bears, but they wouldn't let her. Said she was too old."

"That's okay. I get the picture." I changed the subject. "What about Walter Lawrence? Did he make the rounds like she says he did?"

"Let's put it this way, if you were alive and female, Walter Lawrence was interested."

"Any special girlfriends that you know of?"

"Rita Henry. But you already know about her."

"Anyone else?"

"Quiet. I'm thinking." She pounded her forehead

72

with her fist. "It seems I heard rumors, but I forget who it was."

"What about Norma Rothenberger?"

"What about her?"

"She's alive and female."

"Right on one count. But her wick burned out a long time ago. I can't even imagine Walter Lawrence being interested in her."

"She seems to be interested in him."

"Maybe so. Stranger things have happened." She took a bite of her sandwich and washed it down with a drink of milk. "But I'll say this. If he was interested in Norma, it's two to one he was playing some angle. Though don't ask me what."

"Thanks, Ruth. I'm on my way to work."

"There's summer sausage in the refrigerator if you want."

"No, thanks. I'll eat at the Corner."

I'd almost made it to the door when the phone rang. I went back to answer it. "Garth here."

"Garth! I was afraid I'd miss you."

"Who's this?"

"Karen Wilson. Don't tell me you've forgotten me already."

"It doesn't hurt to try."

"What's that supposed to mean?"

"I'd forgotten you were married. Or conveniently ignored it. Your husband reminded me this morning."

"Don't pay any attention to that," she said lightly. "Maynard's always a bear in the morning, a pussycat by afternoon."

"And a werewolf by night?" I couldn't help adding.

"How'd you guess?"

"Let's just forget it, huh? While we're both ahead." And alive.

"Who's ahead? I haven't even gotten to know you yet. I'd at least like to know what I'm missing."

I sighed and looked at the ceiling. No help there. Life was a lot simpler without a woman in it. Mine anyway. What the hell would it be with two of them? "You might have a point."

"I thought I did. So why don't you have a drink with me tonight, say around six?"

"Where?"

"Montivideo. I'm staying over tonight."

"You have an apartment there?"

"Yes. How'd you guess?"

"Kidneys."

"I'm sure. Will you be there?"

"That depends. Where are we having our drinks?"

"Where would you like to have our drink?"

"A neutral corner. Say a quiet bar with good food."

"I know just the place. Are you familiar with Montivideo?"

"Somewhat."

"The name of it is Clancy's Bar. Turn left just after you cross the railroad track. It's about a block."

"I think I can find it. Thanks."

"Don't be late" were her parting words.

I hung up and said to Ruth, "I won't be home for supper."

"I heard."

That wasn't all she heard either. She had that look on her face, the one my mother used to get when I'd step out of line. The one that said, "Son, you're a skunk, but I love you anyway."

"What should I have done?" I asked.

"You could have said no."

"It sometimes gets lonely alone."

She nodded. "I know."

I went to the Corner Bar and Grill, ate a beef manhattan with macaroni salad on the side, and drank a glass of iced tea. From there I went to my office and spent the afternoon alternately writing and doodling on my

74

desk. On several occasions I picked up the phone to tell Karen I wasn't coming, only to put it down again.

It wasn't a clear choice. Nothing had to happen, that was true. We could both drink our drinks, have some quiet conversation, and go our separate ways. But was that what I really wanted to happen, when she had her own apartment nearby and might want to share it for the night? Christopher Robin's words came back to me. "Silly Old Bear," of course it wasn't.

8

At five-fifteen I walked home, got in Jessie, and drove toward Montivideo. Tonight Jessie started on the first try. She sometimes did that to confuse me.

It was my favorite time to drive through the country. Though still high in the western sky, with at least three more hours of daylight to go, the sun had started to soften, sending out long rays and creating long shadows that draped the road with the coolness of evening.

A half-grown rabbit popped out of the weeds, hopped alongside of Jessie, then ducked back into the weeds again. A covey of quail ran across the road in single file ahead of me. Two crows routed a redtail hawk from a telephone pole and chased it into a woods. A newborn calf wobbled stiff-legged through one of the greenest pastures I'd ever seen, then stopped beside its grazing mother to nurse. All within the space of a country mile.

I came into Montivideo, crossed the railroad track, and turned left. A block later I found Clancy's Bar and parked in front of it. Karen was already there. She got out of her Volvo and walked toward me. She wore a tan suit, a light blue blouse open at the collar, gold earrings the size of basketball hoops, and a smile that made me feel welcome.

We went into Clancy's. I saw several heads turn in our direction as we did. I knew they weren't looking at me. We found a table, and I held her chair for her as she sat down. How long had it been since I'd done that? Before Diana even. Back in the dark ages.

I looked around the room. The walls had been finished with old barn siding that still had some of the nails left in them, along with termite trails, wasp nests, and bits of harness the boards had gathered over the years. The walls had also been decorated with the tools and metal advertising signs of years gone by. All of which made me wonder what my generation would hang on its walls to celebrate its past—if plastic cups and microchips would evoke the same nostalgia?

"You come here often?" I asked.

"Not often," she answered. "Occasionally with clients."

"I like it," I said.

"So do I," she answered. "But by midnight I won't."

I knew what she meant. By midnight, when you looked through the smoke and patter, past the band and the glassy-eyed drunks, into the heart of loneliness itself, all bars looked and felt the same—like the day after Christmas.

The bartender came to our table, and Karen ordered some Chablis, while I ordered a Manhattan up. The bartender soon brought our drinks. I tasted the Manhattan. It was just right. I raised my glass in appreciation. The bartender smiled and went back to her bar.

"So how did your day go?" she asked.

"Not bad. How about yours?"

"I've had better. I spent too much time thinking about you."

I took another drink. Already I could feel the glow. Or maybe it was the company I was keeping. "Same here."

"It's funny, isn't it, how we've been practically neighbors all this time and never met? Now when we do, it's like we've known each other all our lives. At least that's the way it is for me."

"We *have* known each other all of our lives," I said. "You used to throw gravel at me when I rode by on my bicycle."

Her smile widened. "I did not!"

"It was either you or one of your sisters. Talk about kids today. I never went by your house without the flaps down and the tires smoking. Even then I still got hit sometimes."

"It must've been my sisters." But the twist in her smile said it wasn't. "What were you doing in our neighborhood anyway?"

"I used to ride by there on my way to Hattie Peeler's, or sometimes on my way to Phillipee's Pond."

She gave me a strange look. I couldn't decipher it. "I didn't know you were from Oakalla."

"I'm not. My Grandmother Ryland had a farm a couple of miles northwest of town. She still does, only I own it now. I used to spend a lot of time with her. When I'd get bored on the farm, I'd ride into town. I usually found something to do."

"I see." Whatever she saw, she didn't sound enthused.

"Did I say something wrong?"

She looked wistful as she said, "When I ran out of things to do, the only place for me to go was into my room, into a book or magazine. Or inside my head. For a time I had the Morgue, but then it burned down."

"The Morgue?"

"It was an old building just down the alley from our house. I don't know who owned it. It was vacant all the time I knew it. But on a rainy summer day, it seemed the only place on earth to be."

"Why did you call it the Morgue?"

78

"My sisters named it that. At one time it belonged to a doctor or veterinarian. At least we found a lot of empty pill boxes and other stuff like that lying around. I think we even found a syringe once. That's when my sisters started calling it the Morgue. Either then or when we found the dead cat under the floor."

"Describe it for me."

"The cat?"

"No. The Morgue."

Her eyes glistened as she did. "Well, for one thing it had this peculiar smell to it, even before the cat died. It was sort of a dead smell. You know—thick and sweet—and . . ."

"Sticky?"

"That's it! The kind that clings to you and won't let go. Then there was a stairs. A rickety wooden stairs with no railing on either side, so you never knew when it might come tumbling down with you. And the loft. That's where all the pill boxes were. It had only one window, which faced the south. That's where I used to like to sit and watch the rain." She cocked her head and thought about it some more. "What else? The floor. Did I tell you about that? The boards were all loose and you could see the ground between them. I was always afraid I'd get my foot caught between two of them and then not be able to get it out again. I almost did once. I left my shoe there as it was."

"It sounds like a good place to stay out of," I said.

"It was. I guess that's why it fascinated me. I always felt daring when I went in there. It was something not even most boys would do. That and the fact it was my own private place. If I wanted to be alone, to just sit and think, I could always go there."

"And dream?"

She gave me a gentle smile. "That, too. I'll never forget the night it burned down. I felt betrayed, like my

79

best friend had died. It made both me and my world seem a lot smaller."

"It sounds like we have a lot in common," I said.

She again gave me a look I couldn't decipher. It might have been respect. It might have been affection. Then, too, she could have been laughing at me. "It does at that."

We finished our drinks and ordered the house special, which was a breaded tenderloin with everything. The bartender should have brought them to us in a wheelbarrow. Karen nearly fell out of her chair laughing while watching me eat mine. Never a delicate eater to begin with, I ended up wearing most of it.

"That was fun," I said when I finished, dropping my tenth napkin on my plate. "What's for dessert?"

"They have a fudge cake that's out of this world. Or . . ." Her hazel eyes were bright and bold.

"Or what?"

"We can have something at my place."

I didn't have to think it over. "Let's have something at your place."

Again her curious look. "I was hoping you'd say that."

We'd started to get up when we saw the bartender approaching. "Are you Karen Wilson?" she asked.

"I am," Karen said.

"Phone call for you."

I sat back down while Karen followed the bartender behind the bar to where the phone was. I saw Karen nod a couple times, as the smile left her face. I felt myself slowly sinking into my chair. It all began to make sense now. I'd been set up. The timing was too perfect for anything else. I didn't know why, but I'd been had—from her phone call this afternoon until now. And it hurt like hell.

What hurt even more was that I'd gone running off to Montivideo to see Karen Wilson when I should have been back in Oakalla tending to business. Frieda Whitlock was dead. Walter Lawrence was missing. And Rupert was headed for trouble. While here I sat with a Manhattan on the brain and a goofy smile on my face, playing the fool. But then I'd had a lot of practice.

Karen returned to the table. She didn't sit down. "I'm sorry, Garth," she said. "I have to go."

"Trouble?"

"Yes, but none I can't handle. One of my clients. I'll tell you about it later."

"When later?"

"I'll let you know."

I gave her a hard look. "I'm sorry it didn't work out."

"So am I." She was in a hurry. She didn't want to hear this.

"I didn't mean us. I mean your little diversion, if that's what it was. But at least you gave it the old college try."

"I don't know what you're talking about."

"That's okay. I'm a big boy now. I knew what I was getting into. But every time you bend the rules, you pay for it, one way or another. I should have learned that by now. I haven't."

She was suddenly angry. "So what does that make me?"

"Nothing. You're married. That's all. And I'm supposed to be in love with someone else. Put the blame on both of us."

She gestured helplessly and left. I had half a mind to follow her, but instead I stayed for another round. I shouldn't have. Clancy's didn't wait until midnight to turn into a pumpkin.

I didn't see too much on the drive home. I was too busy recounting the mistakes of a lifetime. It seemed I should be getting smarter as I got older. It worked for everybody else. I wondered why it didn't for me?

I rounded a curve and met a car. It looked at first like a Volkswagen. Perhaps Ruth was coming after me, to save me from myself. I smiled. She was a day late and a dollar short.

81

But it wasn't Ruth. This was a green Volvo and looked very much like the one I'd seen parked in front of Clancy's Bar earlier this evening. But it had two people in it. I knew the legal profession was changing. But when did it start providing taxi service?

By the time I got turned around, the Volvo was long gone. By the time I caught up to it, it was parked outside an apartment. I watched a light go on inside and left. I figured I'd already had enough for one evening.

9

The next morning at breakfast Ruth tried hard not to say "I told you so." But she didn't succeed.

"Okay, you were right and I was wrong," I said. "You don't have to kick me while I'm down."

"There's no right and wrong involved," she answered. "There's smart and unsmart. For a smart man, you do some of the stupidest things I know of."

"True, but I work at it."

"You'll get no arguments there."

The phone rang. I hoped it would give me an excuse to leave. "Garth, Rupert here. Your side of the street just warmed up."

"What do you mean?"

"Last evening somebody stole the skull from Doc Airhart. He tried to call you, but nobody was home."

"What time last evening?"

"Between eight and nine. Right about dusk."

About the time I met Karen Wilson driving back to Montivideo. "He have any idea who took it?"

"You'll have to ask him. He was too steamed up to talk to me about it."

"You went over there?" I asked.

"No."

"Why not?"

"I had other fish to try." He paused, then said. "You'd be surprised how many stars there are in the sky. I'd almost forgotten."

"Come again?"

"Never mind." He hung up.

I stopped by the Marathon on the way to Doc Airhart's. Danny was out on the drive, directing a gasoline tanker around the pumps in preparation for a fill up. Sniffy Smith sat on his stool by the window watching the proceedings. He looked small and sad sitting there at attention, like an old groundhog who could still smell the clover growing the next field over, but could no longer get there.

"Morning, Garth," Sniffy said.

"Morning, Sniffy. What's new?"

"Not much. I was hoping you could tell me."

"About what?"

"Frieda Whitlock."

"You know as much as I do."

"Do you think Joe did it? Everybody else in town seems to."

"Sheriff Roberts doesn't," I said, trying to cheer him up.

"Then he's the only one. Him and me and maybe Danny. If it was the old days, he'd been lynched by now. Especially the way Harvey Whitlock's been going about him. Calling him a murderer and worse. No wonder Joe's afraid to show his face around town."

"Where's Joe now?"

"Home, I guess. That's where I'd be."

"Why isn't he in school?"

"His school ended for the summer a couple of weeks ago. He won't go back before September."

"What about last Thursday? Was he off then?"

"Until one o'clock. That's when he came to work."

I filed that away for future reference. "Were you here last night, Sniffy?"

84

"Until closing. I'm usually up at the Corner playing cards, but the guys up there were bad-mouthing Joe. I wanted no part of that."

"Joe hasn't by any chance told you where he went last Thursday when he left here?"

"No, he hasn't."

"But he did go south before he went north?"

"No. He left here on the run and headed north right away."

I studied him. He wouldn't look at me. "That's not what you told me Saturday."

"Well, that's the way it was. I remember now."

"You might have to swear to that in court."

He turned to face me. He looked like a cornered old groundhog now, very capable of defending himself. "If it comes to that, I will. I told Sheriff Roberts that, too."

"When was that?"

"Last evening when he stopped by here."

"Did you happen to see which way Sheriff Roberts went from here?"

"North. Up Fair Haven Road."

"What time was that?"

"Along about dark. He had his headlights on."

"Was he alone in the car?"

"No, he wasn't. Fred Pierson was with him."

"What was Fred doing with him?"

"Getting a ride home I guess. Fred's jeep had broke down and Danny was in the process of putting a new fuel pump on it. You know how things are around here at night. For every minute inside you spend fifteen on the drive. I guess Fred got tired of waiting for it."

"Where is the jeep now?"

"Gone. I guess Fred came back early this morning and picked it up. It was gone when I got here."

"Thanks, Sniffy."

I left the Marathon and walked to Doc Airhart's. He was outside, still at work pulling the weeds from around his roses. At the moment he had a thorn in his thumb and a scowl on his face.

"Don't you ever stay home?" he asked, picking at the thorn. "I nearly wore the phone out last night, trying to get hold of you."

"I had a date." I said.

"Hell of a time to have a date. What with the town falling down about you." He stuck his thumb out at me. "Here. See what you can do about this. I can't seem to get my fingers to work right."

I found the thorn and pulled it out, along with a bead of blood Doc wiped on his pants.

"Thanks," he said.

"You're welcome."

He went back to weeding. "I suppose you're here about the skull," he said. "But I can't help you. I don't know who took it."

"When did you discover it was missing?"

"When I heard my back door slam. I was out front watering my pansies at the time. I beat it around there, thinking it was the neighbor kids playing a trick on me, like we do on each other, when I saw somebody, a woman it looked like, leaving my yard and heading east. I took off after her with the hose in my hand. Thought maybe I'd cool her down a little."

"But you never caught her?"

He never cracked a smile, but his blue eyes twinkled at me. "Might have, if I hadn't run out of hose."

"That would be a problem."

"It's a fact."

"No idea at all who she was?"

"No. It was light enough to see her outline, but too dark to make out her features. She looked like a woman. That's all I know."

"What would somebody want with that skull?" I thought out loud.

"Hard to tell," he answered. "But without it you're going to have a hard time proving anything."

"Who besides us knew it was here?"

"If it's like everything else that goes on in this town,

86

who didn't? You probably told Ruth. I told Sniffy Smith. That's two more than it usually takes."

I nodded my agreement.

On the way to my office, I stopped to ask Doc's neighbors if they'd seen anyone entering or leaving his yard last night. No one had.

I spent the day working on this week's edition of the *Oakalla Reporter*. For once there was some hard local news to report, Frieda Whitlock's death in particular, and as distasteful as it was to me, my readers would want to read about it. My problem was that I didn't know where to start or end, or how much to say. Maybe I'd know by Thursday.

Instead, I decided to go through all the back issues of the *Reporter*, and its predecessor, *Freedom's Voice*, for the past seventeen years and see if I could profile Frieda Whitlock's life. I didn't know what I'd find. Maybe nothing. Maybe more than I could use. And in the end I didn't know what would be served. But too often in a case like this the person was lost, and only the brutal facts of her death remained. If I could help it, it wouldn't happen to Frieda.

By the end of the day I had the facts laid out, like boards and nails, ready to assemble. I knew when she was born, what she weighed at birth, the date of her christening and who was there. I knew her favorite flower, the violet, the name of her dog, Bowser, and her cat, Tugs, and that her "best friend in the whole wide world" at age seven was Jennie Garriott. I had pictures of her in pigtails and prom dresses, leading cheers and selling Girl Scout cookies, and my favorite, as the urchin Topsy in *Uncle Tom's Cabin*. I had almost everything one would want to know about Frieda Whitlock—except who killed her and why.

I stood, walked stiffly to the window, and looked outside. Each time the phone had rung, I'd picked it up on the first ring, hoping it was Karen calling to apologize. I was wrong each time. But that hadn't slowed my arm down any. In Skinner's classroom I would have been labeled a slow learner and given an extra volt or two to wake me up. By the time the day was over, I would've been wired directly to the socket.

I looked out the window. The sun was nearly down. It was about time to leave.

I walked to my desk and reread the notes I'd made. Frieda Whitlock wasn't Oakalla's only star. Walter and Maxine Lawrence's boys had done quite well for themselves, too. Their youngest was student council president and salutatorian of his high school class. The middle son excelled in science and mathematics and was a National Merit Scholar. The oldest was an all-star catcher for the American Legion and had gone to Madison on a basball scholarship.

I wondered, if and when he left home, Walter Lawrence had any idea his boys would turn out so well, and if it would have made any difference if he had? Probably not. Walter seemed a child in heart and mind, someone who followed his impulses wherever they took him without too much concern where that was. And his murder, if that's what it had been, probably came as a surprise to him. In that respect he and Frieda Whitlock were alike. Both were innocents in their own way, vulnerable to evil because neither would recognize it.

Perhaps life had been too good to each of them. Walter had his wife, Maxine, to raise his sons and pay his debts and dry his tears when things got too hard for him. Frieda had her family and friends, even the people of Oakalla themselves, to adore and look after her. When life is so good, why question it? Why indeed? I didn't, not until it bloodied my nose a few times.

At sunset I started home. I was still on Gas Line Road when I saw Rupert's patrol car approach from the south, cross Jackson Street, and head north out of town along Fair Haven Road. By then I knew where he was going and why. I wished he weren't going alone. More, I wished he weren't going at all.

10

It was a restless night, filled with bad dreams, bad vibes, and bad thoughts. I ended it sometime before dawn and went downstairs and put on a pot of coffee, and waited for the sun to rise. When it finally did, the sky went from ash to red to blood orange.

I went to my office and worked throughout the morning organizing the material I'd found yesterday. Occasionally I'd glance out the window to look at the sky. To its credit, the sun was hard at work, clearing away a patch of blue, only to have the clouds fill it again. The end result was that by afternoon the sun was cloaked in a milky haze, and the air had begun to stick to everything, including typewriters and door handles and the skin inside my shirt. I walked outside and took a long look at the western sky. No storm was in sight. But I was willing to bet we'd see one before morning.

I didn't plan to go to Frieda Whitlock's funeral, but when the time came, I just went. I took a seat beside Rupert. Frieda's grey metal coffin sat four rows away.

I pulled at the collar of my shirt, trying to loosen my tie. The air inside this small room was hot and dense, saturated with death and roses and grief. It clung tightly to all of us and wouldn't move.

I took a look around, at the faces of her parents, her friends, her sweetheart, saw nothing new. The death of a child always left those behind broken and bewildered. It was God's hardest question to answer. Why, God? Why?

And it was especially at these times that I was glad to be a mere mortal. Because I couldn't answer that question and didn't know anyone else who could either. I'd heard preachers try. I'd heard them speak of suffering and faith and salvation. They'd read the Twenty-third Psalm and spoke of the glory of the resurrection. They'd praised and promised and prayed, but in the end still laid it in God's lap. Said some things were beyond our understanding. I couldn't have agreed more.

After the funeral, the procession made its way to Fair Haven Cemetery. Fair Haven? I imagined it was at one time, when the brown brick church was new and the hills and dales surrounding it were speckled with the first green of spring. But it had changed through the years, as the church had closed and reopened, closed and re-opened, been boarded and unboarded and remodeled until I wasn't sure just who or what was there anymore. While at the same time the hills had become increasingly cluttered with fat tombstones.

Though even now, amidst the crypts and flags and plastic flowers, if you shut your eyes and listened to the wind in the trees and the tumbling brook beyond, you could catch a glimpse of what it once had been.

A brief graveside service began. I thought the pall that had followed us from the mortuary would lift once we were out here in the open. It didn't. If anything, it intensified.

The tension, too. I could see it on Harvey Whitlock's face. So could Rupert. He'd strategically moved between Harvey and Joe Turner. It was a good thing he did, because as soon as the service was over, Harvey went after Joe.

Rupert blocked his path. Harvey tried to step around him. Rupert blocked it again. Harvey stepped back and drew back his fist.

"Go ahead," Rupert said. "If you have to hit someone, hit me. I might hit back."

Meanwhile I'd gone after Joe Turner and led him out of the line of fire. He offered no resistance. It seemed the past few days had broken every fiber of his being.

"You need a ride back to town?" I asked.

"No. I've got my own car." He looked back to where Rupert and Harvey faced each other in a standoff. "He's right, you know. I should be locked up."

"Why. Are you guilty?"

He didn't answer right away. He was guilty of something, though I didn't know what. Then he looked beyond Rupert and Harvey at someone I couldn't see. Immediately I saw his resolve stiffen.

I asked again. "Are you guilty? Did you kill Frieda?"

"No." But he wasn't convincing.

"Then shut up about it. If Sheriff Roberts hadn't stuck his neck out for you, you'd be in jail right now. Don't undo what he's already done and make a fool out of both of you."

He was half listening to me, half looking for someone in the crowd of mourners. Finally he gave up looking and turned his full attention on me. "I don't plan to, Mr. Ryland. Where I come from, if a man goes out of his way for you, you go out of your way for him. It's the only friendship I know."

"Just don't go off half-cocked," I warned. "And keep a low profile. In other words, stay out of Harvey Whitlock's way."

"Don't worry, Mr. Ryland. He's the last man on earth I want to see right now."

"Who's the first?" I asked on impulse.

91

"In my own time . . . in my own way" was all he would say.

On my way to Jessie I saw Josh Henry standing alone in the graveyard. He wore jeans, a light-blue T-shirt with a pack of cigarettes in the pocket, and a pair of scuffed work shoes. He seemed to know that he wasn't dressed for a funeral and kept a respectful distance from everyone else.

"Afternoon, Josh," I said. "What brings you here?"

"Hi, Coach," he said with a smile. "You clean up pretty good. I didn't recognize you from a distance."

"It's my funeral suit," I said. "It's about the only place I ever wear it."

He walked with me toward Jessie. "I'm supposed to be at the school," he said. "But I figured it wouldn't hurt to take a few minutes off to pay my respects."

"What does your boss say about that?"

"Nothing much. I'm sort of my own boss. I pretty much come and go as I please. Have to. If something needs fixing and I don't have it there at school, I have to go after it or it doesn't get fixed."

"Sounds like the kind of job I ought to have."

"Hey, Coach, don't kid me. You like what you do."

"Most of the time," I said. "Not today."

He nodded like he understood.

"How well do you know Joe Turner?" I asked.

He shrugged. "I see him around town every once in a while. At the Marathon. Sometimes at school when he was there to pick up Frieda."

"Did you see him there last Thursday afternoon?"

"No. I don't remember if I did."

"Can you think of any reason why Joe might want to hurt Frieda, other than what Harvey Whitlock is saying?"

He looked away from me. "I wouldn't know nothing about that."

"Are you sure?"

His face reddened. He was either angry or embarrassed. "Joe never said one word to me about Frieda, or to

92

anybody else I know of. As far as he was concerned, she was nobody's business but his."

"But have you *heard* something?" I persisted.

"I heard something," he admitted. "Pictures that somebody had. Joe was talking to Danny about it up at the station. I didn't aim to, but I overheard them."

"What kind of pictures?" I asked.

"I don't know. But Joe seemed upset about them."

I thought I could guess what kind of pictures. "When was this, Josh?"

"First part of last week. Tuesday, I think, when I came in for a fill-up." He looked so serious I had to take him seriously. "But I wouldn't want you to say anything to Joe about it."

"Why's that?"

"I asked Frieda out once. I didn't know she was Joe's girl or I wouldn't of done it. He hasn't liked me since."

"Frieda was a little young for you, wasn't she?"

He hung his head. His thick blond hair billowed out as he did, making him look about fifteen. When I thought that he and Karen Wilson were contemporaries, it boggled my mind. Not even Henry Higgins could bridge the gulf between them.

"I guess I knew that," he said. "But sometimes it gets lonely, with no one there but me. Frieda was my neighbor. I'd known her all of her life. Otherwise, I wouldn't of asked her."

"Did you tell Joe that?"

"I tried. He didn't seem to want to listen. Like I said before, where Frieda was concerned the subject was closed. He didn't talk about her and didn't want no one else to either."

"Thanks, Josh. I imagine you'd better get back to work." Whether he thought he was his own boss or not, he wasn't. And sooner or later someone was bound to miss him.

He suddenly turned as sullen as the day. "That's just

93

what Grandpop would say. He never did let me think for myself."

Probably with good reason. "Do as you like, Josh. You're free, white, and twenty-one." Something Frieda Whitlock would never be.

I drove home, changed my clothes, and walked to the Marathon. Sniffy Smith was there on his stool watching the drive. But I didn't see Danny Palmer, the owner.

"Danny around?" I asked Sniffy.

"Nope. He just got a call to go pick up a car. He left in the wrecker not five minutes ago."

"Then who's in charge here?"

"I am. I'll pump the gas for them. If they need anything else, they can wait until Danny gets back."

"Where did Danny go?"

"He didn't say. He said he'd be back in about an hour."

Too long for me to wait. "Maybe you can help me, Sniffy. Did Joe Turner ever say anything to you about some photographs?"

"What kind of photograhs?"

"I was hoping you could tell me."

"No. He never said nothing to me about anything like that."

"Did he get a call here the first part of last week that seemed to upset him?"

A car slowed and appeared headed into the station. Sniffy breathed a sigh of relief when it drove on. "Monday or Tuesday he did. He wasn't himself the rest of the night."

"Do you remember which night? It's important."

He watched another car slow and turn the corner into Fair Haven Road. He smiled as it did. "I must be living right. What was your question again?"

"Which night did Joe get the phone call?"

"I told you, Monday or Tuesday."

"Can you come any closer than that?"

"Monday then. Because I wasn't here Tuesday. I was up at the Corner playing euchre."

That seemed to coincide with what Josh had told me. I didn't know why that came as a surprise. Probably because he was capable of making the whole thing up, just as he had about the Plott. "Thanks, Sniffy. I don't know what I'd do without you."

Normally that would have brought a smile. Today it didn't. "Did you get her buried?" he asked.

"We got her buried," I answered.

"Seems a damn shame. Pretty girl like that. "

"It is a damn shame."

He nodded and I left.

I spent the remainder of the afternoon working on the *Reporter*. I knew what I wanted to say about Frieda Whitlock's life, but I still couldn't write about her death. I told myself it was because I didn't yet have all the facts. But I knew it was more than that. Her death touched me in a profound way that went all the way back to my own childhood. It was as if, before she tasted her first bowl of real porridge, Goldilocks had been killed and eaten by the Three Bears.

The telephone was mercifully silent, so I didn't have to wonder each time who was on the other end. I thought about calling Diana to cheer me up, but lately our phone conversations, like our letters, had too many starts and stops, too many sighs and pauses, and too many words between the lines. I knew I'd feel worse, instead of better, after we finished talking. What I needed to do was to go see her and feel her reaffirm what we once had, but I wasn't sure just what that was any longer. Some days the world seemed too sad a place to keep on turning.

At six I left and walked to the Corner Bar and Grill for supper. Ruth wasn't home. Her bowling team had qualified for the playoffs, and tonight were the semifinals. I'd offered to go with her, but she said don't bother, that I made her nervous. To prove her point she brought out a worn score sheet. Her lowest game in the last five years, a one twenty-one, had come the only time I was in the audience. So much for moral support.

I glanced at the sky. The sun had finally gone under for good, and the sky now had a greenish cast, about the color of my face after I swallowed my first tobacco juice. To the west clouds rose slowly through the green, like black dough. Overhead, martins and swallows dipped and darted in a feeding frenzy brought on by the early twilight. People came to their windows and doorways to watch the sky. Everywhere was the feeling of apprehension, that something was going to happen.

The Corner Bar and Grill was nearly empty. Harvey Whitlock, Hiram the bartender, Mildred the cook, and I were the only ones in the place. Harvey sat at the bar with a glazed look on his face. It really didn't matter to him what the weather was, if the heavens opened and the house came tumbling down upon him. He might even have preferred it that way.

I took a seat beside him. I doubted I'd be welcome, but he looked like he needed somebody to talk to. He glanced at me and went on drinking his beer. As far as he was concerned, I wasn't there. Fine with me. I could keep my own counsel. Had for a long time now.

"There's a storm warning out," was the first thing Hiram said to me. "From now until midnight."

"Storm *watch* out," Harvey corrected him. "They ain't seen the storm yet."

"Whatever," Hiram replied. "How does it look out there?"

"Spooky," I said. "Like the end of the world."

"I've seen worse," Harvey said.

"So have I," I answered. "But not much."

He grunted in answer to that.

I ordered a shrimp basket and a tossed salad and a draft of Miller to drink along with it. Then I sat hunched at

96

the bar staring into the mirror. Tonight the fellow across from me looked his age. Maybe he'd look better tomorrow.

"You have any kids?" Harvey asked me.

"No." I'd had one and lost him. But that was a long time ago. It hardly hurt anymore.

"Then I'm probably talking to the wrong person."

"I don't see anyone else around."

"You can't know what I'm feeling. Nobody can."

"That won't stop me from listening."

Harvey sighed, picked up his glass, looked at it a moment, then set it down. "She was all I had. All I ever wanted. Now that she's gone there's a big black hole out there where my life used to be. There's nothing I want. I've done it all. Everything I wanted was for her."

"What about your wife? You might find a need there."

"She's young, Garth. She's got most of her life ahead of her, a lot of places she ain't been, a lot of things left to do she ain't tried yet. She feels Frieda's loss. In ways I never can. But there ain't a big X across her horizon like there is mine."

"You could always have another child."

"We could. But I might not live to see her grow up. What would be the point in that?"

"Someone once said, it's not the end, but the journey. You can't know how things are going to turn out. So you place your bet and spin the wheel and hopefully die with no regrets."

"When you lose your only child, that is the end. There's no wheel left to spin. Not for me anyway."

"Then I can't help you, Harvey."

"I never thought you could. But thanks for trying."

"Sure."

I drank my Miller, ate my supper, and went home. Harvey was still at the bar when I left. I had the feeling he'd be there until closing.

11

I sat in the dark watching the sky. So far we'd had one strong gust of wind and a sprinkle of rain, but nothing else. The phone rang.

"Garth, is that you?" It was Clarkie on the other end.

"It's me. What's up?"

"There's been a shooting."

"Where?"

"Maynard Wilson's."

It took me a minute to get my breath. "Anybody hurt?"

"I don't know. I'm on my way now."

"Does Sheriff Roberts know?"

"No. I can't get ahold of him. That's why I called you. Do you know where he is?"

I thought I did, but it wouldn't help us now. "No. I'll meet you at Maynard Wilson's."

I hung up and left. I didn't even try Jessie. By the time she decided whether she was going to run or not, I could already be there.

Clarkie beat me by a block. His siren was off, but his red light was flashing for all to see. Maynard Wilson sat on his patio in a lounge chair, holding a wet towel up to his right ear. In his burgundy slacks and yellow golf shirt, he looked as dapper as ever and more than a little embarrassed by all the attention. He was trying to tell Clarkie that everything was all right, that as former county prosecutor he knew what to do and could handle it from here. But Clarkie wasn't so easily persuaded. He didn't know for sure what to do, but he had a good idea of what Rupert would not do—and that was to let Maynard Wilson run the show.

I looked at the patio door. It had a single bullet hole through it. Evidently the shot had come from outside. I asked Maynard Wilson.

"Yes," he answered curtly. "I've already told Barney Fife here all about it. I was standing at the counter stirring a drink when I heard a shot and felt something sting my ear. I thought for a moment a bug had bitten me, until I reached up and felt the blood. Then I saw the bullet hole in the patio door."

"You say you heard a shot?" I asked.

"Yes, for the third time. Though I don't see what business that is of yours."

I took out my wallet and showed him the special deputy's badge that Rupert had once given me after an evening with Jack Daniels and friends. It appeared to be worth more than it actually was.

"Since when?" Maynard asked.

"For a long time now."

He shrugged. "You learn something new every day."

"Close or far away?" I asked.

"What was that?"

"The shot. Did it come from close or far away?"

"It's hard to say. The night's so still it could have come from farther away than it seemed."

"Did you jump?"

"What?"

"Did you jump when you heard the shot?"

It pained him to admit it. "Yes, I guess I did."

99

"Then it probably came from fairly close range. What did you do next?"

This hurt him even more. He hated me at that moment for making him admit it. "I hid behind the bar, waited a few minutes, then called Deputy Clark."

"A natural reaction," I said, trying to let him off the hook.

"Maybe for you," he answered. "Not for me."

I let that pass. I was busy counting the minutes to myself. Even pushing it, it was at least a half hour to Montivideo. And having driven there on several occasions, I knew you couldn't push it too hard. You could, but you'd likely end up in a ditch.

"How many minutes were you behind the bar?" I asked.

"Five at the most," he answered.

I looked at my trusty Timex. That meant the shooting occurred less than a half hour ago. "Is Karen home?" I asked.

"Do you see her?" he answered.

"Is she in Montivideo?"

"I assume she is, yes."

"Do you have her number?"

"I do, but I'll call her later myself, thank you."

"Later might be too late," I said.

"For what?" Then he smiled grimly as he caught on. "You don't trust anyone, do you?"

"No more than I have to."

"Wait until she hears this," he said almost gleefully. "That should rub the sleep from her eyes."

I didn't tell him my real reason for wanting to call. I wanted Karen to be there in Montivideo. I didn't want to have to suspect her. I'd had a hard enough day the way it was.

He gave me the number, and I called Montivideo. Karen answered on the third ring. She didn't sound out of breath.

"Karen?"

"Yes, who's this?"

"Garth Ryland."

"Garth!" she exclaimed. "I thought I'd never hear from you again."

"Funny, I was thinking the same thing."

"How did you get my number? It's unlisted, you know."

"No, I didn't know." I took a deep breath. However this came out, I was going to lose. But it was too late now. "There's been a shooting here at your house. Nothing serious. Maynard just lost the tip of his ear, that's all."

"What kind of shooting?"

"It wasn't suicide, if that's what you're asking. Someone took a shot at Maynard from outside. At least that's the way it looks from here."

There was dead silence on her end. When she did answer, there was no mistaking the sound of her voice. She was bitterly and deeply hurt. "And you think it was me, right?"

"Wrong. I hoped it wasn't you. That's why I called."

"Whoopee! Now your conscience is clear. Good night, Garth. Tell Maynard I'll call him later."

"Would you rather I hadn't called, and wondered?"

"I'd rather that you knew me well enough not to wonder."

"We never got that far, remember? A client got in the way."

"Damn you!" she said a fraction of a second before she hung up on me.

I felt the hairs on the back of my neck start to prickle. It meant someone was staring at me. I turned to see Maynard Wilson. I expected to see him wearing a smug smile. He wasn't. He looked tired and vulnerable, like an old politician who's just lost his first election.

"What did she have to say?" he asked.

"She said she'd call you later."

101

He nodded and walked away.

While Clarkie dug for the slug in the wall of the family room, I went around the neighborhood to see if anyone had seen who'd done the shooting. No one had, though most had heard the shot and agreed it came from close to the house.

When I returned, Clarkie held the slug in his hand and appeared to be studying it, so intently he didn't see me come in.

"Any ideas?" I asked.

His head jerked up. "About what?"

"Where that came from?"

"Not yet. I'll have to run it through my computer."

"How long will that take?"

"Not long, once I set up."

"Will you give me a ride first?"

"Sure. Where?"

"Home, for starters. I want to pick up a raincoat."

"Where to from there?"

"To look for Sheriff Roberts."

Clarkie stared straight ahead out the window of his patrol car. He was half willing and half afraid. "I knew you were going to say that. He's not going to like it."

"No. He probably won't."

We stopped in front of my house, and I went in and got my raincoat. On my way out the door I saw the storm in the southwest. It looked like a beaut.

"They just had a tornado touch down about fifty miles west of here," Clarkie said when I got in the car. "It's coming our way."

"Yeah, I saw it. How much of a touchdown?"

"They're not sure. They think it hit a trailer court."

"That's not good."

"No," he agreed.

Clarkie drove, while I showed him the way. He kept the radio on, listening for further weather bulletins. What he got was a lot of static and the occasional crackle of lightning. Finally in self-defense I reached over and turned the radio off.

I didn't need it to tell me where the storm was. All I had to do was to look out the window. It didn't seem to be moving, just growing larger and more intense. The lightning never stopped. Neither did the thunder, one continuous murmur, like the grumbling of a mute giant.

When we pulled into Fred Pierson's drive, Rupert's car was there, but Rupert wasn't. Neither was Fred Pierson, nor his coon dogs. Together or apart, they were all somewhere out in Mitchell's Woods.

"What do we do now?" Clarkie asked.

"We go looking for him."

Clarkie was staring at Mitchell's Woods. "In there?"

"In there."

"We'll never find him."

I opened the glove compartment and took out Clarkie's flashlight. "Probably not. But I'm going in anyway. You can stay here if you like."

He thought it over. "I hate the dark," he admitted. "And Mitchell's Woods is the darkest place I know. But I'd be more scared here alone than in there with you."

"Then let's go."

I led the way. I hadn't gone ten feet into the woods when I tangled with a greenbrier. I caught it squarely in the face and lost some flesh getting untangled. Then the mosquitoes found me. They were so thick I couldn't breathe without sucking them into my mouth and nose. Too many even to try to kill. The best I could do was to wave my arm in front of my face and try to keep them out of my eyes.

The storm had started to move. The lightning was closer, more vivid, the thunder coming in volleys that shook the ground under our feet. Mitchell's Woods began to close in around us, so tight and so thick it was hard to breathe, the woods scent so bold it seemed I could reach out and touch it. There was something else in the air, too,

103

something that hung poised, like the blade of a guillotine, over all of Mitchell's Woods. Something, for want of a better word, I called death.

Clarkie was about a yard behind me when we heard it. He froze in his tracks. I froze in mine. We stood there suspended, waiting for something to break the spell.

There are sounds, and there are sounds, but this sound squelched every living thing around it, crawled inside my skin, and stayed. It sounded like a bobcat's cry, wild and fierce and without mercy. But it wasn't a bobcat's cry. It was something else again, something practiced, controlled, and strangely human.

In the silence that followed, when even the storm seemed to pause, I could hear the yip-yip-yip of the coyote pack come from somewhere deeper in the woods. They seemed not to have heard the cry, or if they did, paid no attention.

I heard a shot, followed in rapid succession by two more. They sounded like pistol shots. They also sounded like a call for help.

That broke the spell.

I took off northeast and Clarkie followed as best he could. Every few feet I'd stop, hoping to hear more shots, but didn't. Keeping the storm directly behind me, I kept moving. Finally I heard a groan. Swinging my flashlight to the left, I saw Rupert sitting on the ground, leaning against a tree.

He smiled in recognition as I knelt beside him, but then his eyes flickered as he fought to stay conscious. He was smeared with blood from his face down to his belt. It was hard to tell in how many places he was bleeding.

One tear on his upper arm seemed the worst. Blood was pumping from it rather than seeping as from the others. I put direct pressure on it and held tight. I could feel his pulse in my hands.

Meanwhile Clarkie caught up to me. "Jesus Christ, what happened?" he asked.

"I don't know."

"What are we going to do?" Clarkie's voice shook as he spoke. He was about to lose it. So was I. But I didn't tell him that.

I took a deep breath and tried to get my mind to work. "I don't know," I repeated.

"It might come back."

"What might?"

He was looking down at Rupert. "Whatever did this."

"You're right. We've got to get him out of here."

But neither of us moved. I couldn't. My hands still covered Rupert's wound, holding back the blood. Clarkie was frozen with fear. It wasn't until the thunder boomed, shaking him to life, that he bent over and picked up the flashlight.

I waited until the bleeding slowed, then tightly wrapped Rupert's arm with my shirt. He was still conscious, but too weak even to talk.

Draping Rupert over my shoulder, I began to follow Clarkie through the woods. Clarkie didn't know where he was going, but with the storm approaching from the southwest, the direction we were heading, it was hard to get lost.

I stopped to examine Rupert. His eyes were closed. I leaned close to make sure. Yes. He was still breathing. I lifted him back to my shoulder. He felt unnaturally light, rough and dry like a cornstalk. I hoped he still had some blood left in him.

A wind sprang up and shook the tops of the trees, pelting us with leaves and small branches. In his haste to beat the storm, Clarkie grew careless and brushed a low-hanging limb. I caught it right in the face and it made the tears run. But at least it momentarily chased the mosquitoes away. Then they returned with vengeance, whirling around my head in an ever-thickening cloud until I could barely see. I yelled at Clarkie to slow down. He didn't hear me. By the time he missed me, I was already out of the woods.

The full force of the storm hit us on our way back to Oakalla. It rocked the car with wind and thunder and dropped a wall of rain in our path. Clarkie couldn't see to drive. I couldn't see to tell him where to turn. But somehow we made it.

Clarkie had called ahead and when we stopped outside the emergency room door, we were met by a nurse and the resident on duty. Both were young and competent. And caring. I felt better already.

Clarkie went to call the dispatcher, while I sat down on a red plastic chair in the waiting room. I saw the nurse come out of the room where Rupert was. She looked worried. I got up and intercepted her on the way to the desk.

"Problems?" I asked.

"None we can't handle." So be a good boy and go sit down.

"What kind of problems?" I persisted.

"Blood problems. We're out."

"How in the hell can you be out? This is a damned hospital!" I yelled at her.

"Look, I know how you feel. But your friend's not the only one who's had a rough night. A tornado tore up a trailer park west of here. Then there was an accident on I-90. Multi-car, lots of blood spilled. We sent them some of ours."

"But not all of it, for Christ's sake?"

"No. Not all of it. But all of our B-negative, which is what your friend needs."

"You don't recognize him, do you?"

"No. Should I?"

"My friend is Rupert Roberts, sheriff of this damned county. He's given his sweat and blood for the past eight years to keep it going and now you don't have a damned drop for him when he needs it. That's irony, but I'm not

106

buying it. You can use my blood, all you need short of killing me."

"It's not that simple. I said we need B-negative."

"Well, I'm O-negative. That's close enough."

"You're right. You'll do. Follow me, please."

She prepped me and wheeled me into the room where Rupert was. "How long before you get more blood?" I asked.

"It's already on its way."

"Good. I'd hate to make a career out of this."

As she inserted the needle and began to draw my blood, I had a crazy thought, one that made me smile in spite of myself. Rupert and I would now be blood brothers, just like Tonto and the Lone Ranger. My smile broke into a laugh. The nurse gave me a funny look. Ugh, Kemo Sabe, please don't die on me.

It was still storming when they wheeled me back into the waiting room. I got to ride as far as the red plastic chair, where I got up and immediately sat back down again.

As I sat watching the rain lash the windows, listening to the cannonlike volleys of thunder, I felt at a distance like I was somewhere else and this wasn't really happening. Life no longer had the urgency it'd had only a few minutes ago. I was becalmed, adrift and floating above the torrent, and very much at peace with one and all. I wondered if death was like this. If so, when the time came, it might be hard to resist.

12

I dozed off and on for the next few hours. Once I woke up sweating. The next time I awakened I was so cold my teeth were chattering. Someone must have heard me. The last time I opened my eyes, I was covered with a blanket.

I thought I remembered telling Clarkie to call Ruth and tell her where I was. I hoped he had. I knew he had when she walked into the waiting room, handed me a tray with my breakfast on it, and walked out again. She knew I wouldn't want any company. I waited best when I waited alone.

I tried to eat my breakfast, but I didn't have much luck. The juice kept burning my nose, and the toast kept catching in my throat. I tried not to think about what I was trying so hard not to think about. But it still kept coming up. It said my best friend might be dying and what would I do then? That if I thought it was hard to bury Frieda Whitlock, what would it be like to bury Rupert? My eyes burned as I looked from the tray to the day outside. Damn you, Diana! Where are you when I really need you? What in the hell is it all for if there's nobody there to catch your tears?

The nurse from last night came into the waiting room.

She looked tired and beaten. I was expecting the worst. "Sheriff Roberts would like to see you," she said.

I nodded numbly. No doubt some last words.

"He's out of danger," she said.

It took a moment for that to sink in. Then I shoved the tray aside, stood up, and hugged her. She felt stiff and awkward in my arms. Nothing like Diana.

"Thanks," I said.

She managed a smile. "To you, too. He owes his life to you."

I returned her smile. "Don't tell him that. He might change his mind about getting well."

I started to go into the room where I'd last seen Rupert. "He's not in there," she said. "Try two thirty-seven."

I waved and ran for the elevator.

In room two thirty-seven Rupert was lying in bed, looking out the window. He looked even worse than I remembered. What wasn't bandaged, which wasn't much, was purple and yellow and swollen. Even his eyes had a yellow tint to them. Out of danger? From what? I wondered.

He raised his head and turned slowly to look at me. It was a great effort.

"How do you feel?" I asked.

"About three sheets to the wind. Like I've been shot full of dope, which I probably have." Never a fast talker, he spoke even more deliberately than usual. His voice sounded like it was coming through a long tunnel.

"You look fine."

He tried to smile, but couldn't. His face was too swollen. "I'll bet."

"By tomorrow you'll probably be back to your old self again."

He laid his head back on his pillow. "That's good."

"Maybe you'd better rest. I can come back later."

109

He raised his arm in protest. "No. Pull up a chair. You need to hear this. Somebody does anyway."

I pulled up a chair. "Would it help if I asked the questions and you answered them?" I said.

He nodded.

"Where should I start?"

"With how many nights I was in Mitchell's Woods."

"Okay, how many nights were you in Mitchell's Woods?"

"Three."

"But nothing happened the first or second night?"

"No."

"What did you do differently the third night, if anything?"

"Borrowed a sock."

"From whom?"

"Betty Pierson."

"Betty Pierson is dead."

"I know that. Take my word for it."

"Why did you want one of her socks?"

"To lay a trail. I wanted to see . . . what was out there." He had to stop to rest.

"You thought that whatever it was might have deliberately trailed and killed her, instead of just happening upon her?"

He nodded.

"That's even worse."

He nodded again.

"So you laid a trail with her sock. Then what? Sat down with your back against a tree?"

"The biggest one I could find. Then took out my gun, cocked it, and rested it on my knee."

"But nothing happened?"

"No. I could hear the coyotes off in the distance. Then I thought I heard something following my trail, working its way toward me, but I never did see it."

"Had anything followed you the first two nights?"

110

"No."

"What happened next?"

"I looked up and saw the storm coming. I didn't want to be in the woods when it hit, so I started out. I never made it. He jumped me from behind before I knew he was there."

"A man?"

"No. A wolf. I guess it's a wolf. It's too big for a coyote."

"And there's only one of it?"

"Yes. Once he had me down, he went right for my throat. He'd have had it, too, if I'd let him."

"How did you finally get him off of you?"

He looked away, hiding the tears in his eyes. Instead of proving himself in Mitchell's Woods, he'd been humbled by it. That hurt both of us.

"I didn't," he said. "He was all teeth and fury. As much as I wanted to live, he wanted to kill me more. I'd just about reached my limit when something shrieked in the night. He left just like that."

"Do you remember what the shriek sounded like?"

"It made him stop. That's all I remember."

I wondered if it was the same one that Clarkie and I heard. "That's when you fired the shots?" I asked.

He nodded. "Without hope," he said, "of anyone ever hearing me."

"'To the Open Water,'" I said.

"What's that?"

"It's a short story about a man who goes duck hunting alone in winter. He feels that if he can just get to the open water where the ducks are, he can shoot one. He makes it to the open water, but in the process falls out of his small boat and can't get back in it. Gradually the weight of his clothes and the icy water pull him down, and he knows he's going to die. His last conscious act is to scream, even though he knows no one will hear him."

"Does anyone hear him?" Rupert asked.

111

"No."

"Then I guess I got lucky."

I put the chair back where I found it. "I'll be back later for a second installment." But Rupert wasn't listening. He'd turned to look outside at the bright June day unfolding. "Don't take it too hard," I said. "You'll be out and about before you know it."

"That's not it," he answered. "There was something else."

"It'll come back to you." I was ready to go. He needed to rest more than he needed to talk to me. Then I remembered one of the reasons I'd gone to Mitchell's Woods last night. "Maynard Wilson," I said. "Do you know anyone who's out to get him?"

"No. No one comes to mind. Why?"

"Somebody took a shot at him last night."

"Hit or miss?"

"Near miss. It nicked his ear."

"Then two of us got lucky."

I nodded, hoping we hadn't used up our quota.

He turned back toward me. It was painful to watch him, even more painful to think how close he'd come to death. It made me determined to do something about it.

"Be careful," he said. "I thought I was. You can see what happened to me."

"Aren't I always?"

"No."

I called Ruth and had her bring me home. I shaved, showered, and went to bed. I thought I'd sleep a week. I slept an hour.

I went out to the garage and tried to start Jessie. Nothing. She wouldn't even stutter, let alone turn over.

I asked Ruth if I could borrow the Volkswagon and she said yes, for today. Tomorrow she had a lot of places to go—including grocery shopping, her least favorite thing to do.

I drove north to Fred Pierson's house. The sky was

deep blue without a cloud in sight. The streams along the way ran bank-full, fed by sewers and ditches that had now started to recede from last night's storm, leaving a swath of flattened grass in their wake.

Fred Pierson was home. He was outside sawing and stacking the tree limbs that had fallen in the storm. I would have liked to watch him work. He handled the chain saw so effortlessly he made it look easy. But there wasn't time. Whatever was out in Mitchell's Woods might now be on its way to Oakalla. Or already there.

He shut off the saw and walked over to where I was standing. "What's on your mind?" he asked.

"A couple questions, that's all."

"About dogs?"

"Dogs and coyotes . . . and wolves."

He shook his head. I didn't know whom he was trying to convince, him or me. "No wolves around here."

"You sure?"

"As sure as I am about everything." He gave me a hard look. "Who said there were?"

I wondered how much I should tell him, how much he already knew. Maybe I wasn't telling him anything he didn't know already. "Something took Sheriff Roberts down last night and almost killed him. He thought it might have been a wolf."

"In Mitchell's Woods?" He didn't want to believe it.

"I'd say not over a mile from here."

His face darkened to match his thoughts. "Not a wolf," he said.

"What then?"

His look grew darker as he stared into the woods. "I don't know."

"Any ideas?"

"Some." He picked up a dead branch and threw it in the direction of Mitchell's Woods. It caught in a tree and hung there. "I lost a two-year-old female the first part of last season. She was coming into heat, so I left the males at

113

home. I didn't want to breed her until this year. She struck a coon, or what I thought was a coon, and started it north toward that old barn that sits in the heart of the woods. That was the last I heard of her. I looked for her most of the night, and when I didn't find her, I figured she was treed somewhere. When she didn't come in the next morning, I went looking again. I found her about noon laying next to a den tree. Her throat was torn out. Coyotes. That was my first thought. Then I remembered hearing a bobcat in the night—or what sounded like a bobcat to me. Except a bobcat would've torn her up more than that. So would a pack of coyotes."

"Which leaves what?"

"I don't know." His voice had gone dead. He was thinking of someone else besides his lost coon dog. "Whatever it was, it was big and silent and deadly. She never had a chance."

"Betty?"

"Her either. After I lost the female, I told Betty to stay out of the woods. Not to go in unless I was along. Something was in there that hadn't been before. She just laughed at me. She'd been raised in that woods, she said. She knew what was in there and what wasn't."

"Then it wasn't coyotes that found her?" I already knew that. I just wanted it confirmed.

"Nothing found her," he said quietly. "Something killed her. Hamstrung her, then tore out her throat. But that's not for publication."

"What was she doing in the woods anyway?" I asked.

"She was on her way home from her mother's. It was a short cut."

"Was it after dark?"

"It was in the evening. Near dark. At least when she left her mother's."

"And it was snowing?"

"Yes. It had just started."

"But there was no chance of her getting lost?"

"No chance at all. She knew the way by heart."

"Then she travelled that route often?"

"Two or three times a week. Why?"

"A thought I had."

"Why don't you share it?"

"If you'll tell me where you were last night."

His dark eyes narrowed with anger. He didn't like the question, nor its implications. "What's it to you?"

"A good friend who almost got himself killed. That's what it is to me. He shouldn't have been out there alone, but he was. I just wondered, where were you?"

"The north end of the woods."

"What were you doing there?"

"Hunting."

"Coon hunting? They're not in season."

"I never said they were." He looked through me into the woods beyond. His eyes said he wished he were there. "I haven't rested, not a night in the past six months," he admitted. "And still I haven't found it yet."

"What is it? The Coy-Dog?"

"Who told you that?" he asked sharply.

"I've heard rumors."

"That's all they are. Rumors."

"Then you've never seen it?" I asked.

"What's that?"

"The Coy-Dog?"

"I didn't say that." He didn't want to talk about it.

"What are you hiding, Fred? Why won't you tell me all you know?"

"Because it's not your concern. That's my woods, my wife that was killed in it. Whatever happens it's between me and it. Nobody else."

"Frieda Whitlock was killed in it, too. And I'd explored Mitchell's Woods before you were even thought about. You have to count us somewhere."

He never wavered "Maybe you do. I don't."

I couldn't argue with him. In Mitchell's Woods he saw

an adversary older than either of us. Like Faulkner's bear, once it was gone, his life would never be the same again.

I shrugged. I had little more to ask. He had little more to say. "Does anyone else hunt Mitchell's Woods?"

"Josh Henry," he said. "I see him up here every now and then."

That was a surprise to me. "Isn't he a little far from home?"

"I think he is. I've told him as much. But you have to go where the game is." A strange smile creased his face, made him look somehow evil. "You might check with Josh. He might know something I don't."

"That's my next stop. Thanks for your time."

"You said you had a theory," he reminded me.

"Not a theory, a thought."

"Which is?"

"Maybe he was waiting for Betty."

"Who was?"

"Whoever killed her."

"It wasn't a who," he said. "It was a what."

I drove back to Oakalla and stopped at the high school, a two-story brick building in the south end of town that had been here since 1926, the date on the cornerstone. Remnants of the past year, pop cans and cigarette butts, littered the schoolyard. Cellophane wrappers fluttered in the ivy like nesting birds.

Josh Henry sat near the bicycle rack in the sun, eating an early lunch. His head back, his eyes nearly closed, his blond hair glinting in the sun, he looked content. Evidently litter didn't bother him the way it did me.

"Morning, Josh."

He sat up with a start. "Morning, Coach. You sure gave me a scare."

"I thought you saw me coming."

"I should have. I guess my mind was somewhere else. He put the sandwich he'd been eating back in a brown sack. "What can I do for you?"

116

"Keep on eating. You don't have to stop on my account."

"It's just peanut butter and jelly," he said. "Now or fifteen minutes from now it'll still taste the same."

I sat on the steps facing him. "You ever hunt in Mitchell's Woods?" I asked.

"A time or two. Why?"

"I just wondered. Have you seen anything there that maybe shouldn't be there?"

"Like what?"

"A wolf?"

"There ain't no wolves in there."

"That's what Fred Pierson says."

"He ought to know."

"What about the Coy-Dog?"

"What about it?"

"Have you ever seen it?" I asked.

"Once."

"When?"

"A year ago this summer. I had the Plott out there getting him acquainted when I saw something staring at me. Mean-like, like he was thinking about taking me. It was the Coy-Dog. I'd bet my life on it."

"How big was he?"

"Big. About the biggest I've ever seen."

"As big as a wolf?"

"At least that."

"What did the Plott think about him?" I asked.

"He was nowhere around. That's why I was scared."

"What happened then?"

"I yelled and the Coy-Dog took off. But not far. I could hear it shadowing me all the way back to my truck. I waited there for the Plott to come in."

"Did he ever come in?"

"Sure. When he was good and ready. There ain't nothing he's afraid of. Including me."

I remembered the Plott with a chill, how his blue eyes

had measured me. With his size, strength, and intelligence, there wouldn't be much for him to fear—including the Coy-Dog, no matter how big and mean he was. Which gave rise to an interesting thought. "Do you think you could train the Plott to track down the Coy-Dog?"

"Sure! Give me enough time, I could train him to track down anything."

"How about by tonight?"

He shook his head. "Not a chance. I'd need at least a week."

I didn't have that long. "Well, it was an idea," I said.

"I'll tell you what we can do," Josh said. "We can take the Plott out there and see what happens."

"What good will that do?"

"The coyotes. If the Coy-Dog is running at the head of them, maybe the Plott will bring them in close enough for us to get a look at him. It's worth a try at least."

"Have they followed the Plott before?"

"Sure. All the time when they're in the area. But they usually keep their distance. Probably because I'm along."

It seemed the shoe was on the other foot, that they kept their distance because they either weren't hungry or foolhardy enough to take on the Plott. I didn't blame them. If I were a coyote, I'd stand back and yip at him from a distance, too.

"I guess it's worth a shot," I said.

"What time?" he asked.

I thought it over. "I've got a paper to print tonight. But I should be through by midnight. Why don't you stop by the *Reporter* office and pick me up then? If there's a change in plans, I'll give you a call."

"That doesn't give us much time," he pointed out. "It starts getting light early these days."

"It's about all the time I have," I said.

"What about Friday night?"

"Friday might be too late. Let's make it tonight." I got up and dusted off my jeans. "One other thing, Josh, now

118

that we're on the subject. Fred Pierson doesn't seem to want to talk about the Coy-Dog. Do you have any idea why?"

He was only half-listening to me. His mind was already on tonight. "What doesn't Fred want to talk about?"

"The Coy-Dog. Do you know why?"

"I've got an idea."

"What's that?"

"I think he raised it. At least I saw him hunting it one evening. I asked him what kind of hound *that* was, and he said it was none of my business. But it sure could tree coons. Though it had the funniest bark I ever heard on a dog."

"What kind of bark?"

"I can't describe it. It sounded almost like a cat. When I told Fred that, he told me to get the hell out of his woods and not come back. I didn't either. Not for a long time after that."

"Do you know why he got rid of it, let it go back into the wild?"

"His wife, I think. She made him. At least that was the story he was telling up at the Corner."

"Do you know her reason?"

"No. I didn't hear. It might be because she was afraid of it. Women don't usually take to hunting dogs much, especially one that's half coyote."

"Thanks, Josh. You've been a big help."

"Anytime, Coach. You know where to find me."

I left for uptown. The last I saw of him he was reaching inside his sack for his peanut butter and jelly sandwich.

13

I parked Ruth's Volkswagen in front of the Corner Bar and Grill and went inside, but before I ordered, I went into the bar to talk to Hiram, the bartender. Usually he worked nights. That day they were short-handed, and he was helping out, quietly and efficiently, as was his style. If there was a prototype of the perfect bartender, Hiram was he. He poured good drinks, listened when you wanted to talk, and called a friend when you were too drunk to drive home. He knew almost as much about Oakalla as Ruth did, and she was second to none. But he didn't gossip and only half-listened when you did. That made him okay in my book.

"Morning, Garth," he said. "What can I get you?"

"A ticket to Alaska. One way."

"Been one of those weeks, huh?"

"Yeah, and it's not getting any better."

"How can I help?"

"Josh Henry just told me something. I'd like to know if it's true."

"You mean you don't believe everything Josh says?"

I smiled at him. "Do you?"

He smiled back and shook his head. "About half.

120

Though sometimes it's hard to know which half, he spreads it on so thick."

"And so well," I thought to myself.

"What is it about Josh you want to know?" Hiram asked.

"It's not about Josh. It's about Fred Pierson. Did he ever say anything to you about a dog of his, one his wife, Betty, made him give up?"

Hiram nodded. "That night was the only time I ever saw Fred drunk. He loved that dog so. He hated to give it up. It ate at him for months after that."

"Did he ever talk to you about the dog?"

"Only what the dog was up to, and how proud he was of it. He called it something. His . . . Gloria. Something like that."

"His Glory Hound?"

"That's it! His Glory Hound."

"Did Fred ever say why Betty made him get rid of it?"

"No. He never said. And I never asked. I figured it was none of my business."

"Thanks, Hiram."

The phone in the bar rang. Hiram answered it and held the receiver out for me. "Garth Ryland here," I said.

"Rupert Roberts here." He spoke slowly and with effort.

"How did you know where to find me?"

"I called Ruth. She said to call here." I waited while he caught his breath.

"That piece of straw you found in Frieda's hair—it came from Harvey Whitlock's barn."

"Are you sure?"

"That's what the coroner just told me. He matched it to a straw I took from the barn myself."

"Thanks, Rupert. Now get some rest."

"I plan to."

If he did, it'd be the first time.

I hung up. My stomach still said eat, but I wasn't in

121

the mood anymore. I got in Ruth's Volkswagen and drove out to Harvey Whitlock's.

On the way I noticed that Hattie Peeler's grass was getting high. Also, the storm had put down several limbs in her yard, but so far she'd made no move to pick them up. That wasn't like Hattie. Usually, when a limb fell, she was there before it ever hit the ground.

No one was home at Harvey's. The pickup was there, but the car was gone, so I guessed he and Dora might be out at Fair Haven. On my way back to town from Fred Pierson's, I'd seen a car that looked like theirs pulling into the cemetery. Probably the first of many visits.

I walked to the barn and went in the side door, chasing a cat into hiding as I did. I was in a narrow passageway that led to the main section of the barn. To my left were a couple of empty stalls, a pile of empty feed sacks, and an old barn swallow nest that still clung tenaciously to the ceiling. To my right was a wall that I followed until it opened into a straw mow.

I went into the mow and stood for a moment, letting my eyes adjust to the dim light. Sunlight was streaming in the north window. The straw seemed to smoke. It smelled hay-musty in here, the way Grandmother Ryland's barn used to smell.

A few minutes later I found a nest in the straw toward the east wall behind a stack of bales. It included a blanket, a portable radio, and a box of tissues, and looked like it had been used recently. I found something else I wasn't expecting. It was Frieda's purse.

I opened it up and looked inside. Along with her billfold and makeup and comb and a nail file, and a dozen other things I could only guess the use of, I found two sets of pills—one set in a package, the other in a bottle. I was sure I knew what those in the package were for. My former wife used to take some like them. But I didn't know about those in the bottle. I would have to get a second opinion.

Taking Frieda's purse with me, I got in the Volkswagen and drove back toward town. On the way I again noticed the limbs in Hattie Peeler's yard. I stopped in the middle of Gas Line Road and backed all the way to her drive. Hattie might by chance leave a limb in her yard if she weren't feeling well, but never in her garden. And that's where a large maple limb lay.

I parked in Hattie's drive and walked to the porch. It, too, was covered with leaves and small limbs from last night's storm.

I knocked on the screen door. When no one answered, I went inside.

The house smelled like it had been closed up for at least a day or so. I walked through the living room into Hattie's bedroom. Her bed was made, her dresser dusted, and all of her clothes, except for a red nightshirt hanging on her door, were put away. I bent down and looked under the bed just to make sure. She wasn't there.

Back in the living room, everything seemed to be in place—couch under the north window, fern stand and fern by the east window, Hattie's recliner and footstool snugged into the southeast corner, her floor-model Philco radio to the right of the recliner, her pipe stand within an arm's reach to the left.

Except Hattie's pipe and tobacco were missing from the stand. I looked around the room, but didn't see them anywhere. She only smoked her pipe when she sat down to read. And she only read after supper and only then when the last dish was dried and put away.

Had the last dish been dried and put away? I went through her small dining area into the kitchen to find out. A plate, glass, serving spoon, two forks, and two pans were sitting in the draining rack. I turned them over, then back again. They'd all dried a long time ago.

Stepping from the kitchen onto her sun porch, I stood a moment staring into the sheep pasture behind her house. Nothing there but sheep and thistles and butter-

123

flies. No sign of Hattie anywhere. And no sense in looking further. The leaves on the porch had told me that.

On the way out I stopped by the garage just to make sure. When I couldn't get inside, I went around to the south side to the only window. It was glazed over with dirt and hadn't been washed for years. A curtain covered the window from the inside. Whatever her reason, Hattie didn't want anyone looking in.

But I knew Hattie used her garage. I'd seen her come in and out of there many times. And if I remembered right, she never kept it locked when I was a boy.

A search of her house turned up no keys, just a growing sense of time. It seemed to be running out on me, perhaps on Hattie as well, and the dead quiet of her house only magnified that fact.

Walking back to the garage to break out the window, I discovered a small brown circle in the grass about five feet from the door. Underneath was a glass jar with a key inside. The key opened the garage door, revealing a 1968 maroon Bonneville hardtop. One that, according to the registration, belonged to Walter Lawrence.

The keys were in the ignition, and there was an empty gas can and funnel sitting behind the Bonneville. It appeared someone had tried to start it recently. Without success, since the battery was dead and the Bonneville still there.

But no Hattie in the trunk. That was something at least.

From the house I called Rupert at the hospital. He sounded worse than he had this morning.

"You okay?" I asked him.

"Okay. But if you want to talk, you'd better hurry. They made me take a pill. I'm about to fade out." He'd already started to slur his words.

"I'll keep it short. You had a caller who saw Frieda Whitlock walking along Gas Line Road. Could the caller have been Hattie Peeler?"

124

He didn't answer right away. I was afraid he'd fallen asleep. "Rupert, you still there?"

"Still where?" he mumbled.

"Still with me?"

"Barely. What is it you wanted to know?"

"Hattie Peeler. Was she your informant?"

"I think so. It sounded like her."

"Did you ever ask her?"

"What?" He was fading fast.

"Did you ever ask Hattie if she called you?"

"Tried. Couldn't pin her down. She kept changing . . . the subject."

"Thanks. You can sleep now."

I could have saved my breath.

Thinking things over, it appeared that with Hattie, the past and the present, Rupert's case and mine, had just crossed paths.

I tried to call Clarkie to ask him about the slug he'd dug out of Maynard Wilson's wall. But Clarkie was nowhere to be found. That in itself didn't bother me. The fact that I needed him did.

I drove uptown and parked in front of the drugstore. Spencer Davis, the pharmacist and owner of the store, was wiping off the counter. He still served lemon cokes and chocolate sodas the way he used to when I was a boy, but the look of the store had changed since then. The aisles were wider and more streamlined, with more to buy, but less to interest me. The comics were gone, along with the paraffin teeth and mustaches, and the balsa airplanes you could buy for a dime. Everything now was pack-aged—overregulated and overpriced until the joy was squeezed out of it and you were left with a piece of hard plastic that might last until you got it home.

Spencer looked up at me, then continued wiping. He liked to see me come in, but hated to see me leave, since we spent most our time commiserating about the "good

125

old days." Therefore, until he knew I was there to stay, he kept busy and tried to ignore me.

"Nice day," I said.

He nodded, but didn't look up.

"The storm do any damage here?"

"Got the floor in the back wet. That's about all." He glanced up at me over the rim of his glasses. "You here to chat or are you here on business?"

"Business, I'm afraid."

"Then get on with it," he said brusquely.

I laid the package of pills on the counter in front of him. "Can you tell me what these are?"

He glanced sharply at me. "Is this official?"

"It's official. I can even show you my badge if you like."

"That's not necessary. I heard Sheriff Roberts was hurt. I figured you'd take up the slack."

"What else did you hear about Sheriff Roberts?"

"Nothing. Nobody's doing much talking."

Good, I thought to myself. The less people know about what really happened, the better. That certainly hadn't been my tune a few short days ago.

"You haven't heard anything about the particulars, have you?" Spencer asked.

"No. All I know is what I read in my newspaper."

"I figured," he said. Then he picked up the package and handed it back to me. "They're birth control pills."

I set the bottle of pills on the counter. "What about these?"

He picked up the bottle and examined it. When he read the name on the label, his face went white. "Where did you find these?"

"In Frieda's purse. Where I found the others."

He stared at me. He wasn't so angry with me, as at the times. "Nothing's sacred anymore, is it?"

"Not much, I'm afraid."

"Why do you have to know what's in that bottle?"

126

"Because it might tell me how Frieda Whitlock died. Or why."

"Epilepsy," he mumbled.

"What was that, Spencer?"

"Frieda had epilepsy. These pills helped her control it."

"How bad a case?"

"Not bad. The pills did their job. Hardly anyone in town knew." He handed the bottle back to me. "But now they will, won't they?"

"Would it matter if they did?"

"It might. It might take away from who she was and what she did. To most people in town Frieda was the perfect little girl. Their minds might change once they learn the truth. Some extremists might think her death was warranted."

I hated to admit it, but he was right. It somehow eased our minds when we could find a flaw in the victim, made our perfect selves seem less vulnerable.

"If it helps any, unless there's no other way, this stops right here with you and me."

"What about Sheriff Roberts once he finds out?"

"He's Frieda's godfather. He won't say anything more than he has to either."

Spencer went back to wiping the counter. "That's some comfort at least."

I left the Volkswagen in front of the drugstore and walked to the Marathon. The scene was a familiar one. Danny was busy on the drive. Sniffy was sitting on his stool, staring out the window.

"Where's Joe?" I asked Sniffy.

"He never came in. Said he had somewhere to go."

"Is he at home?"

"Was last time I heard from him. You might call down there and see before you walk all the way."

It was a good idea, because there was no answer.

"You have any idea where he might be?" I asked.

"No. Unless he took his mother to the doctor."

"What's the matter with her?"

"Nerves, most likely. She flies off the handle at the least little thing. All in all, I'd say this probably ain't been too good a week for her."

"Any of us, for that matter," I said.

"Amen to that."

"What about Joe? How are his nerves?"

"No better or worse than most, I guess. What are you getting at?"

"Have you ever seen him panic? Completely lose his head?"

"What are you getting at, Garth?"

"The truth, if I can learn it."

"Why do you keep coming through me?"

"Because if Joe has a friend in this town, it's you. You know things about him that no one else does."

"All the more reason to keep my mouth shut. At least that's the way I figure it."

"I don't. Not this time. There's too much at stake."

"Go on. I'm listening."

"I can't tell you all of it, Sniffy, because I don't know all of it. But I can tell you this much. If I don't find out who killed Frieda, somebody else will surely die. Maybe as soon as tonight."

He thought it over, then said, "What was your question again?"

"Have you ever seen Joe panic, completely lose control?"

"I did once. And over nothing at that. Him and me were in here by ourselves one night. It was summer, and we had all the doors in the place open trying to keep cool. Well, a kitten snuck in and got to messing around behind those tires over there and got itself trapped somehow. Then it commenced the most pitiful howling you ever heard. I was all for leaving it there, seeing how it found its way in, it could find its way out. But Joe would have none

128

of that. He ran over there like a wildman, throwing tires right and left until he found that kitten. And with two cars on the drive to boot." Sniffy shook his head sadly. "He could have saved himself the trouble. That kitten didn't last the week around here."

"What happened to it?"

"Joe killed it. Accidentally, of course. He was coming in to close up and hit the button for the overhead door, never thinking that kitten might take it in its head to go out then. It was one of those once in a lifetime things, but the kitten tried to squeeze through just as the door came down. It never made it. We like to never got it away from him to bury it."

"He seems to take those things to heart," I said.

"I guess we would, too, if we'd watched our old man burn up in a truck the way Joe did."

"What's that?"

"It happened when Joe was nine or ten. Danny told me about it, and he wouldn't of known if Joe's mother hadn't told him. Joe's old man was a trucker. He used to run between Dallas and Nashville, I think Danny said. And he and Joe were real close. He used to take Joe along whenever he could. They had an accident one night. I don't know the particulars, but Joe was thrown out, and his old man was trapped in the cab. It caught fire and burned. Joe must've watched it all happen. But he doesn't remember any of it."

I turned to watch the drive where Danny was still busy pumping gas. Things were starting to add up, but I wasn't yet sure to what. "You like Joe, don't you, Sniffy?"

"You know the answer to that."

"If what you say is true, he might need help, and not the kind you've been giving him."

Sniffy sat up straight on his stool and blinked at me, like the eagle in him had just been awakened. "What are you saying, Garth, that I'm still hiding something about Joe?"

129

"Yes."

"You don't beat around the bush, do you?"

"Not when something's this important."

"And Joe isn't?"

"Of course he is, Sniffy! But he's carrying enough guilt to break the back of any man. First his father, then the kitten, then Frieda . . . Even if he didn't kill her, he somehow acts like he did. . . ."

"He always acts like that," Sniffy interrupted. "Guilty, like you said. It didn't start with Frieda, so it ain't nothing new."

"That's my point. Joe needs help. Professional help. But he'll never get it the way we're going. Don't you understand that?"

"Suppose I do? What kind of help is he going to get in prison? Or maybe the gas chamber is your idea of professional help!"

"He's not going to the gas chamber! He's not going anywhere that I know of."

"How do you know that?" Sniffy crossed his arms and stuck out his chin defiantly. "You know what they're saying around town, that he killed Frieda rather than have her go off to college and leave him, that it was the only way he could make sure she stayed here. The worst part about it is, knowing how much he loved her and how bad he wanted to hang on to her, I halfway believe them."

"Only the truth will tell us for sure."

Sniffy gave me a sad look, one that welled up from his soul. "What the hell is the truth? You tell me that? That we could all get blown up tomorrow? That's the truth for you. But who the hell wants to believe it?" Then he sighed and looked away. "What is it you want to know?"

"Which way did Joe go when he left here last Thursday?"

"He went south, like I told you the first time."

"What time was that?"

"Between three and three-thirty. I'd seen the school buses go by, but they hadn't picked up the kids yet."

"When did you see Joe come back north?"

"I didn't," he admitted. "I didn't see his car again until I met him on Fair Haven Road on my way home from here. I was heading north. He was heading south."

"What time was that?"

"Close to suppertime. That's why I was heading home. To a TV dinner," he added. "That's about all I cook."

"I wonder why he was gone so long?"

"I asked him the next day. He said he got lost."

"Did he say where?"

"No. He didn't say."

I noticed Danny was heading our way. "Thanks, Sniffy. I appreciate your help."

14

I walked to the Corner Bar and Grill and ate a late lunch—pork steak and dressing, pea salad, iced tea to drink—but no dessert. I noticed Clarkie sitting at the bar with his uniform on. That was unusual. For one thing, Rupert didn't allow himself or any of his deputies to drink while on duty. For another, Clarkie wasn't known for his drinking. A large slice of rum cake put him under once.

I finished my dinner and walked into the bar. Clarkie was nursing a beer, trying hard to get it down without choking. He'd had one glass and was pouring a second.

"I need your help," I said.

"Sorry," he answered, pointing to the bar where his badge lay. "There's my star. I just quit."

"Why?"

"I can't take it no longer. As Aunt Norma says, if you can't take the heat, get out of the kitchen." He took a drink of beer and made a face. "Hell of a lot she knew. She should've got out of the kitchen a long time ago."

"Do you mind explaining that?"

"I ran an I.D. on that slug I dug out of Maynard Wilson's wall. It was a .32 caliber. Does that tell you anything?"

"Not offhand. No."

"Well, it does me."

"Maybe we should go somewhere and talk."

"What's wrong with right here?"

"There are too many ears around," I said.

"Hell, I don't care who hears it."

"I do." I took him by the arm and tried to stand him up. "Come on, Clarkie. Let's go."

He jerked away from me and sat hunched over his beer, like a dog guarding a bone. "I'm staying until I finish my beer."

"The way you're going, that could take until Christmas."

"I don't care. I've got time. Lots of it now . . ." I was afraid that one sad song on the juke box and he'd cry me a river.

"I guess the strain of command is just too much for you," I said, trying to put some starch in his spine.

It worked. Momentarily anyway. He straightened and took another drink of beer. His eyes didn't even water this time. "It ain't that. I'm fit to command, as fit as anybody in this town besides Sheriff Roberts. Otherwise, I wouldn't be." He took another drink of beer. "Personal reasons. That's why I'm resigning."

"What kind of personal reasons?"

"The personal kind. What other kind are there?"

We weren't making much progress. If he drank the rest of his beer, I'd have to carry him out of here. "Have you told Sheriff Roberts yet?" I asked.

He gave me a guilty look and reached for his beer. "No."

"Then let's go do it, so he can appoint somebody else to your job."

His hand closed around the glass. He squeezed it hard without realizing it. Too hard. It shot from his hand and slid off the bar. Clarkie never even noticed. "I can't face him."

133

"Sure you can. You've done it before."

"I was just mad at him then. This is different. This is for keeps."

"Then why don't you tell me about it? Somewhere else."

I helped him to his feet. This time he let me. We went outside and began walking south. Clarkie lived on the corner, the first house south of the City Building. We sat down on his back stoop. I noticed he'd picked up his badge and now had it in his hand.

"Why don't you put it back on?" I said.

"I can't."

"Why not?"

"Because I'm an accessory."

"To what?"

"Attempted murder."

"Why don't you start at the beginning?"

He turned away from me and coughed. He looked a little green around the gills. I hoped we'd get through this before he got sick. He coughed again. Nothing came up.

"I don't know where the beginning is," he said. "I just know I gave Aunt Norma a .32 caliber Smith and Wesson as a present a year ago last Christmas. She kept asking me for one. Said she wanted it for protection."

"Maybe she did. For a lot of people it's either that or get a guard dog."

"She might have," he agreed. "That's not the point."

"What is the point?"

"I think she used it last night to try to kill Maynard Wilson."

"Why do you think that? There are a lot of .32 caliber revolvers around."

"Maybe a few, but not a lot. Not in Oakalla."

He had a point. Most of the people I knew owned shotguns or rifles or pellet guns. A couple owned .44 Magnums, but I tried to stay out of their neighborhood.

"Okay, I'll grant you that. Why else do you think it was your Aunt Norma who shot at Maynard Wilson?"

"For one thing, I tried to call her last night about the storm, just before Maynard called me to report the shooting. She wasn't home. That's not like her. She never goes out at night, especially when it's threatening to storm. For another, she's had it in for Maynard for a long time."

"How long?"

"I'd say the last fifteen years."

"How about the last seventeen years?" Which was as long as Walter Lawrence and his fifty thousand dollars had been missing.

"It could be that long. Yes."

"What does she have against Maynard?" I asked. "You have any idea?"

"No. She's never said. Just dropped hints here and there."

"What kind of hints?"

"That she suspected him of something she couldn't prove."

"Then why did she keep on working for him?"

"To get the evidence that he did whatever it was she suspected him of."

"But she never did?"

"Nope. At least not until now."

He leaned away from me and coughed some more. He appeared to be growing sicker by the minute. "You okay?" I asked.

"Not really."

"Have you told your Aunt Norma what you suspect?"

"No."

"Have you searched her house?"

"No. I couldn't. Not legally. Not without a search warrant."

"How about illegally, since you're not a deputy anymore?"

"I couldn't. I still am at heart."

"Then you always will be, so you might as well put that badge back on."

He didn't answer. He moaned and leaned away from me. I was up and gone before the first volley was ever fired.

Two blocks later I walked east along Jackson Street toward Norma Rothenberger's house. She lived in a grey two-story frame house about a block from the Marathon. The house had a large concrete front porch where a swing hung perennially, winter and summer, fair weather and foul, like the plastic flowers on the porch sill.

I went around to the back door, glanced over my shoulder to see if anyone was watching, and went inside. I was in Norma's utility room, which looked like it might have once been a summer kitchen. Long and low with a row of windows facing the north, it was piled high with everything from canning jars to mops to a pair of five-buckle overshoes. There was a red corduroy cap hanging on a nail beside the door, and under it was a green corduroy coat that looked like it had seen more years than I had.

I stood a moment examining the coat and cap. They reminded me of the coat and cap Grandmother Ryland used to wear when she went out to feed the chickens and milk the cows. That put Norma Rothenberger a notch higher on my list.

There was a white wooden door between the utility room and the kitchen. I knocked twice, then waited for an answer. When none came, I gave a "Yoohoo!" and went on in.

It smelled stale in there, just as it had at Hattie's. But this staleness seemed more permanent, with a thicker crust, like it had been building for years. Norma's bedroom was the first room at the top of the stairs. It was a cheerless room with a dark walnut floor, a dark walnut dresser and washstand, a dark walnut bed, a dark walnut baseboard, and dark green wallpaper.

136

In the top dresser drawer was a .32 caliber Smith and Wesson revolver. There was an empty shell still in the chamber. It smelled like it had been fired recently.

In the bottom drawer of the dresser, wrapped in pantyhose, was Walter Lawrence's skull. A nice touch. At least Walter would have approved.

I went outside into the sunlight. The day seemed particularly bright, the storm-washed air unusually clean. A swallowtail drifted into Norma's garden and drifted out again—dark and fluttery like my thoughts.

When I was twelve, I'd spent most of one summer at Grandmother Ryland's farm. To earn spending money, I sometimes mowed yards in town. This had been one of the yards I'd mowed—by hand—for a dollar. It seemed every bit of ten acres then, Norma Rothenberger hell's handmaiden, with a magnifying glass in one hand and a bullwhip in the other.

Today it looked much smaller. Norma had shrunk, too. To what, I didn't know. But the loss, like the rest of childhood's drama and grandeur, was irretrievable.

I walked uptown and climbed the stairs to Maynard Wilson's law office. Except for Norma, it was empty.

She looked up from her typing and gave me a worried smile. "I'm sorry, Garth. Maynard's not here. He's taken the afternoon off."

"That's okay. I didn't come to see him. I came to see you."

"I'm very busy today. Perhaps tomorrow." She resumed typing, her thin fingers dancing shadowlike across the keys. She looked like a shadow herself, too light to even stay in her chair.

I walked over to her desk and stood right in front of her where she couldn't ignore me. "It won't take long."

She typed even faster. "I said I'm busy. Come back tomorrow."

"If I do, I'm bringing Walter's skull with me." In truth, I had it right outside the door in case I needed it.

137

That stopped her. Her fingers locked and tightened into fists. But her arms kept moving, shadowboxing above the keys. She looked up at me. Not exactly murder in her eyes, but something close. Desperation perhaps, like that of an alcoholic who finds his last hidden bottle empty.

"Don't do that," she said thickly.

"Then don't make me."

Her arms stopped swinging and came to a rest on her desk. "What do you want from me?"

"I want to know why you took a shot at Maynard Wilson."

"Because he killed my Walter!" She burst out.

"*Your* Walter?"

Her face softened, became defensive. "*My* Walter. It was me he loved, no one else."

"He told you that?"

"He didn't have to. He brought me flowers, bought me candy, touched my hand when no one was looking. He didn't have to tell me. I knew!"

"And what did you do for him?"

"Nothing!" she snapped. "It wasn't like that between us. He didn't want . . ." she could hardly say the word ". . . sex from me. He wanted understanding and affection—something that no one else ever gave him."

That didn't sound like the Walter I'd come to know. His wife gave him all the understanding and affection any man would need, plus more forgiveness than he had a right to expect. It was sex that Walter craved—and probably what got him killed.

"How did you give him your understanding and affection?"

"By listening. Something you could take a lesson in."

"There are a lot of things I need lessons in. Both of us."

"Meaning what?"

"You figure it out. But I'll tell you one thing. The odds are that Maynard Wilson never laid a hand on Walter Lawrence."

138

Her lip began to tremble. She was on the verge of tears, but fighting them back. "That shows you what you know."

"I'm all ears."

"You knew Walter withdrew a great deal of money the day he disappeared?"

"I heard that."

"You also know the money was never seen again, just like Walter?"

"I heard that, too."

"Then where did the money go?"

"I don't know. That's what I'm asking you."

She smiled smugly as she dropped her bomb. "It never went anywhere. It stayed right here."

"You know that for a fact?"

She retreated a little. "No. I never saw the books. But it stands to reason."

"Why?"

"Maynard Wilson. He was a changed man after Walter left. He smiled, he spoke civilly to me, he took new interest in his practice. It was like he'd been at death's door and something gave him a reprieve." She paused to make her point. "That something was Walter's fifty thousand dollars!"

"His wife said he took it with him."

"She would." Judging by the scowl on Norma's face, I'd opened a new can of worms. "She's in Maynard Wilson's pocket."

"How so?"

"It's as plain as the nose on your face. She put three boys through college. With what, you tell me that? And now for the last four years she hasn't lifted a hand. She quit her job at the market. She even quit cleaning my house after ten years. You tell me where her money's coming from."

"Maybe her sons are helping her out."

"Of course they are! But that doesn't explain where

that new Buick of hers came from. Or how she could afford to go to Hawaii last winter. Or that new color television set. No. It's conscience money from Maynard Wilson. *Walter's* money!"

"Her money, too," I pointed out.

"And what did she do to earn it?"

"She scrubbed your God damned toilet for ten years!" I yelled. "And put three boys through college! And kept a smile on her face the whole time! Something you might take a lesson in. Along with compassion."

She looked guilty and distraught, like a proper little girl who'd just dripped strawberry jam down the front of her new Sunday dress. But not defeated. If Norma Rothenberger was nothing else, she was a survivor. When I thought of it, so was a cockroach, though I didn't put Norma in that class. She was like a lot of us. She'd spent too much time alone, dwelt too long on her own aches and pains, and come to all the wrong conclusions.

"What happens now?" she asked. "To me, I mean?"

"I honestly don't know."

"Does anybody else know what I've done?"

"Clarkie does. It's eating him up inside. He's resigned his job because of it."

"I never intended for that to happen." Then she had to add, "Even though I've always said that job is beneath him."

"He happens to like it."

"What does he know, at his age?"

"From one sinner to another, what do any of us?"

15

I walked south toward the railroad tracks and Willard Coates' house. The shadows had started to lengthen and now reached the middle of the street. The day was fast getting away from me. Not a comforting thought.

Willard sat at his desk, working on his books. I looked for moss growing on the north side of him, but saw none. This time I didn't wait for him to acknowledge me. I laid Walter's skull on the desk in front of him.

"Where'd you find that?" he asked without looking up.

"In Norma Rothenberger's dresser."

"What was Norma doing with it?"

"That's what I'd like to know."

"Sorry. I can't help you."

"For God's sake, Willard, what's it going to hurt?"

"Probably not a thing. It's principle."

"I can get a search warrant."

He folded his hands behind his head and put his feet up on the desk. "Then get it."

"Word will get out," I said. "That we're auditing your books. What are your clients going to think?"

I didn't ruffle a feather. "Probably not much. It

141

happens every couple years anyway. I've come up clean every time for the past fifty years."

I should have known I couldn't bluff Willard. It'd been tried before by experts, Rupert included. Once he'd left here spitting at children and talking to himself. I'd have to try something else. But not my first thought, which was to choke him to death.

"I need your help," I said.

"I know you do, but that doesn't change principle."

"What does change principle?"

"Nothing. You should know that. You're a man of principle yourself."

He had me there. At least I always thought I was. "This is a life and death matter. No clear principle applies."

"Whose life? Whose death?"

"A lot of lives. Walter Lawrence's death . . . among others."

"What others?"

"Betty Pierson's, Frieda Whitlock's."

"Are you saying they're connected?"

"I'm saying they might be. But until I look at your damn books I'll never know."

"What do you expect to find—in my damn books?"

"I'm not sure."

He shook his head. "That's asking too much on faith."

"But I'll know when I find it."

"What if you don't find it?"

"Then what have we lost?"

"The principle. The simple trust people have put in me. It's what makes anything work, simple trust in each other. Once you lose that, you lose everything. Nothing works anymore. Not me, not you, not government, not civilization as we know it. Without it, we're right back in the cave, starting over."

"I can't argue with you, Willard."

"Then don't."

"But there's another principle involved. Call it truth if you want. What is. What's real. Ignore it and no matter how much trust you have, it'll step out of Mitchell's Woods one night and eat you alive!"

"Is that what happened to Betty Pierson and Frieda Whitlock?"

"Yes. And to Sheriff Roberts last night. Though he's going to survive."

"I wondered. I heard he was laid up. But I didn't catch the details." He thought about it long and hard. Finally he said, "Okay. I'll show you the books you want, but on one condition. You have an hour and I won't answer any of your questions."

"That's two conditions," I said.

"Two conditions then. Whose books are you interested in?"

"Can I change my mind once I get into them?"

"No. Not once I drag them out here."

"Then give me Maynard Wilson's for the past twenty years and Karen Wilson's for as long as you've been keeping them."

He left and a few minutes later returned with the books I wanted. One glance told me it was more than an hour's job. "You might as well take them back," I said. "It'd take me an hour to count the pages."

"I'll make it easier for you. Maynard Wilson didn't get well when Walter Lawrence disappeared seventeen years ago. I know that's what Norma Rothenberger says, but the books say different. He didn't get well until a lot later. And that was from hard work."

"He could've salted it away and fed it in gradually."

"He could have. I don't think he did."

"Why?"

"If I knew the answer to that, Garth, I wouldn't be here. I'd be telling fortunes on television. Something inside me knows, that's all."

"Then I'm wasting my time looking at Maynard's books?"

"I'd say so, yes."

"What about Karen Wilson's books?"

He suddenly changed his tune. "I've helped you all I will, more than I said I was going to."

"Thanks, Willard, for this much."

"Tell that to my conscience."

"If it helps any, when this is all over, I think your conscience will rest in peace."

I began looking through Karen's books. Willard left to go to another part of the house. I didn't see him again.

Forty-five minutes later I left. I didn't have all the answers, but I had enough information to know where to look.

For the past four years Willard had been writing monthly checks on Karen's account to the Bywalter Foundation. The checks were for eight hundred dollars, written the first of every month. When I thought about it for a while and put two and two together and came up with "Bye, Walter," I was sure I knew where the checks were going.

But there was one other check that puzzled me. It was for ten thousand dollars in cash, endorsed by Karen herself two years ago. The timing bothered me.

While waiting for Maxine Lawrence to answer her front door, I glanced inside the garage, which was open. It was about the neatest garage I'd ever seen, and made mine look like the rat's nest it was.

Then I saw something in the near corner that caught my eye. It was a catcher's mask and shin guards, no doubt those of her all-star son. I wondered where his bat and glove were. He must have taken them to college with him.

When no one answered the door, I walked around back. Wearing a painter's cap, bib overalls, a white long-sleeved blouse, and tennis shoes, Maxine was busy trimming the hedge. Her movements were bold and energetic, almost exaggerated. She truly seemed to be enjoying what she was doing, that here was where she

144

really wanted to be. I hated to interrupt her, especially with what I'd come for.

"How does it look?" she asked, taking off her cap to wipe her brow.

"Good."

"I never had time for it before. I do now."

"Time is important."

Her face grew reflective. She seemed to be counting every grocery item she ever sacked. "About the most important thing we have. Next to our kids."

"Than I'm one for two."

"No time?"

"No kids."

"Cheer up. You're a young man yet."

I shook my head. "No. It's not in the cards. Maybe once upon a time. Not now."

"And maybe somebody will change your mind."

"Maybe. But I doubt it. Not the somebody I have in mind."

"Do I know her?"

"Diana Baldwin."

She smiled. "Pretty lady."

"Agreed."

"But I haven't seen her around lately. Has she moved?"

I felt my chest tighten. "Temporarily. She's gone back to school in Madison."

"You miss her, I bet."

"Like crazy."

"When is she coming back?"

"I don't know. Maybe never."

She reached up and clipped off a twig she'd missed. "Well, even if she doesn't, you'll survive. I did. It was hard, though. Awful hard."

"I'm learning that."

She lowered the trimmers. "Would you like a glass of sun tea? I made it fresh today."

"Maybe later. I've got a couple questions I need to ask you first."

"About Walter?"

"In a way. It's about the checks you've been receiving the first of every month." I could have stopped there. Her face told the tale. Maxine Lawrence wasn't good at hiding anything.

"You mind if we sit down?" she asked.

"I was about to suggest that."

We walked around to the side of the house and sat on green metal lawn chairs in the breezeway between her house and garage. It was cool and shady there. She took off her cap and set it on the concrete, then sat with her hands folded primly in her lap, as if awaiting for the judge's verdict. None would be forthcoming. Not from me anyway.

"I knew it had to end someday," she said. "I just hoped it wouldn't be so soon."

"You never questioned where the checks came from or why?"

"I knew where they came from. Willard Coates' signature was on every one of them. As for the why, I didn't think too hard about that. I wanted to think they came from Walter, that he'd set up some kind of trust for me. But that's impossible, isn't it? Because Walter's dead."

"How do you know that?"

"I guess I've always known. In my heart of hearts as they say. Lately I've heard rumors that his body was found in Phillipee's Pond. Is that true?"

"Yes. I'm afraid it is."

"Why didn't you tell me? Somebody anyway?" She wasn't angry. She was just asking. She had a right.

"I didn't tell anyone. I didn't want anyone to know."

"Why? Was he murdered?"

"It looks like it."

"Am I a suspect?"

"No. Not to me you aren't."

146

"I had reason to kill him. Probably more reason than anybody else."

"I know that."

"Then why aren't I a suspect?" She seemed to want to be.

"Because you're too good a person."

It took her a moment to digest that. I wasn't sure she believed it as much as I did. "Good persons run out of patience sometimes. God knows I did with Walter. I think I might have killed him, if I'd been smart enough to figure out a way."

"I'm glad you didn't."

"I guess I am, too. Now. Ten years ago, when I was down on my hands and knees scrubbing kitchen floors, I wasn't. I wished I'd killed him when I had the chance." She looked at me. "Do you know who did kill him?"

"No. But I'm working on it."

"Maynard Wilson had reason. Though I won't say he did it."

"What was Maynard Wilson's reason?"

"I think Walter was stealing money from him. Clients anyway. It's the same as money."

"How was he stealing clients?" I asked.

"Norma Rothenberger. She was their secretary. She still is Maynard's. She made sure that Walter got the lion's share of the business."

"How did she manage that?"

"Easy. If a new client called or came into the office, she referred him to Walter. She always said Maynard's case load was full."

"Which it wasn't?"

"No. It was the other way around. Walter had so much to do he couldn't handle it all. And what he did handle, he handled poorly. He was losing business for the firm right and left."

"What did Walter do for her in return?"

"Nothing much. Bought her a few things, that's all. Paid attention to her when nobody else would. He told me

147

all about Norma. It was the ones he didn't tell me about that worried me."

"Such as?"

"Rita Henry. But you probably already know about her."

"Was he paying her support for Josh?"

"I think so. But it wasn't her he was paying. She ran off and left Josh here. He was paying Buck Henry, Josh's grandfather."

"Was he paying anyone else for support?"

"Not for support. For favors maybe."

"Sexual favors?"

"Yes."

I thought about it, then finally asked it. I had to know. "Karen Wilson?"

"Yes again. Though I never breathed a word about it to anyone. She used to sit with our boys. Our youngest. The older two were close to her age. He really didn't need a sitter, and I told Walter that, but he insisted on Karen. So much so I didn't call him on it."

"Did he take her home afterwards?"

"No. She lived right across the street."

"That's right. Then what was the purpose in having her sit?"

"To see her, for one thing. To touch her whenever possible. For another it gave her an excuse, if her mother ever wondered where her money came from."

"What about her father?" I remembered I'd been compared favorably to him.

"He was dead by this time. He was a lineman. He got hit by a high-voltage wire during a storm and that was that." She bit her lip and looked away from me. "I followed them once. Walter's car. I didn't know who he had in it. I was at Opal Starcher's house when I saw it creep by and make the turn onto Gas Line Road. I followed it on foot, never thinking I'd catch up to it. But I did."

"Phillipee's Pond."

"How'd you know?"

"As someone once told me, I'm a good guesser." Though at the moment I wished I wasn't. I stood, trying to get my legs to work.

"There's more to it," she said.

"I know. Karen was in the car with him."

"I didn't watch what happened. But I think I know."

"I wouldn't bet against it."

"Did I say something wrong? You look upset."

"No. You told me what I came for. Sometimes I learn more than I want to."

"Is is about Karen?"

"Yes."

"Karen is a beautiful woman. It's natural men would be attracted to her." You included, her smile seemed to say.

"Beauty is as beauty does." To quote Grandmother Ryland.

"Don't be too hard on her. You were young once yourself."

"I thought you said I still was."

"I guess I did, didn't I?"

I waved and started to leave.

"Garth? Will the checks stop now?"

"I don't know, Maxine. I wish I did."

"Well, if they do, it was sure nice while it lasted."

I walked south to Maynard Wilson's. He was sitting on his patio in the shade, drinking a gin and tonic. He looked about like I felt, lower than an ant's ass. "Have a seat," he said.

I did, taking the lounge chair beside him.

"So, what are you here for today—to question, to gloat, or to give fraternal solace?" Maynard was well on his way to being drunk. I would have liked to have joined him.

"It's not to gloat."

"To question then?"

"Only a couple. Did you kill Walter Lawrence?"

"No."

"Do you know who did?"

"No."

"You had every reason to kill him."

"I know. But I didn't."

"I'm glad."

"Are you really? If I were you and after my wife, I wouldn't be. I'd like to see me put away for a long, long time."

"What would that prove?"

"Who's the better man. You would be—by default."

"I might be anyway. I don't need you out of the way to prove it."

"Sure of yourself, aren't you? Wait twenty years. You won't be."

"Why wait that long? Twenty minutes might be long enough."

That made him smile. "You know, Ryland, you're not half bad. Under other circumstances we might even be friends." He rose unsteadily, taking his glass with him. "Would you like one?"

"No, thanks. I've got a long night ahead of me."

"With Karen?"

"With the *Oakalla Reporter*. It comes out tomorrow." Maybe.

"Suit yourself." He went into the house and came out a few minutes later with another gin and tonic. Another gin anyway. He looked like he was running low on tonic. "You're still here, I see."

"Still here."

He held onto his drink and flopped into his chair without spilling a drop. He was still a class act, even when three sheets to the wind. "Seen Karen lately?" he asked.

"No. I haven't seen her all week."

"She was here earlier, checking up on me. Then she went back to Montivideo."

"She say why?"

"A case she's working on. She wouldn't say what it is."

"Does she usually say what it is?"

"That depends on what she's working on. Sometimes she does, sometimes she doesn't." He took a drink, draining half his glass. "Why all the questions about Karen? Why don't you ask her yourself?"

"I might have to."

"I would think you'd want to."

"Then you don't know me very well."

"You're a strange a bird, you know it?" he said. "Just when I think I've got you pegged, you're somewhere else."

I rose, nearly upsetting the lounge chair as I did. "The story of my life."

He picked up his glass and sat staring at it. "Any luck finding out who took that shot at me?" he asked.

"Some. I think I know who did it."

"So do I."

That surprised me. "For how long?"

"Since last night."

"You saw her?"

He nodded ever so slightly.

"Why didn't you say something?"

He raised his glass and drained it. "She missed."

I walked uptown, picked up Ruth's Volkswagen, and drove to the hospital. Rupert was awake, but groggy. He sat up in bed trying to focus on me, but first one eye, then the other would droop. "Should I come back tomorrow?" I asked.

"No. I'm listening," he mumbled. "I just can't seem to keep my eyes open."

"How will I know when you've stopped listening?"

"I'll tell you."

Somehow I doubted that.

"Go on," he said. "While I'm still in the mood."

151

I pulled up a chair beside him. "This might take a while."

"I'm not going anywhere. Except to sleep, if you don't get on with it."

I smiled. He was starting to get surly. He must be feeling better. "Okay, first I'll tell you what I know. Then I'll tell you what I think. Then if you're up to it, you can tell me where I'm wrong."

He nodded.

"I know Frieda left school somewhere around three-thirty, or maybe earlier. I know she got at least as far as Gas Line Road where Hattie Peeler saw her walking. I know Joe Turner left the Marathon sometime between three-fifteen and three-thirty and drove south toward the school. I know he came back north again, but I don't know when. I know he was seen coming into town from the north somewhere around six o'clock. I know he and Frieda had a love nest in her straw mow where I found her purse. I know Frieda was taking birth control pills and that she was mildly epileptic. I know Joe watched helplessly while his father burned to death and is carrying enough guilt to grow dragons. I know Fred Pierson once owned a strange dog that his wife, Betty, made him get rid of. I know Fred has been out every night for the past six months hunting for whatever killed Betty. I know it wasn't coyotes."

Rupert was looking at me with both eyes open. "Go on."

"That's all I know."

The faintest of smiles creased his swollen face. "That's good. I was sure in the next breath you'd say I was Lazarus and you were the Holy Spirit come down to earth. And the way you were going, I'd have had a hard time doubting you."

"Did I belabor the point?"

"No. You made one. You're better at this than I am. It's time I admitted that and learned to live with it. Not

152

that you'd make a better sheriff. Because you're not near as good at the things I do that occupy ninety-nine percent of my time, like seeing drunks home and keeping Hershel and Liddy Bennett from killing each other. You don't have the patience for it. But when it comes to asking the right questions, you stand head and shoulders above anyone I ever met. And if I had it on, I'd take my hat off to you."

"At least we agree on one thing," I said.

"What's that?"

"You make a better sheriff than I would."

"You don't take praise easy, do you?"

"Nor criticism. One embarrasses me, the other makes me angry enough to chew nails."

"Then how do you know when you're on the right track?"

"Something inside tells me. It's something I know when I look in the mirror."

Rupert's eyes strayed to the bouquet of roses in the vase beside his bed. "Elvira tells me. Always has. I hope always will."

"Then you're a very lucky man."

"You mean that, don't you."

"From the bottom of my heart. I've never known anyone well enough to trust her that much. Sometimes I doubt if I ever will."

He nodded. He understood—well enough not to ask me to explain myself, something I didn't want to do. "You told me what you know," he said. "Tell me what you think."

So I told him. Essentially it was that Frieda had somehow gotten out of school early, called Joe and told him to pick her up on her way home, which he had. They'd gone to the barn to make love as they had in the past. But something had gone wrong. Perhaps Frieda had forgotten to take her pill, or something had set her off, and she'd suffered an epileptic fit, possibly lapsing into a coma. Thinking he'd killed her, Joe panicked and ran, taking Frieda with him. He got as far as Mitchell's Woods where he decided to hide. From there it was hard to guess what happened. Knowing Joe and his past, it didn't seem likely he would have abandoned Frieda under any circumstances. It was more likely he discovered she was still alive, though unconscious, and went in search of water. In the meantime she awakened, wandered off, and became lost. Or he lost his way and couldn't find her again.

"Then why did he come back to town?" Rupert asked.

"He might have reached a point where his mind blanked out, rather than admit what had happened. I'd guess that even now he has no memory of it."

"You might be right. When I asked him where he'd been on Thursday, he told me Mitchell's Woods. He said he'd gone out there to jump somebody's car."

"But he never said whose?"

"No. He said the car was gone when he got there."

"Did Fred Pierson see any other cars in the area?"

"No. The only one he saw was Joe's."

"Parked at Mitchell's Woods?"

"No. Driving south, on Joe's way home."

"What about the rest of it? Do you think it could have happened as I said? Frieda could have had a seizure of some kind?"

He took some time to think about it. "It's possible. Stranger things have happened. Frieda had slept with someone the day she was killed. And she'd also been thrashing around in Mitchell's Woods awhile, before she was killed. The scratches on her legs showed that."

"Could she have been raped?"

"No. At least the coroner doesn't think so, and he's usually right about those things." He studied me. He usually knew what I was about. "Is there a reason for that question?"

"I was thinking about a phone call Joe got last Monday. It really seemed to disturb him. I don't know how to explain it, unless it was from Frieda. You know, a lover's quarrel. It might have continued into Thursday. Joe forced himself on her, and that's when her seizure came."

"From what I know of the boy it's not in him," Rupert said.

"I don't think so either. What did set her off then?"

"Maybe she thought she heard her dad coming home. Harvey would've killed both of them if he knew what was going on. Joe anyway. He figured they were up to something, but not there in his own barn." He noticed the look on my face. "Does that bother you?"

"In a way it does. Frieda's death, if it happened like we think. Kids her age and younger committing suicide. It seems such a waste—none of this need happen if, damn it, we'd just learn how to talk to each other. But then, there wasn't anything Diana and I couldn't, or didn't, talk about. Now she's in Madison and I'm here, and we seem to be drifting farther apart every day. So what's the answer, Rupert? I'm fresh out of them."

He suddenly looked and sounded tired. "I don't know, Garth. I don't think that hard about it. I have enough to do, trying to keep a lid on this county, without trying to solve the problems of the world."

"The world's problems are our problems."

"Only some of them, Garth. Only some of them."

I drove home. Ruth was frying hamburgers when I got there. She had the potato salad already made. I sat down at the table and watched her work. I'd learned long ago not to try to help.

"You're home early," she said. "Supper's not even cold."

"It's been a long day."

"How's Rupert?"

"Doing okay at the moment."

"What was it you said happened to him?"

"I didn't say."

"Then somebody better. Rumors are flying hot and heavy. They're saying he was attacked by everything from a pack of coyotes to the abdominal snowman."

155

"I think that's abominable."

"I know what it is. They don't. What I'm saying is that somebody ought to set the record straight before it gets out of control."

"Namely you?" I asked.

"Namely *you*."

"I don't know what happened to him."

She stopped frying long enough to glare at me. "I thought you said you were there?"

"I was. I just don't know what attacked him."

"Then something *did* attack him?"

"Yes. Though this is as far as I want it to go."

"Any ideas?"

"Rupert thinks it was a wolf, Josh Henry a coy-dog, and Fred Pierson's not saying."

"What's a coy-dog?"

"Half dog, half coyote. Sometimes they interbreed."

"What do you think?"

"I don't know. I just know I'm afraid of it."

"That's comforting. What am I supposed to say when somebody asks me?"

"Stay out of Mitchell's Woods."

"That's what my mother used to tell me." She smiled at the thought. "But not for the same reason."

"Too bad. I've had a lot of fun in the woods."

"I'll bet you have." She opened a bun and put a hamburger in it. "You ready to eat?"

"As I'll ever be. Are there any onions cut?"

"I thought you'd sworn off onions."

"I said I should. I didn't say I had."

She gave me her "got you" smile and took a plate of sliced onions from the refrigerator.

I smiled in return. When everything around me started going crazy, I could at least count on Ruth to stay sane. Then, before I forgot, I called Karen Wilson.

16

After supper I walked to my newspaper office. It was an orange and cloudless evening, and pale blue above the orange. It seemed all of Oakalla was outside tonight, either working in their yards, or tending their gardens, or playing tag and baseball, or just sitting down and enjoying themselves. There was the smell of new-mown grass in the air, the sweet scent of honey locust in flower. It was that spring evening you always remembered, the one you put in your heart and gave your grandkids one day.

I sat down at my typewriter and thought about what I was going to write. I had the story of Frieda Whitlock all ready to go. I just didn't have a beginning or ending.

I pushed my chair back and stared out the window. This wasn't going to be easy. Saying too little about Frieda's death would lose my readers' trust in me, a trust that had been six years in the making. Saying too much, which in this case was the bare facts, would put Oakalla in an uproar and turn every television camera in the state our way. It seemed I couldn't win. I was damned if I did and damned if I didn't.

Finally I decided the hell with it. I'd rather lose my readers than the integrity of Oakalla and the sanctity of

157

Mitchell's Woods. As Harry Truman so eloquently and succinctly said, the buck stopped here.

I was halfway through the second paragraph when Karen Wilson walked into my office. She wore sandals and jeans and a University of Wisconsin sweatshirt with cut-off sleeves. She wore no makeup and her hair looked like a squirrel's nest. She still looked good to me.

"Have a seat," I said. "I'm busy at the moment."

She had a seat. I returned to my writing and had just finnished the paragaph when the phone rang. It was Diana. When it rains, it pours.

"I thought I'd find you here," she said.

"Where else? How are you?"

"Not bad. How are you?"

"A little frazzled at the moment. I could use a back rub."

"Funny I was thinking the same thing. Should we make an appointment? I'll do you if you'll do me."

"Best offer I've had all day. When?" I asked.

"Is tomorrow too soon? I'd really like to see you."

"Same here. But I can't tomorrow."

"Then how about Saturday?"

I was tempted, but Saturday was still an unknown for me. "How about a week from Saturday?"

"I'll have started summer school by then."

"What difference does that make? You have all summer to school."

"It's a five weeks course. They cram a lot into it. I don't want to get buried."

"How far behind can a back rub put you?" I asked.

"I thought we might make a weekend of it."

"You could always come here. My door's always open," I said.

"So's mine. But you haven't walked through it very often lately."

"I could say the same."

"Should we just forget it then?" She was hurting. I

158

could tell by the sound of her voice. So was I. As she'd told me on the eve of my last departure, long distance relationships are hell.

"Is that what you want?" I asked.

"No."

"Me either."

"So what do we do in the meantime?"

"Hang in there."

"How can we if we don't ever see each other? Some days I even forget what you look like."

"I'm not the one who moved away, who doesn't know if she's ever coming back."

"So it's my fault? Is that what you're saying?"

"It's nobody's fault. You're there. I'm here. It's hard to make it work."

"Then why don't we give it up?"

"I don't know. Call me back tomorrow. I might have an answer for you then."

"Bye." She hung up.

I sat looking at the receiver. My first impulse was always to call her back and apologize. For what I didn't know. I just felt like we left too many things unsaid. Except in trying to say them, we usually tried too hard, got too deep, and then couldn't dig our way out.

"Friend of yours?" Karen asked.

I looked up, saw her staring at me. I'd forgotten she was in the room. "Yes."

"Who? If it's any of my business?"

"Diana Baldwin."

"I know her. She's a beautiful woman."

"Yes, she is. Probably the most beautiful woman I've ever known." I smiled at her. "No offense."

"None taken." She got up and stood beside me, reading over my shoulder. I could feel her presence, imagine how good the rest of her would feel. It made my shoulders ache. "What is it you're writing?"

"My column for tomorrow's paper."

"Do you mind if I read it?"

"I'd rather you wait until I finished."

"How long will that be?"

"An hour or two, depending on how it goes."

"I'm not sure I can wait that long. I *do* have to get back to Montivideo tonight."

"You been home yet?" She still stood behind me. I kept waiting for her to touch me, but she didn't.

"No." she answered. "I came right here."

"Maynard could use some company tonight."

"Since when did you start worrying about Maynard?"

"I just know how I feel."

"Aren't I company?"

"Yes. But you're not my wife."

"And I'm not Diana, right?"

"Right."

She returned to her chair. "Go ahead. Type," she said. "I won't bother you again."

I swung my chair around to face her. "I'm out of the mood."

"What are you in the mood for?"

"Conversation."

"Talk's cheap."

"Not where I come from."

She looked at me with those big hazel eyes of hers. I felt overmatched. "So what do you want to talk about?" she asked.

"Walter Lawrence."

"What about him?"

"I want to know if you killed him."

Her gaze never wavered. But I couldn't have hit her harder with a club. She took a sharp short breath and held onto the arms of the chair for support. "You don't waste any words, do you?" she said.

"Like you said, talk's cheap."

"And I thought I was being clever."

"You were. I got lucky."

She laughed, releasing some of the tension between us. "It wasn't luck, Garth, not after seventeen years. You're damn good, that's all. I'm sorry I won't find out how good."

"So am I."

"I wish I could believe that."

"Believe it. It's true."

She smiled and shrugged. She didn't believe it. "Should I call my lawyer?" she asked. "The last time I talked to him he was drunk on his ass."

"No. I'm not charging you with anything."

"Then why did you call me?"

"I wanted some answers."

"I thought you had all the answers."

It was my turn to smile. "Not nearly all of them."

"What answers are you missing?"

"What happened and how it happened. I know you and Walter sometimes went to Phillipee's Pond. I know Walter was killed and dropped in the pond. I know he had fifty thousand dollars on him, which you've started to pay back to his wife, so I assume you took it. But I'd like to think I know you well enough to know that you're neither a murderer nor a thief. So I'd like to know what happened, how Walter died and why you took his money."

"How will that help?"

"I don't know. It might make you innocent."

"I've never been innocent, Garth. Not for a long time anyway."

"Less guilty then."

"That's better. That's language we both understand."

"So we're neither one a saint. I like people with a little tarnish on them. It shows they've rubbed elbows with life."

"Then why don't you like me?"

"I do. Perhaps too well."

"You wouldn't care to explain that, would you?"

"No. I wouldn't."

161

"You'd rather have my version of what happened at Phillipee's Pond?"

"Walter's dead, or I'd ask him."

"Would it help to say it was an accident?"

"It'd help. But I'd still like to hear the rest of it."

"This isn't on tape, is it?"

"I'm not even taking notes."

She stood and walked to the window. The moon was on the wane, about three-quarters full. It shone with a white light through the trees along Gas Line Road. I wished I were out in it, walking, letting my thoughts unwind, until there was nothing left to think.

"It was in May," she said. "The last week, I think. We'd just gotten out of school for the summer. Walter called me at home and said he had to see me. He sounded excited, but then he always sounded like that when he called. Walter was easily excited."

"Especially where you were concerned?"

"I guess so. Though I wasn't the only woman he ever chased."

"Were you the only woman he ever paid?"

"Who told you that?"

"It doesn't matter. Is it true?"

"Sometimes he paid me. Sometimes he didn't. I was flattered—by the attention of an older man. I didn't care if he paid me or not. I just wanted his company."

"Was he good company?"

"I thought so at the time. Now, who knows? My taste in men has changed, like everything else."

"Welcome to the club. But go on."

"As I said, Walter called. He picked me up in the alley behind my house, and we drove to Phillipee's Pond. We'd just gotten there when he took off his money belt and told me to look inside. It was full of one hundred dollar bills. Then he told me to count it. I did. It came to over fifty thousand dollars. I asked him what he was going to do with all of that. He said *we* were going to Mexico. When, I asked? As soon as I could pack. For how long? Forever, he answered." She'd been watching the moon. She turned to look at me. "It was tempting," she said. "I was going nowhere here, and I didn't have the money to go to college as I wanted. But I at least wanted some time to think about it. I told Walter that. He said we didn't have any time, that he'd be in trouble the minute someone discovered he'd withdrawn all that money. In fact, he might be in trouble already. I said he should have thought of that beforehand, that I wasn't going to run off and leave my family without at least thinking about it first." She turned to watch the moon some more. "There was one thing I'd forgotten about Walter. His persistence. He wouldn't take no for an answer. First he pleaded, then he cried, then he begged. When that didn't work, he used force. He grabbed me by the arm and at the same time tried to start the car. I jerked away, got out of the car, and started running. He ran after me. I made a circle of the pond and had started up the hill toward town, when I didn't hear him behind me anymore. I looked around to see where he was, and he was nowhere in sight. I should've gone on home, but I didn't. I went looking for him. I found him at the edge of the pond. He was dead." She said it quietly, without emotion, as if reciting a liturgy.

"What had happened to him?"

"I don't know. It looked like he'd fallen and hit his head on something. The back of it was all bloody and mushy. And his clothes were mussed, like he'd rolled down the hill." She turned back to me. Her eyes said believe it if you will. That's the way it happened.

"What did you do then?"

"I didn't know what to do—whether to run and just keep on running until someone caught me, or call the sheriff and tell him what happened, or get rid of Walter and take my chances that no one would find him. I didn't think about the fifty thousand dollars, not until I was

163

driving out of there in Walter's car and saw it lying on the seat."

"So what did you decide to do about Walter?"

"That's obvious. I decided to get rid of him."

"That sounds pretty mercenary to me."

"The hell with you!" she said, her voice coming to life. "It's not you we're talking about. I was seventeen years old, barely graduated from high school, and looking *what* in the face? I didn't know. I did know I didn't want to spend the rest of my life paying for something I didn't do."

"You went there with Walter, don't forget that."

"Which makes me guilty of what?"

"Nothing. But it seems like you owed him more than a swim in the pond."

"I gave him what he wanted. He gave me what I wanted. It was a fair trade. No more. No less."

"Not to Walter."

"I'm not responsible for his feelings. I never asked him to fall in love with me."

"What about your own feelings? Or don't you have any?"

She looked away from me, back to the moon. The tears in her eyes answered my question. "Screw you," she said.

"I'm sorry. That was uncalled for."

"Yes, it was."

"But so is murder," I said.

She wheeled around to face me. She was so angry she couldn't get the words out. "I didn't . . . murder . . . Walter Lawrence!"

"Doc Airhart says someone did."

"That old quack! What does he know?"

"He knows that Walter died from a blow of such force that it couldn't have been accidental. And he's not an old quack. He's about the best there is."

164

"He's an old quack if he says I killed Walter Lawrence! Because I didn't!"

"You don't have to shout. I'm right here."

"Go to hell! I didn't just call you a liar!"

"I didn't call you a liar. I said Walter Lawrence was murdered. I didn't say you did it."

"I was the only one there. Who else could have done it?"

"I don't know. Let's pass on that for a moment. What did you do with Walter after you decided to get rid of him?"

She stopped a moment, swallowed hard, and when she spoke again, she had control of her voice. "There was a boat out there at the pond. It had an anchor in it. The boat didn't look like it was used anymore. It was full of holes. I barely got out and back with it. I dragged Walter into it, wrapped the anchor rope around him, rowed out to the middle of the pond, and dumped him overboard. It wasn't easy. I rocked the boat and nearly went out myself. Then I rowed back to shore, got in Walter's car, and started driving back toward town. On the way I saw Hattie outside in her yard. I pulled into her drive and told her what had happened. She didn't even think twice about it. She said she'd hide Walter's car for me. I asked what I should do with the money. She thought about it a moment and said, 'Use it, child. But use it wisely.' That's what I've tried to do."

I thought about the consequences. She'd gotten an education and was now was living the good life, if there was such a thing. Maxine had been forced to scrub floors and clean toilets and sack groceries to give her boys the same education. Now she was getting paid back a month at a time and starting to live the good life. Had the money been used wisely? If it bought somebody some peace of mind along the way, I guessed it had.

"Was it Hattie who called when we were in the bar in Montivideo?" I asked.

"Yes. She told me to get you out of town and she'd do the rest. She planned to drive Walter's car as far as Phillipee's Pond and leave it there. That way she wouldn't have to answer any of your questions when you finally found the car in her garage, which she was sure you would. Except she couldn't get the car started. So since she couldn't move it, she moved herself into my apartment until we could decide what to do with it."

"What did you decide to do with it?"

"Nothing. We thought that was perhaps the best. Hattie would come home and try to keep you out of her garage as best she could. Meanwhile it might all blow over." She gave me a look that was half smile, half frown. "Fat chance, with you involved."

"How is Hattie by the way?"

"About to go crazy, and drive me crazy besides. She can't wait to get back to her house and garden. I can't wait to let her."

"Keep her at least another day."

"Why?"

That was a good question. I wasn't sure I had an answer for it. "I just think it'll be better for all concerned."

"What's the point? You already know what happened to Walter. The only thing another day with me will do is drive us both up the wall."

"It's not Walter I'm thinking about. Hattie might be a witness in the Frieda Whitlock case."

"She never said anything to me."

"She probably won't either, so don't press her on it. I want to wait until I can at least talk to her."

"Why can't you talk to her here?"

"I could, but I don't want to take any chances."

"What chances?"

"That something might happen to her." Which surprised me, because up to now I didn't think she was in danger. But something was gnawing at me, something

166

that said all the pieces in the Frieda Whitlock puzzle didn't quite fit.

"Are you sure you aren't trying to get even with me?"

"For what?"

"Leaving you in Clancy's Bar."

"I did have my hopes up. Among other things."

She gave me an all-knowing look. There was a smile inbedded in it. "So did I. Pity it didn't work out the way I planned. I'd even changed the sheets at noon."

I took a deep breath and slowly counted to ten. There she stood in her jeans and baggy sweatshirt with no makeup and a squirrel's nest for hair. She'd set me up for one fall and could just as easily set me up for another. Not to mention the fact that she was married. And had possibly killed a man. Still I was having a hard time staying in my chair. I would have liked to make love to her right there on the office floor.

In self-defense, I changed the subject. "Two years ago you endorsed a check for ten thousand dollars. Where did that money go?"

"None of your business."

"If it has to do with Walter, it is my business. Is Maxine Lawrence blackmailing you?"

"No. She has no idea where the money is coming from. She won't either, if I can help it."

"How long do you intend to support her?"

"As long as I can afford it."

"That might be the rest of your life. Or hers."

"What's that to you?"

"Nothing. Except it's not necessary."

"You mean it won't change what I did? I know that. But it still makes me feel better to give her money."

"What if she asks for more?"

"I told you. She doesn't know where it's coming from."

"Then where did the ten thousand go?"

"I don't know," she said. "That's the truth."

"Josh Henry?"

She gave a pensive look. "Is there anything you don't know about me?"

"A lot of things. Was it Josh?"

She glanced away, then back at me. "I always thought so."

"Why?"

"The way the letter was written. Crude and backward, the way I remembered Josh from high school. He said he had pictures of me screwing Walter Lawrence, that if I didn't want my husband to see them, I'd leave ten thousand dollars in the hollow stump at the south end of Phillipee's Pond. I ignored him of course."

"Why?"

"I knew Walter and I had been spied on, but I was sure no one had ever come close enough to take photographs of us."

"Spied on by whom?"

"Buck or Josh Henry. A couple of times I caught him looking at us. I couldn't see his face, but I could his cap and shirt. He left in the direction of their cabin."

"Could it have been Buck who wrote the letter?"

"No. Buck had just died. I remembered thinking good riddance."

"What happened after you ignored the letter?"

"I got another one. This one I paid attention to. It told me he knew what I'd done to Walter Lawrence. If I didn't want the rest of Oakalla to know, I'd pay him the money he asked for."

"Did he up the ante the second time?"

"No."

"Did you pay it as he asked?"

"Yes. I knew it was a mistake, that he'd surely ask for more later, and then what would I do? But so far he hasn't."

"If it's any consolation, I don't think he will. He got what he wanted with the ten thousand."

"Which is?"

"A dog," I said without thinking.

"A dog! What kind of a dog?"

That was the question I didn't have an answer for. I gave her what I did have. "A hunting dog. A coon dog, to be exact."

"A coon dog! What kind of a coon dog is worth ten thousand dollars?"

"A good one. A great one is worth ten times that."

But she wasn't listening. "Half the world is starving and I pay ten thousand dollars for a coon dog! Someone ought to shoot me."

"Given the chance, someone might try."

"What do you mean by that?"

What did I mean by that? I didn't know. It seemed my mouth was ahead of my brain tonight. Not so unusual for me. "Nothing. But Hattie's not the only one I want to stay in Montivideo tomorrow. I want you to stay there, too."

"Why?"

I ignored her question. My mind was somewhere else. "Did Josh Henry ever ask you out?"

"When? Lately?"

"When you were in high school?"

"He asked. Several times. I didn't go. Why?" she repeated.

"Thanks for stopping by. I'll be in touch."

"That's all? Now I'm dismissed? Like a good little girl or bad little girl, which is it?"

"Neither. But I have a column to write and a paper to print. I'll be busy. You'll be bored."

"Why don't you let me worry about that?"

I started typing. "Suit yourself."

"Thanks. I will."

So she stayed and when I finished my column, I handed it to her to read, while I took a walk outside. When I returned, she was sitting where I'd left her, and the column was lying on my desk. She had the same look on her face that I'd seen in Clancy's Bar. I would have given a lot to know what it meant.

"Well?" I finally asked to break the silence.

"I think it's the best thing you've ever done," she said quietly.

"Thank you. I appreciate that."

Again silence, as she sorted her thoughts. "It would have been a mistake, you know, to have slept with you. I'm glad now it didn't happen."

"I'm not."

"Please, Garth. I'm trying to make some sense out of this. What I feel for you is too strong for a romp in the hay, yet not enough to chuck it all, including my marriage, for you. I like who I am and what I have, and I plan to go on liking it. I'm not a boat-rocker at heart, though I suspect you are."

I smiled at her. "It's been a long day, Karen, and it's not over yet. I don't want to talk about it, okay? I do enough of that with Diana. If you want me, fine. If you don't, fine. But don't feel you have to explain yourself."

"What about you? What do you want?"

"I don't know, and I'm too tired to think about it. I do know one thing, though. If you do have to think about it, and convince yourself that it's right, it's not."

"That sounds like a man's point of view."

"I'd hope so. Goodnight, Karen."

"Goodnight, Garth."

"You going home?"

"Not tonight. Maybe tomorrow."

"Then have a safe trip back to Montivideo."

"Thanks. I will," she said and left.

17

 Josh Henry was a half hour early. That was fine with me. I was ready to go by then.

I called my printer, then stepped outside into the night air. It was cooler than I expected. I was way underdressed for a night in Mitchell's Woods.

I got in the cab with Josh. I guessed the Plott was in the camper in the back. "Stop by my house a minute, will you?" I asked.

"Sure. Why?"

"It's cooler than I thought. I need something more than I've got on."

"I've got an old hunting coat in back. It don't smell too good, but it'll keep you warm."

"Sounds fine to me. Thanks." As tired as I was, once I climbed the stairs to my room, I might decide to stay.

We drove north on Fair Haven Road, then west, then north again toward Mitchell's Woods. Josh meanwhile had taken a pinch of snuff and begun spitting in the Pepsi can he kept on the dash for that purpose. The cab soon began to smell like dog and evergreen. I cracked my window to let in some air.

"How much did you say you paid for the Plott?" I asked.

"I didn't say," Josh answered. "At least I don't remember saying."

"I thought you told me ten thousand dollars."

I had him there. I thought I saw him squirm a little. "I might have. I just don't remember it."

"It doesn't matter. It just seems like a lot to pay for a dog."

"Not this dog!" Josh was quick to defend. "Hell, that ain't even close to what he's worth! You'll see. Once we get out to Mitchell's Woods."

"What did your grandfather think of him?"

"He didn't. Grandpop died before I ever bought him. Shame, too. Grandpop never thought I was worth a shit, not without him telling me what to do. And here I went out and bought the best damn dog in the country—all on my own. I bet Grandpop's doing flipflops over that."

I gave Josh the smile he wanted. "I bet he is."

He went on, "To look at him, the Plott don't look like much, those blue eyes and all. But I knew the first time I saw him hunt that was the dog for me. So I began putting away every penny I could save in hopes of buying him someday. Never thinking, of course, my dream would come true."

"If he's such a good dog, why did his owner sell him?"

Josh was indignant. "He didn't know what he had, that's why!"

"I thought you said he was a world champion."

He retreated and gave me his boyish smile. "Well, I stretched the truth a little there. But he could be a world champion, if I wanted to make him one."

"Don't you?"

"No. It's too much trouble going around to all the hunts all over the country. Then you got to pay an entry fee every time. It just ain't worth it to me. I hunt for the plain fun of it. I don't want it to seem like work."

"A point well taken," I said.

We parked at the south edge of Mitchell's Woods about a mile or so east of where Fred Pierson lived. We got out of the truck, and I stretched and shivered, while Josh opened up the back and handed me his hunting coat. He was right. It didn't smell very good. But at least it was better than being cold.

Then the Plott appeared on the tailgate. Up close, he was even bigger than I remembered him. He yawned, showing me all of his teeth, but otherwise took no notice of me. Josh put on a lead strap, the Plott jumped down from the truck, and they walked around to the cab, where Josh took his shotgun down from the rack over the back window. I counted as he put five shells into the gun, then injected one into the chamber. I noticed, by the red showing, that the gun was off safety. I told Josh this.

"I know," he said. "I always keep it that way when I'm in here. You never know about this place." There was caution in his voice, and just a hint of terror.

"Then I'd rather you walked ahead of me."

"Have to anyway. We only have one light. I intended to bring Grandpop's, but I forgot."

The more I thought about it, the less I liked what I was about to do. It was bad enough to go into Mitchell's Woods at night, but without a light, with a scared, trigger-happy companion, and a man-eating something on the loose, it almost seemed suicidal. I was thankful for the Plott at least. He seemed the calmest of all of us.

We walked into the woods a short way and Josh turned the Plott loose. Already I could see the hazard of not having a light. If I stayed close enough to Josh to use his light, I caught the branches he clipped on his way through. If I hung back a few feet until all was clear, I couldn't see what was in front of me. And Josh wasn't by nature a slow walker. I almost had to run to keep up with him.

"What do we do now?" I asked after he turned the Plott loose.

"We wait until he strikes a track. Then we'll have to move with him. Otherwise, he might run it out of hearing."

So we waited for the Plott to strike a track. In the meantime I listened for the night sounds of the woods. I heard a few of them, a nearby tree frog, some peepers way off to the north, and the occasional trill of a nightbird I couldn't identify. But Mitchell's Woods seemed hushed, on tiptoes, like it had last night, as if death were stalking it once more.

The strike bark wasn't long in coming. It was sharp and close at hand and sent a shiver up my spine. The hunt was now on.

But Josh didn't move. I asked him why. "There's no need," he said. "The Plott just tapped a tree. That coon won't be far off."

He'd no more than said it when the Plott began to bay. He had a deep resonant voice that rolled from his chest like that of a practiced baritone. It was rhythmic, musical, and hit all the right notes, but like the portfolio of a good journeyman seemed more style than substance.

He did have a coon, though, which Josh was quick to point out to me. It was a kitten coon, no more than half grown, and sat huddled on a bare limb barely ten feet above the ground. Given a little better nose and enough time, *I* could have treed that coon. But Josh didn't care. He lavished praise on the Plott like he'd just treed Old Ridgerunner himself, the one coon that eluded Buck Henry to his dying day.

Then Josh snapped on the lead strap and tried to pull the Plott away from the tree. The Plott was reluctant, however. He knew the coon was still there. That was obvious. He could see him. And this might be his one and only claim to fame. Finally, though, the Plott relented and let Josh lead him a couple yards deeper into the woods, where Josh released him again. I was sure the Plott would turn around and head right back to the same tree, as I'd seen other dogs do in the past. But to his credit, he didn't. If he was nothing else, he was clever, clever enough to go on fooling Josh indefinitely.

"What do you think now?" Josh asked.

I didn't want to tell him that on first impression I thought his dog was overpriced—almost nine thousand nine hundred and fifty dollars worth. Instead, I said, "He's one for one."

"You ain't seen nothing yet!"

He was right. Nothing was what we saw at the next tree. Josh shined it for about a half hour before he gave up, saying the coon was there, he just couldn't find it.

I didn't argue. The Plott had treed in a huge white oak about a hundred feet high and a hundred feet wide. Even in daylight, a coon could have been hiding in there and we'd have never seen it. Clever, I thought again. If you had to pick one, pick a tree too big to shine.

I thought the Plott would be happy to be on lead again, satisfied he'd put on a good show. But he wasn't. He looked almost insolent as Josh roughly led him away and started him hunting again. His eyes seemed to say, "I know that damn coon is up there. Why the hell don't you?"

The next tree was an old den tree. I could see a well-used hole about thirty feet up. Josh was determined to climb up to it and show me there was a coon in the den. I told him it wasn't necessary, that I believed him. But I could tell he didn't believe me. Worse, he was beginning to doubt the Plott. When the Plott wouldn't leave the tree willingly, Josh beat him with the lead strap until he did, though grudingly, and more insolent than before. And we hadn't even heard from the Coy-Dog, which is what we'd come for.

The next track took the Plott almost out of hearing before he treed. Instead of running to keep up with him as before, Josh hung back and sulked, then waited several minutes before he even started for the tree. Though his behavior seemed childish, I didn't try to tell him what to do. It was his dog on trial, not mine. If I'd been in his shoes, I might have felt as he did.

On our way to the tree I heard a familiar sound. It was the yip-yip-yip of the coyote pack. Though they were still far to our north, it sounded like they were heading our way. In fact, it sounded like they were heading for the tree where the Plott was.

Josh heard them, too. He stopped and turned to look at me. As he did, the light on his red hard hat swung into my eyes, temporarily blinding me. "Did you hear that?" he asked.

"Yes! Now turn that damn thing off!"

"Sorry, Coach. I was just making sure you were back there."

"Why wouldn't I be? This is what we came for, isn't it? A chance at the Coy-Dog?"

"That's right. I forgot."

But he didn't sound convinced. And the closer we came to the tree, the closer the coyotes came to us, the more tentative he became. When we reached the foot of the tree where the Plott was, I noticed his hand was shaking, so badly he couldn't even snap the lead strap on the Plott. He set the shotgun down to use both hands.

"What are you doing?" I asked.

"Catching him while I can."

"Aren't you even going to shine the tree?" It seemed we owed the Plott that much.

"What's the use? There ain't nothing there. He's only bluffing, just like he's been all night."

"Then give me your light and let me shine it."

"I said what's the use! He's my dog, ain't he? I ought

176

to know when he's bluffing!" His voice was shrill, nearly hysterical.

I looked at the Plott. He didn't look like he was bluffing to me. He looked dead serious, like he wasn't going to be put on lead this time without a fight. To prove his point, when Josh reached for him again, he grabbed Josh by the wrist and held on. Josh screamed in pain, trying to fight his way to the tree where the shotgun stood. The Plott, however, wouldn't let him. He wasn't trying to hurt Josh, just teach him a lesson. And when he did let go, he was gone before Josh even touched the shotgun.

"The sonofabitch!" Josh snarled, waving the shotgun around, looking for something to shoot. "Wait until I catch up to him!"

A bad night was fast deteriorating. I wondered what I could salvage from it. "Give me your light, Josh," I said, looking up the tree.

"Why?"

"Just give me your light. I want to show you something."

He took off his belt and battery and shoved hat, cord, belt, light, and all at me. Holding the belt and battery in my hand, I put the hat on and turned the light to high beam. As I swept the tree with the light, I saw the coon where I thought I'd seen it before. It was a large coon and smart enough not to look at me when the light was on.

"You want to see for yourself," I said to Josh.

"See what?"

"The coon."

He was still sulking. "I've seen coons before."

"It's a big one."

"How big?" I'd gotten his attention.

"Come see for yourself."

Finally he did. Then he smiled and said, "I guess I owe old Mike an apology. Though he had no call to grab

177

my wrist like he did." It was the first time I'd heard him call the Plott by name.

"He could've broken it," I pointed out. "But he didn't."

"He could at that," Josh agreed. And seemed satisfied. Though for how long, I wondered. We still weren't out of the woods yet.

We sat down and waited for the Plott's next strike. It was a long time in coming, so long I began to get cool sitting there, even with Josh's heavy hunting coat on. I hadn't heard the coyotes for a while. They seemed to have forgotten about us. At least I thought so until Josh turned on his light and swept the woods around us. I counted ten or more pairs of eyes staring at us.

Josh picked up the shotgun and brought it to his shoulder. The shotgun shook as he did. But when it reached his shoulder, it was rock steady.

"What are you doing?" I asked.

"I'm going to kill me a coyote."

"Don't."

"Why not?"

"Because the Coy-Dog might be out there somewhere. I at least want to get a look at him."

"What's looking at him going to do?"

"I don't know. Maybe tell me he's real."

"I seen him! I know he's for real!"

"I know you did. But he's not real to me until *I* see him."

"You think I'm lying, it's another one of my stories?"

"No, Josh. It goes deeper than that. I want to see him for myself. Not through somebody else's eyes."

I didn't expect him to understand, but he lowered the shotgun. Then he said, "Sort of like me and Grandpop. I always had to take his word for things, even when I knew I was right."

"Yes, sort of like you and Grandpop."

Josh kept his light on and slowly turned his head,

stopping at each pair of eyes in turn. I saw none that stood out from the rest, that were either larger or fiercer or more cunning. Gradually the eyes winked out one by one, leaving us alone in the dark. Had I seen the Coy-Dog and not known it? Possibly. But I didn't think so.

We never did hear the Plott strike the track. After what seemed hours we heard him treed somewhere far to the east. His voice faded in and faded out, like a late-night radio station, just on the threshold of hearing. I couldn't even be sure it was the Plott. It might have been Godzilla mumbling to himself.

"Aren't you going after him?" I finally asked Josh.

"Can't," he said. "I must've twisted my ankle somehow. It's really starting to hurt me."

"Then what are we going to do?"

"Wait for him to come in."

"What if he doesn't come in?"

"Go on back to the truck. I'll leave my coat there on the ground. He'll be there when I come back for him tomorrow."

"You've done it before?"

"Sure. I do it all the time. With him you practically have to. Once he's treed, he ain't about to leave it, not until he's sure you ain't coming. And maybe not even then."

"Can't you call him in?"

"Yeah. But he has to hear me first. The way he's carrying on now, there ain't a chance of getting through to him"

"So we just sit here?" I asked.

"Unless you've got a better idea."

"Why don't I go after him?"

"Alone? Hell, Coach, you'd fall into a sinkhole and break your neck."

"There aren't any sinkholes in this part of the woods."

"How do you know that?"

179

"I know Mitchell's Woods. Part of it anyway. I used to roam here as a kid."

"You never told me that. Here I thought you were a greenhorn to the ways of the woods. That's what Grandpop always used to say about me. 'I'd be okay if I didn't have this damned greenhorn along.' I didn't know who he was talking to. I was the only one there."

"It sounds like your grandfather was pretty hard on you."

"He was, Coach. But you know something? I miss that old man. I miss him a lot." He sounded like he meant it.

The long and short of it was that I went after the Plott myself. I left Josh with the light and shotgun, thinking he needed them worse than I did. I wasn't as daring as I felt. The moon was still high and white, and the night as clear as a night could be. I'd follow the Plott's voice to him, and once on the lead strap, he'd take me back to Josh.

My real concern was getting him on the lead strap. He hadn't exactly been willing the last time Josh tried it. That and the fact that the Coy-Dog might be out there somewhere. Better I didn't think about that.

I'd been travelling about fifteen minutes when I stopped to listen. I could hear the Plott more plainly now. At last I was finally sure it was the Plott, not somebody's yard dog barking at the moon. No mistaking that smooth mellow voice of his that seemed more style than substance—until you had a chance to watch him work.

Then I heard something moving in the brush a few yards away from me. It wasn't shuffling, like a coon or possum, or scampering, like a smaller animal would do, but seemed to be taking slow, deliberate steps. Not a man. The steps were too light for one. Something four-footed. And solitary. At least I didn't hear any companions.

My mouth went dry. And suddenly Josh's hunting coat seemed to weigh three hundred pounds. I didn't know whether to stand still or move, walk or run, or find the nearest tree and climb it.

I decided to walk. Slowly. Keeping one eye behind me and one eye ahead, stopping every few feet to look and listen.

I'd gone about a hundred yards when I stopped to catch my breath and help hold my heart in my chest. Those hundred yards seemed a mile long, and the night seemed to grow darker with every step. Still he was there, somewhere behind me. I could feel him rather than hear him. Bold, yet wary, he seemed a paradox—totally wild, yet comfortable within a stone's throw of man. The Coy-Dog? It had to be.

I listened to the night sounds around me. They were hushed, like whispers in church, but not unnaturally so. They seemed to say to go on, that I had nothing to fear. So, my heart now in my shirt pocket, I went on.

The Coy-Dog shadowed me almost all the way to the tree where the Plott was. We were within two hundred feet with only a small hollow to cross when I heard him growl. I stopped. That's what the growl seemed to say to me. Stop, Garth. This is my first and last warning. Go no further.

"Show yourself then," I said out loud. "And I'll be satisfied."

No answer. I waited a moment, then took a couple steps in the direction from which the growl had come. I could have saved myself the effort. The Coy-Dog was no longer there. If I hadn't heard him growl, I might have convinced myself he was never there.

The tree on which the Plott was leaning was a huge beech with a massive twisted trunk that had grown out instead of up, entangling itself in several nearby trees until they formed a single dense canopy that stretched for hundreds of feet. I might have shined it with an airport beacon and found the coon, but I didn't even have a match. I hoped the Plott would understand.

181

He didn't. When I bent down to put the lead strap on him, he stiffened and growled. It was a low threatening growl, telling me to keep hands off, that he meant business.

But so did I. I'd spent most of the night in here already. I didn't intend to spend the rest of it. I could never find my way back without the Plott—at least not until daylight.

"Look, damn it," I said. "You know there's a coon up there. I know there's a coon up there. The coon knows there's a coon up there. But he's not coming down, and I'm not going up after him. So unless you plan to climb the tree yourself, we're going to have to leave him there."

The Plott turned to look at me. The shadow of his huge head tilted as if he were thinking it over. Then he seemed to shrug and say, "Okay," and he walked over to me and held his head up for the lead strap. I knew at that precise moment this was no journeyman dog, that I'd misjudged him at first, that he was in fact a world champion. The question was, how did Josh get him for only ten thousand dollars?

With the Plott leading, we started back through the woods to where Josh sat. I was now certain that the Plott was smarter than Josh was. It seemed only a matter of time before he'd shoot the Plott in a fit of rage, and that would be that. There was also one other possibility, one I didn't like to consider. If Josh shot at and by chance missed the Plott, I'd bet on the Plott from there on, that he'd be the one, instead of Josh, who walked out of the woods alive.

We were nearing the place where I'd left Josh when I heard the shotgun boom. Silence. Then followed the same cat cry I'd heard last night when Rupert was attacked. It had the same effect on me. It raised every hair on my body and stopped my heart for a full beat.

The Plott, however, had a different reaction. Immediately he took off toward it, dragging me along behind

182

him. I couldn't have stopped him if I wanted. I didn't even try. I let go of the lead strap and let the Plott go on alone. When I saw him next, five minutes later, he was licking Josh Henry's hand.

"Didn't you hear it?" I asked.

"Hear what?"

"Whatever it was that just screamed. It sounded like it came from right over your head."

Josh smiled broadly. "Just a little old bobcat, that's all. He's not going to hurt anybody."

"Is that what you were shooting at?"

"No. One of those coyotes came back. That was his first and last mistake."

"You killed him?"

"I never went to look. But I bet I did."

I went to look. The coyote lay about thirty yards away. Most of his muzzle had been shot off, along with both ears. It looked like a direct hit. I stood for a while in the silence, listening to Mitchell's Woods. Death was still about. The hushed woods seemed to know that. The question was, was it waiting here for us when we came in, or did I bring it in with me?

18

It was daylight before we left Mitchell's Woods, sun-up before Josh let me off in front of my house. I was so tired I forgot about his hunting coat and wore it into the house with me. It was the first thing Ruth noticed.

"Get that out of my kitchen," she said. "I don't know where you got it, but go bury it somewhere."

"It's Josh Henry's."

"Figures."

There was something I wanted to ask her, but I couldn't remember what it was. It had to do with Buck Henry. I remembered that much. It was something she'd said when we first talked about him. I took the coat outside and laid it on the front porch. Maybe I'd remember after a couple cups of coffee.

The coffee didn't help. Neither did the bacon, eggs, and toast. My eyes still felt like sandpaper and my brain a bowl of mush.

Ruth, however, was banging around the kitchen in her usual Friday morning frenzy. Friday was her shopping day, her least favorite day of the week. So she compensated by trying to get through it as quickly as possible.

"Where to today?" I asked.

"Here, there, and everywhere. Nowhere I want to go."

"I know the feeling."

"I wouldn't know how, since I'm the one who does the shopping. But thanks for trying." She remembered something she'd forgotten and went upstairs to do it.

Folding Josh's coat under my arm, I walked to my office. The grass along the way was soaked with dew so thick it shone like frost in the sun. Another beautiful day.

Welcome. That's how my office felt. Cool and clean and comfortable, with just enough of me sprinkled here and there to show that it was mine, it was my favorite place to be early in the morning before the phone started ringing. Today I was especially looking forward to it. Today it seemed a godsend.

Leaning back in my swivel chair, I'd just closed my eyes when something started crawling down my spine. I stuck my hand down my shirt but couldn't reach it. It crawled a little further, just enough to let me know it was still there.

I stood up, pulled out my shirt and undershirt, and shook them. Relief. Whatever it was fell out on the floor.

Let it lie, I told myself. It'll still be there an hour from now. But it kept insisting, and conditioned by forty-one years of nonstop curiosity, I bent down and picked it up.

It was a piece of straw. It looked very much like the straw I'd seen in Frieda Whitlock's hair, very much like all straw looks.

Suddenly I wasn't tired anymore. I walked to the corner where I'd laid Josh's hunting coat, picked it up, and examined it. Here and there on it, inside and out, were several small pieces of straw like the one in my hand. It started my mind racing through the events of last night's hunt, events that had no connection until now. My hand was shaking when I picked up the receiver to call Fred Pierson. I was lucky. I caught him just as he was about to go out the door.

"More questions?" he asked.

"About dogs again. Do you happen to know who won the World Hunt two years ago?"

"No. I never make it there."

"Do you know anyone who did?"

"You might try Josh Henry. He goes to all the big hunts. Used to anyway."

"I'd rather not ask Josh. Anyone else?"

"Not from around here. But wait a minute. I've got some old copies of *Full Cry* laying around. They might tell who won it. If you'll hang on, I'll go look for them."

"I'll hang on."

He came back on the phone a few minutes later. "His name is Red Callahan. He won it with a three-year-old Plott named Arizona Mike."

I felt my heart start to beat a little faster. Last night Josh had called the Plott, Mike. "Does it say where Red Callahan is from?"

"Somewhere in Illinois. Here it is. Effingham."

"Thanks, Fred. I appreciate it."

"You thinking about buying Arizona Mike?"

"I doubt I could afford him."

"Why the interest then?"

"Just curious. Thanks again."

I hung up, called information in Effingham, Illinois, and drew a blank. No Red Callahan was listed. The operator went through the list of Callahans, and I picked two I liked. I got lucky on the second call.

"Red Callahan?" I asked.

"Yes. Who's this?"

"Garth Ryland. I own a small newspaper in south-central Wisconsin. I think we have a dog here that once belonged to you."

"What kind of dog?"

"A blue-eyed Plott."

There was a pause on his end. "What's the dog done?" I didn't like the question, nor the tone of voice.

186

"Nothing that I know of. I'd just like to know why you sold him for ten thousand dollars. Was he sterile?"

"I don't know. I never got the chance to find out."

"Do you mind explaining that?"

"I don't mind. Except I'm about to be late for work. Could I call you back this evening?"

"You could. But I'd rather know now. There have been a couple of deaths here. I think the Plott might be involved somehow."

"Damn!" he said. "I knew I should've shot that dog! I was afraid something like this might happen."

"Would you start at the beginning? Please. As I said, it's important."

Fortunately for me Red Callahan was an honest and decent man. "What the hell. After twenty-five years I'm entitled to be late once. What is it you want to know about the dog?"

"Anything you can tell me about him."

"He's one hell of a tracker, I'll tell you that. Once he's on your trail, you'll never shake him. I bought him as a two-year-old from a man in Arizona. He was a lion dog then. I saw him in action on a hunting trip out there. He was a holy terror on lions. Fearless. He'd go right into the lion's mouth and come out again. I don't know how he did it, but he did. He put more mountain lions at bay than the rest of the dogs put together. I decided right then I had to have that dog for myself. I offered the man ten thousand dollars cash for him, never thinking he'd take it, but he did. I should've known then something wasn't quite right with the dog, but I was so tickled to get him at that price I didn't ask any questions. I loaded him in my truck and started for home the same day. It took me about a year to finish him. There was no trouble switching him over to coons. Once he saw what I wanted, he took right to it. Smartest dog I ever owned, and that's going some. Too smart in some ways. That was part of his trouble. He didn't want to hunt for me. He wanted to hunt for

187

himself—when he thought he could get away with it. Besides that, he was as closed-mouthed as they come. He'd strike okay when he first hit the track, and he'd tree once he got that far. But between first strike and tree, I didn't know what the hell he was doing."

"Did that ever change?" I asked.

"No. Not much it didn't. That's why I wasn't too sure about hunting him in competition. I was afraid he'd take off somewhere on his own, and I'd never hear from him again. If you've got a good coon dog and there are no coons around, he'll go looking for one, even if it's in the next county. The Plott was that way. Except that he had such a good nose on him, he could cold-trail a coon when other dogs didn't even know it was around. So he didn't get into the next county too often."

"How did he do hunting with other dogs?"

"He ignored them for the most part. There wasn't a one I ever saw that could keep up with him. And when the other dogs finally would come to the tree with him, he'd stay there, close enough so he didn't get any minus points, but he'd let them do most of the barking. And pity the dog that tried to pick a fight with him. One tried when I had him on lead. The Plott had him down and by the throat before the other dog even knew what hit him. If I hadn't been there to pull him off, he'd have killed the other dog sure."

"Could you handle the Plott?"

"As well as anybody could. He'd listen to me and for the most part do what I wanted. But I've got thirty years of dog-handling behind me. Never one like the Plott, though. For a while I thought I had me the Glory Hound."

"After he won the World Hunt?"

"Yes. Though even before that I knew I had me a dandy. It was just a matter of time before he won something big. Huntingest dog I've ever seen. Some dogs are moody, just like people. Take them away from home and put them in a strange place with strange dogs and they won't hunt. Sometimes they won't get more than ten feet away from you or the truck, whichever's closest. Not the Plott, though. As soon as I turned him loose, he was ready to hunt. And he'd keep on hunting until I called him in."

"How did you call him in?"

"A special call. His first owner taught it to me. It was about the only thing he'd respond to."

"How does it go?"

"It's hard to describe. A mountain lion comes the closest thing to it. Or maybe a bobcat. It'll flat take the hair off your head if you're not expecting it. And sometimes when you are."

"Did you teach it to Josh Henry?"

"I think I did. Why?"

"I just wondered." Mainly because I'd heard it in Mitchell's Woods the night Rupert was attacked, then again last night. "What changed your mind about the Plott?"

"You mean why did I decide to sell him?"

"Yes."

"I never intended to. You can bet on that. I planned to keep him at stud a couple, three years and build up a little nest egg, enough so I could retire early if I wanted. Then I planned to hunt him again and let him help me train his pups. That's what I've always wanted to do full-time, raise and train dogs for a living. But I've never quite made it. Either the money or the dog was lacking. With the Plott I thought I had both."

"But you didn't?"

"No. I'm sad to say. It happened with the first female I brought to him. She wasn't worth much. Thank God. She was my hunting buddy's dog, and I was doing it as a favor to him. I didn't even plan to charge him for it. Good thing, the way things turned out."

"What happened?"

"The Plott killed her. I was at work at the time. My

189

wife went out to the kennel and found the female dead. The Plott was standing over in the far corner of the kennel, seeming to not be paying attention to much of anything. My wife thought the least she could do was to go into the kennel and drag the female out. Except she was already afraid of the Plott. She said she didn't like the way he looked at her with those blue eyes of his, that there was something evil about him. I told her she was just imagining things, but that didn't change her mind any. Anyway, she'd started into the kennel when something told her that was the wrong thing to do. She turned around, and by the time she took the one step she needed to get her out of there, he was nearly on her. He hit the gate just as she closed it behind her."

"What did you do then?"

"First I came home from work to find out what had happened. Then I grabbed my shotgun, loaded it with double zeroes, and went out to the kennel. I planned to kill the Plott. I don't know what stopped me. Maybe the way he stood there looking at me—head raised, eyes staring into mine, as if saying go ahead and do it if you want. It's all the same to me." He paused while he cleared his throat. "It's hard to kill an animal like that. It seemed such a waste. So I had my wife cover me with the shotgun while I went into the kennel and dragged the female out. To this day I don't know why he killed her. I guess he just didn't want to be bothered."

"That's when you called Josh Henry?"

"Not right away. I had to think about it first. I'd had a lot of offers for the Plott, anywhere from seventy-five thousand on up, but in good conscience I couldn't take any of them. They'd want to use him at stud, and the same thing might happen to them that happened to me. Then I thought of the Henry boy, how he was so taken with the dog, how he'd once offered me ten thousand for him, more than likely his life savings. He seemed like a nice enough kid and should give the Plott a good home.

190

But more than that he'd hunt the Plott. He wouldn't use him at stud. So I called him one night and asked him if he was still interested. He said he sure was and he'd be here the next day with the money. But he wasn't, nor the following day. A week or so went by and I'd about given up on him. In the meantime I was getting a lot of pressure from people who wanted to breed their dogs to the Plott. I was more than tempted to try it again. It's hard to turn down five hundred dollars a throw. Then the Henry boy showed up out of the blue one day. Said something about his grandfather dying in a hunting accident. That's why he didn't get here sooner. He asked me what I wanted for the Plott. I told him ten thousand dollars, just what I had in him. He said he didn't have the money on him, but he could raise it. I told him to come back when he had. A couple more weeks passed, and I'd about given up on him again, when there he was on my doorstep. He had the ten thousand dollars in a shoebox. He handed it to me just like that and said he wanted his dog. I said I had to tell him a few things about the dog first. So I told him what had happened and warned him to keep the Plott away from other dogs, and women just to be on the safe side, to keep him chained and hunt him alone at all times. He promised he would. He said there weren't no women in his life and he didn't like to hunt with no one else anyway. I believed him, so I let him take the Plott. But as he drove away, I had this sick feeling in my guts that I'd made a mistake, that the boy was no match for the dog. It was like pairing a goat and a tiger. Nothing good would ever come of it."

"You were right about that."

"How much damage so far?"

"More than you want to hear. But thank you for your honesty."

"I told my wife when they drove away that I should've shot the Plott when I had a chance."

"Both of them," I answered. I could still see the Plott

191

licking Josh's hand, the smile on Josh's face after he killed the coyote.

"What do you mean by that?"

"You didn't pair a goat and tiger. You paired something else again, a mutant of some kind. Whatever it is, it has two minds and one soul. If that tells you anything."

"I didn't know. Believe me."

"I believe you. I didn't know either—until now."

I called Ruth. I thought I knew what I was up against, but I wanted to make sure. "Yes, Garth, what is it?"

"How did you know who it was?"

"I just had that feeling. What do you want to know?"

"Josh Henry went to college for part of a year. I think it was Whitewater or Stevens Point, someplace like that. Can you find out for me?"

"Maybe. How soon do you need to know?"

"Yesterday."

"I'll get right on it."

In the meantime I tried to call Fred Pierson, but he wasn't home. I remembered something Karen had told me about a missing sock. Or was it Rupert? Or was it both of them? In any case I needed to check with Fred Pierson.

Ruth called me back a few minutes later. "It was in Cherubusco. He was there all of two months."

"Thanks Ruth. You're a saint."

"Well, Saint Ruth is about to leave for the day. So if you need anything, you'd better ask now. I won't be back before five."

"No. Nothing I can think of." A statement I would soon regret.

I called Cherubusco College and finally reached the equipment manager, but he didn't know where the football coach was. He gave me the coach's home phone number. The coach wasn't at home. His wife gave me the number of the Winding Hills Country Club and said if I hurried, I might catch him in the clubhouse. I hurried. I got lucky. Coach Bo Stackhouse was in the pro shop.

"Yeah, what do you want?" he asked. His voice was gruff, like his tonsils had rusted. Or maybe it was my ears.

"This is Garth Ryland. I own a newspaper in Oakalla and I'm tracking down a story."

"What kind of story?"

"A horror story. But I'll spare you the details. Josh Henry. Does that name mean anything to you? I think he played ball there at Cherubusco sixteen or seventeen years ago. He didn't last long, a couple months at the most. You might not remember him. If you were even around then?"

"Yeah, I was here. I've been here forever it seems. I'll probably die here, if I last that long. But back to Josh Henry. I think I remember him. Blond, well-built kid, not too long on smarts?"

"That's Josh. Do you remember why he left?"

"Yeah. I cut him from the team and took away his scholarship."

"Why?"

"He broke a kid's back, came within an inch of paralyzing him."

"No offense, but doesn't that come with the territory?"

"Sure. But not in this case. It was a cheap shot. The other kid was on his way down. He speared him in the back with his helmet."

"It happens every week on television."

"It wasn't the first time. He also broke a guy's leg, another guy's arm, another guy's collarbone, and hung a manager up on the wall to dry. He wasn't just mean. I'd have kept him if he was. He had all the tools to be a great linebacker. That's why I recruited him. But he was chicken-mean. He'd hurt you when you were least expecting it, and he always picked on somebody smaller than him."

"I'm starting to get the picture."

"That wasn't the only reason I cut him from the team. There was an incident at a women's dorm. He got caught

193

window-peeking. It wasn't the first time he'd been there, the girl said. He came on a regular basis, said things through the window. She lived in real fear of him."

"What kind of things?"

"What he'd do to her if he ever got the chance. Sick things. Things I'd rather not think about."

"Me either. Thanks, Coach."

"What's this Henry boy done, killed somebody?"

"I wouldn't bet against it."

I hung up and looked outside at the bright blue morning. Sad to think that Frieda Whitlock wouldn't see it, or Betty Pierson, or even Buck Henry—God rest his ornery soul. Sad to think that the boy I once had such high hopes for had probably killed them all. And he still called me Coach. That was the hardest of all to accept.

I called Fred Pierson again. He wasn't home. I called Ruth to commandeer her Volkswagen. She'd already left for parts unknown. I called Harvey Whitlock. No one home there either. I got the message.

I walked uptown to the Marathon and I was surprised to see Joe Turner there pumping gas. I thought he'd be home in bed with the covers pulled over his head. Maybe I'd misjudged him all along. Maybe he had the kind of grit that had to weather to show. Mountain grit, like that of his kinfolk.

"Morning, Mr. Ryland," he said as he cleaned Bertha Comer's windshield. "Just passing through?"

"No. I came to talk to you"

"What about?"

"Frieda."

The subject didn't please him. "I'll be with you in a minute." He finished cleaning the windshield, took Bertha's five dollar bill, and came over to where I stood on the service drive. "What about Frieda?" he asked.

I didn't answer right away. He looked bright and freshly scrubbed, like the morning. And out of place amidst my dark thoughts. I almost wished he'd stayed in Tennessee. He probably would have been happier there.

"I think I know who killed her," I said.

He wasn't impressed. "So do I. When I know for sure, I'll kill him."

"And go to prison."

"They'll have to find me first. Back in Tennessee, where I come from, there are hills that even the sun ain't seen." He said it very slowly and quietly, the way he always spoke. I had no doubt that he meant it.

"It's still a poor trade, your life for his."

"One I plan to make just the same."

His mind was made up. There was no use arguing with him. Someday, somehow he'd redress his father's death. This was as good a time as any. Maybe this time the gods would listen.

"That's not what I came for anyway," I said.

"What isn't?"

"To talk you out of it. I need some information. Only you can give it to me."

"What information is that?"

"Where you went the afternoon Frieda was killed and why."

"I went to Mitchell's Woods. But why is my business."

"You went home first. My guess is to get a gun. Then you took the long way around to Mitchell's Woods so no one would see you. Did you intend to kill whomever it was you went to see?"

"Yes."

"But you won't tell me why?"

"No."

"Was it about some photographs?"

Anger darkened his face. I'd scored a bull's-eye.

"Photographs of you and Frieda?" I continued.

"No," he said. "Pictures of Frieda screwing a dog." His voice went dead. He'd spoken the unspeakable.

"But there were no pictures, right?"

195

He shook his head and mumbled. "No pictures. I should have known." He looked at me for an answer. His eyes shown with tears. His face was etched with guilt—deep lines that might never wear away. "I loved her! I should of known!"

"Sometimes love isn't enough."

"If it ain't enough, then what the hell is?" he shouted at me.

"I don't know," I said. "Willard Coates would say trust. I'd say truth. But like love, both are just words. They have meaning only to us, what we put into them and try to live by. They don't cover every circumstance. Nothing does."

"Are you saying you might of gone to Mitchell's Woods, too?"

"We've all been to Mitchell's Woods at least once. It's a part of life, the part we know least about ourselves. I once thought the woman I loved was screwing everybody but me. It turned out she wasn't screwing anybody. But I had a lot of dark thoughts about her. I still have then now and again. I probably always will."

"But a dog!"

"It's happened, Joe, with a dog, horse, sheep, about any animal you can think of. Once it happens, it becomes possible in our minds. We might refuse to admit it, but it's still there. In our minds, even in our fantasies. And it jumps out at us when we least expect it."

A car pulled in the drive. He looked at it, then looked at me. He nodded, like he understood. If he did, he was one up on me. "Thanks, Mr. Ryland. But I've got to get back to work."

"It can wait for one question. Did you make love to Frieda last Thursday noon?"

He nodded.

"In the barn?"

He nodded again. "We usually waited until after school, whenever we were sure her dad would be gone.

196

But I was off school for the summer and Frieda was done with classes. It just happened naturally. It was nothing we planned."

"Why did she leave her purse?"

"We got in a hurry. We thought we heard her dad coming home. She remembered her purse after we'd already left. She said she didn't need it. She'd pick it up after school."

"And you let her off at school?"

"Yes. About twelve-thirty."

"If she was done with her classes, why did she go back?"

"She was helping a teacher grade papers. Besides, she wanted to say goodbye to everyone. She said she might not get a chance on Sunday."

"What was Sunday?" I asked.

"Commencement."

"That's right. I forgot."

The car by the building honked its horn. Joe was on the run before he ever thought about it. But two steps later he slowed to a walk. I took it as a good sign.

I walked west along Jackson Street and saw Harvey Whitlock's green Ford pickup parked beside the Corner Bar and Grill. I looked at my watch. Ten forty-five. A little early for lunch.

I walked into the Corner Bar and Grill and found Harvey sitting at the bar. He didn't look drunk, just lost, like he didn't have anyplace else to go.

"Is this supposed to help?" I asked, taking a seat beside him.

"I don't know if it's supposed to," he said. "But it does."

"You heard what happened to Rupert?"

"I heard something happened to him. I didn't hear exactly what. I thought your paper might tell me, since you're the one in the know. But it didn't."

"I'm sorry you're disappointed."

197

"I'm not disappointed, Garth. I'm satisfied. You said about what I expected, which was nothing."

I smiled to myself. What a fun day I was having. And it wasn't even noon yet. "You win some, you lose some, and some are rained out. But you've always got to dress for the game?"

"Meaning what?"

"At least I'm out there plugging, more than what you're doing."

"Go to hell."

"I would, but I've been there. I didn't like the accommodations."

"When?"

"A few years ago when my son died."

"You said you didn't have any children."

"I don't. The only one I had is dead. So is that part of me. The rest of me goes on."

"Hooray for you." He took a drink of his beer.

"Screw you," I said. "I'm sorry I bothered."

I started to get up. He put his hand on my shoulder and held me down. Its weight alone was enough. "I'm sorry. That was out of line," he said. "And what you wrote about Frieda . . . It was good. Her mother and me . . ." He looked away. "Thank you."

"You're welcome. Like I said, I've been there."

He offered his hand, and I shook it. That was that.

"You been to see Rupert yet?" I asked.

"No. I thought I might go this afternoon."

"I'm sure he'll be glad to see you."

"I'm not so sure. But I'm going anyway."

Then I remembered why I was looking for him. "Would you answer a question about Frieda?"

"What's the question?"

"Did she ever mention losing anything? I mean lately. A sock perhaps, or something like that?"

"She lost one of her slippers. Her mother and I turned the house upside down looking for it, but we never did find it."

"How long ago did she lose it?"

"Sometime this spring. They were a present from her mother and me." He took a long look at his bottle, then swept it off the bar. "Damn! Doesn't it ever get better?"

I stood. It was time for me to go. Harvey would have to answer that question himself. "Mine did."

"How long, Garth? How long?"

"About a thousand years. But it seemed longer."

He nodded and ordered another beer.

I walked to the hospital. Rupert was sitting up in bed eating his lunch. I didn't know why I expected him to look better today, but he didn't. And his movements were painfully slow. It seemed to take his fork five minutes to reach his mouth once it left his plate. Then he had to eat. I found myself working my jaw, trying to help him chew.

"Thanks for the flowers," he said between bites.

"What flowers?"

He pointed to a bouquet of red-and-white carnations sitting in a vase on the windowsill. "Those flowers."

"Thank Ruth. She's the one who sent them."

"I figured." He laid down his fork. "What's on your mind?"

"A lot. How much do you want to hear?"

"It have to do with Frieda?" he asked.

"Her and Betty Pierson. Maybe others we don't know about."

"Then I'd like to hear all of it. But I'd like to finish my lunch first."

"Be my guest. You mind if I use your phone?"

"As long as it's not long distance."

I called Fred Pierson. I waited through six rings and was about to hang up when he answered. "Garth again," I said. "Sorry to bother you, but I have a couple questions."

"About what?" It sounded like he was running out of answers. Or patience. I didn't blame him. As a solitary man, he'd already gone out of his way for me.

"The Coy-Dog. Have you seen it since you released it three years ago?"

"I didn't release him. He ran off. But no, I haven't seen him."

"Not in all your trips into Mitchell's Woods?"

"No. I'm sure he's seen me, but I haven't seen him."

"But he is in there?"

"He is." Of that he was certain.

"Do you think he killed Betty?"

"Don't you?" he asked.

"I did once. I don't anymore. Not unless you change my mind."

"How would I do that?"

"By telling me the Coy-Dog is a killer. That's why Betty made you get rid of it."

"I wish I could, Garth. I can't. When I had him, the Coy-Dog was as gentle as they come. Around us. He was death on coons."

"Then why did you get rid of him?"

"Simple jealousy. I was spending a lot more time with him than I was with Betty. She said one of them had to go. It was the Coy-Dog. It broke my heart, but I did it for her."

I wondered, considering the outcome, if he'd do it the same again? But I didn't ask. "And you say the Coy-Dog ran off. Why did he do that?"

"Because of me. I couldn't drive him away. I didn't have the heart. Besides, it might make him mean. So I did the next best thing. I quit feeding him. Every night, when I'd come out to feed the other dogs, he'd be standing by his dish, waiting for his share. When I walked on by without even a kind word, he'd sort of shrug, then go chew on a stick until I went back in the house. This went on for days, him getting thinner all the time, until I told Betty I was either going to have to feed him or shoot him. She said to feed him, that after all he'd been through he deserved to stay. But that night when I went out there, he was gone. Into Mitchell's Woods, where he's been ever since."

"He never came back?"

"I never saw him. But for the longest time I kept finding dead things on the porch, rabbits and squirrels and chipmunks, things like that. I guess he figured we were so hard up he'd help us out a little."

I was beginning to feel Fred's loss.

"Thanks, Fred. I'm sorry the way things turned out."

"So am I. I raised him from a pup. His mother had been poisoned. I found her at the mouth of her den, along with her litter. They were all dead except for Sam. That's what I named him. He still had enough life left to try to bite me when I picked him up."

"Any chance you'll ever get him back?"

"No. But I keep trying."

I was about to hang up when I remembered something else. "Fred, you still there?"

"Still here."

"Did Betty lose a sock or a shoe or a house slipper, anything like that, shortly before she died?"

"She lost one of her moccasins. We spent a lot of time looking for it. We never found it."

"When was that? Do you remember?"

"A couple months before she died. She had them outside on the porch at the time. I always thought a varmint carried it off."

"Could have been. Thanks, Fred."

But he was stride for stride with me. "It wasn't a varmint, was it, Garth?"

"Depends on your definition. I have to go. Thanks again." I hung up before he could corner me.

"What was that all about?" Rupert asked.

"A man and his dog."

Two for two. Frieda Whitlock and Betty Pierson had both lost shoes shortly before they died. Karen had lost a sweat sock the morning she talked to me along Gas Line Road. Three for three?

I tried to call her at her apartment in Montivideo. No one answered. No one would answer if Karen wasn't

201

there. Especially not Hattie. She didn't answer her own phone half the time. I tried to call Karen at her law office, got a busy signal.

"Sorry, Rupert," I said. "I have to go."

"Where?"

"Montivideo for starters. After that I don't know. If everything's okay there, I'll probably see you back here."

"What's in Montivideo?"

"Karen Wilson."

"How does she figure into this?"

"I don't have time to explain now." I started for the door.

"Garth." His voice stopped me. It had the force of command. "I remembered what I couldn't yesterday morning. The thing that attacked me, it had blue eyes. I remembered seeing them in a bolt of lightning."

"I know," I said. "Just remember that if I don't come back."

"A name, Garth, I need a name."

But I was already out the door.

19

Jessie wouldn't turn over. She buzzed a couple times like she might, but I'd played that game with her before. I put her in neutral, straightened the wheels, walked around to the front of her, and pushed her out of the garage into the alley. My next step was to go get my grandfather's shotgun and shoot her. I'd shoot her inside the garage, but I didn't want to get oil all over the floor.

My neighbor was outside mowing the yard. He saw me pushing Jessie and thought I needed help. He probably saved her life.

He got his El Camino and drove it into the alley beside Jessie. We took out my jumper cables, put positive to positive, negative to negative, and Jessie started on the first try. The trick now was to keep her running. Because once she stopped, I might never get her started again.

I thanked my neighbor and started to drive to Montivideo. Every time I came to a stop sign, I held my breath until I was going again. There weren't many stops between Oakalla and Montivideo, but it seemed a lot more than the last time I drove there.

I found Karen's apartment complex and parked a block away at the top of a hill just in case. Before I got out,

I checked the gas gauge. Between a quarter and a half. I debated a moment, then shut Jessie off. I might need that gas before the day was through.

The apartments were brick, numbered about twenty, ten above and ten below, and were part of a complex named Colonial Mansion. Colonial Mansion? I wondered where they dug up the name? It actually was ten house trailers stacked upon ten house trailers and bricked over. Maybe it seemed the kind of place that a colonial would love.

I knocked on Karen's door. No one answered. I knocked again, louder this time. "Come on, Hattie!" I yelled. "I know you're in there!"

A concerned neighbor stepped outside her door and gave me the evil eye.

"My mother's in there," I explained. "She's nearly deaf."

She left immediately. Probably to call the cops.

Meanwhile Hattie had come to the door. "Let me in, damn it," I said. "It's Garth."

She opened the door and let me in. "I know who it is."

"Is Karen here?" I asked.

"No. She's at work. Did you come to rescue me? If not, I'm walking home."

"You're staying here. That's final."

"You'll have to shoot me first. I've run out of things to read, run out of things to do, run out of clothes, run out of tobacco, run out of patience. I'm going home."

"Have you tried watching television?" I knew Hattie didn't own one. The closest thing she had was the old Philco radio in the living room.

"I tried. Couldn't get interested."

"Not in anything?"

"The knobs. I liked them. Especially the one that said off."

No use arguing. She was going home. I couldn't stop her. "Do you have Karen's office number handy?" I asked.

She walked over to the phone and pointed to a pad of paper. "It's right here."

I dialed the number. It was still busy.

"What do you want to see Karen about?" she asked. "I thought you already talked to her."

"I did. I came to tell her to stay away from Oakalla."

"Why?" Her small dark eyes were quick to understand. She didn't miss much.

"Because she might be in danger."

"Who from?"

"Josh Henry."

She didn't say anything. She just wrinkled her nose, like a rabbit sniffing a lettuce leaf. She didn't seem surprised, but if I'd lived as long as she had, it'd be hard to surprise me, too. "You got a reason?" she asked.

"He does. That's all it takes."

"He killed the Whitlock girl." It wasn't a question.

"I know. You saw him pick her up, didn't you?"

"I saw her walk by. I saw him drive by a few minutes later. Not ten minutes after that I saw him drive by again on his way toward town. That's all I saw."

"Before or after four?"

"Before. The four o'clock whistle hadn't blown at the quarry yet."

"Was she in the truck with him?"

"Something was, sitting in the front seat. But it looked like a dog to me."

That didn't make sense. But then not everything did. I called Karen's office again. I got her secretary.

"Is Karen Wilson in?"

"Who is calling, please?"

"Garth Ryland."

"I'm sorry, Mr. Ryland, but Mrs. Wilson is out of town this afternoon."

"Do you expect her back?"

"No. She said not to expect her."

"Do you know where she's gone?"

She hesitated. "Not exactly."

"I have to reach her. It's urgent. Anything will help."

"Well, she did say if you called, that she went to see a man about a dog. Mr. Ryland, are you there?"

"Barely. How long ago?"

"Not more than an hour."

I hung up. "Got to go!" I said to Hattie.

"You going back to Oakalla?"

"Yes, I am."

"I'm going with you."

"No, you aren't. You're staying here. Karen's life might depend on it. If she calls to check in with you, tell her to come here immediately. And once she walks through that door, don't let her out again. I'll be in touch."

"Ring twice. Then hang up and call again. That's our signal," Hattie said.

"Thanks, Hattie."

"Where's Karen gone?" she asked.

"Right into the jaws of death."

Hattie shrugged.

I turned Jessie's key. She didn't even bother to buzz this time. I pushed her out into the street, turned the key on, and put her in first. About halfway down the hill I popped the clutch. She sputtered, then started. This time I didn't have to stop at all on my way back to Oakalla. I hardly even slowed down.

I went directly to Josh Henry's cabin and left Jessie out front with her motor running. No one answered the door when I knocked. I walked around back. I didn't see anyone. Maybe Karen hadn't come here. Maybe she'd gone to the school instead.

I got in Jessie and drove back to town. Again I left her running and went in the front door of the school. I found Bernice Thompson, the secretary, in the office. She appeared to be the only one here. "Is Josh around?" I asked.

"No. He took this afternoon off."

"Did he say why?"

"No, he didn't."

"Did he by chance get a phone call earlier?"

"Yes. As a matter of fact, he did."

"From a woman?"

"Yes again. You're a good guesser."

True. But this time I wished to hell I wasn't.

I drove back to Josh Henry's. But I didn't plan to stay. I only wanted to confirm something. I walked around to the back of the cabin and looked inside the one remaining doghouse. I was right. The Plott was gone. That meant Josh was all ready to go hunting.

I looked at the gas gauge. Below a quarter now. I couldn't make too many more stops between here and Mitchell's Woods.

As I passed the Marathon, I took a long look its way. I wanted to stop for gas, but I was afraid I'd run out of time before I ran out of gas. I thought about calling Clarkie and asking for his help, but he wouldn't be much help in a case like this. The one I needed was Rupert, and he wasn't available.

I was already two miles out of town when I realized I needed some kind of a weapon. Too late to turn back now. I made a quick detour, stopped at Grandmother Ryland's farm, and ran to the door. It was locked. I ran back to Jessie to get my keys. But I couldn't get them out of the ignition without shutting Jessie off. That meant I had to dismantle my key ring with her running. I finally did, but lost precious seconds in the process.

Panic overtook me. About ten seconds worth, then I got control again and went inside the house. There had to be some kind of weapon around. When I was a boy, I was never without one.

In my old room I found the forty-pound fiberglass bow that I always had trouble stringing and a quiver full of motley-looking arrows. Most were blunt tips and those that still had the tips had a feather or two missing. Two had even been broken and glued back together.

But I found two others that looked sound and the only hunting arrow I'd ever owned. It was like new. Mainly because I'd never used it.

I carried the bow, quiver, and three arrows outside and put them in Jessie's back seat. Now I had a new problem. Jessie's temperature gauge was steadily climbing. It continued to rise on the way to Fred Pierson's.

Fred wasn't home. Neither was his Jeep. I could have used both of them right now.

I looked at the sun. It was on its way down, but had at least four hours to go. Still too early for Josh to start the hunt. Then again maybe not. Josh would probably want to see its climax. He'd want daylight for that.

I drove slowly along the south edge of Mitchell's Woods, looking for Josh's pickup. I found it parked in a stand of small hickories about a mile and a half east of the road that ran past Fred Pierson's. The truck was facing east, away from the sun. There appeared to be two people sitting in the front seat.

I had an idea. It wasn't a great one, but under the circumstances it'd have to do. I could probably make one more trip by there without Josh getting suspicious. And only then if he didn't recognize me.

That's where the sun would come in. It would be glaring against Jessie's windshield, making it hard for him to see inside. It would be hard for Karen to see inside, too, but I was hoping she'd recognize Jessie. If she did, she might read my message.

I drove down to the next road and turned around. The needle of the temperature gauge was almost to the red, the needle of the gas gauge almost to the E. But that was the least of my problems.

I left Jessie running, took the duct tape from the glove compartment, and walked around to the front of the car. "Escape Wisconsin," the sign said. I altered it with the duct tape, blocking out all the letters in Wisconsin, except for the W, the direction I wanted Karen to go. So the sign now read, "Escape W."

It was a long shot, but if she could make it to Fred Pierson's road, I could take it from there. And with luck, Fred would be home any time now. With his jeep and me riding shotgun, I knew damn well we'd get her out of Mitchell's Woods. Even if Fred didn't show up, I could always go into the woods and intercept her. We'd be on our own, but we'd still have a shot at it.

Jessie almost died when I put her in gear. I drove slowly back the way I'd come. The pickup was parked where it was before. I squinted, fighting the sun. Good. They were still there. Maybe I'd get lucky . . .

My heart sank. There were two forms in the front seat all right. One was Josh. The other was the Plott.

I eased down on the gas and drove west to Fred Pierson's road and turned north. Fred still wasn't home. I drove to the north edge of Mitchell's Woods, then east again. Even though I was looking for it, I almost passed the overgrown lane that led back into the heart of the woods. It had been a year since I'd been back here. I'd forgotten how narrow the lane was, how deep its ruts were.

I slowed to a crawl as Jessie tore through a snarl of underbrush that had overtaken the lane. I didn't look at the temperature gauge. Already I could smell the anti-freeze as it boiled out.

Then I came to a small sassafras that had fallen across the lane. Nothing to do but get out and drag it out of the way. When I got into Jessie again, steam was rolling out from under the hood and into the car, and she was running on about three cylinders.

At lane's end was the barn I knew so well. If I could get Karen this far, here was where we'd make our stand. We didn't have a choice. Jessie had gone as far as she was going to go.

I left the bow and arrows in Jessie. They'd only slow me down. They wouldn't be much help against Josh and the Plott anyway, at least not out in the open. In closer quarters it might be a different matter.

I went south toward where Josh's truck was parked. My hope was that Karen would come north, since to her it would seem the direction that offered the best chance of escape. It wasn't. Against a man maybe, but not against the Plott. With him on your trail it didn't matter what direction you took.

The mosquitoes and deerflies soon zeroed in and made life miserable for me. I couldn't move fast enough to shake them. I thought about the six cans of insect repellent collecting dust on my closet shelf. No doubt right above Grandpa's shotgun.

Spider webs, too, were a problem. Strung across every small opening and along every deep path, they caught and clung, itched and burned, until I was clawing my face, all the while on the move, ducking vines and low-hanging limbs.

I stopped to catch my breath, as a cloud of deerflies descended on me, each and every one trying to draw blood. I slapped my head and nearly knocked myself silly, but had the satisfaction of killing two of them. I slapped again. Two more. But one bit me on the ear. A maddening welt began to grow.

I moved on, crossing my favorite trout stream and stopping long enough to splash my face with water. I felt better. For the moment at least the cobwebs were gone. Not the deerflies, though. They took the opportunity to bite me twice more. One on the arm, the other dead center between my shoulders, and right where I couldn't scratch it.

I heard the Plott make one deep bellow—his strike bark. A chill passed through me. It meant the hunt was now on.

I stopped and waited under a low limb where the flies

couldn't get at me. The Plott's bark had come from directly south of me and not that far away. Karen should be coming along soon. Sooner than I thought. She nearly ran past me.

"Oh!" she cried, when I stepped out from behind the tree and grabbed her. Then she tried to kick her way free.

"Stop!" I whispered. "It's Garth!"

She stopped. But she didn't relax. Not even when she recognized me. Already her white cotton blouse was torn at the shoulder and she'd lost one of her Hula-Hoop earrings. Her shoes were gone, too, and her feet were bleeding. Only her khaki slacks looked intact.

"We've got to get out of here!" she hissed, trying to pull away from me.

"I know we do. But not the way you're going about it. Get on my shoulders."

"Garth!"

"Don't argue. Get on my shoulders. We can't outrun the Plott. Either one of us." I didn't tell her I thought the Plott was still on lead. Otherwise, he'd have caught her by now.

"Then what's the point?" She tried to tear away again.

I shook her. She whipped like a reed in my hands. "Get on my shoulders, damn it! I don't have time to explain!"

She got on my shoulders. She didn't want to, but she did.

"The point is," I said a few minutes later when I stopped to rest, "the Plott's smart, but he's not human. He's been trained to follow your track. That's where your sweat sock went. But he hasn't been trained to follow mine. It'll take him a while to figure it out."

"But he *will* figure it out?" she asked.

"I'm afraid so. He's a world champion."

"A world champin what?"

I didn't answer. I'd just heard the Plott bark again. Farther away than the first time, but too close for comfort.

I bent down, she got back on my shoulders, and away we went. I soon came to the stream where I'd washed my face. I walked downstream, so our scent would be carried ahead of us, not trail along behind. Also, if Josh Henry was close, which I imagined he was, I didn't want him to see our muddy trail washing back downstream. We needed every second we could get.

After about a hundred yards I set Karen down. "Once the Plott gets this far," I said, "he'll have it all worked out. So let's make tracks."

"To where?"

"Follow me."

I ran at a slow jog, my upper limit. Karen followed as best she could. Her long legs and long stride, which were so graceful on the open road, were a liability here in Mitchell's Woods. She couldn't take a step without tangling in something and losing her balance. Besides, she was barefoot. Both feet were bruised and swollen, and bled every step of the way. Her face, too, was scratched, and spotted with welts from the deerflies.

But she didn't complain. She ran with a grim determination that was all heart. She ran until we reached the barn, and she collapsed against me.

"No farther," she gasped. "I can't go any farther."

"You don't have to."

But she didn't hear me. She'd seen Jessie. She straightened and started limping toward her, like a thirsting legionnaire toward an oasis, or in this case a mirage.

I caught her arm and tried to hold her back. "Don't get your hopes up. She got me in here, but she won't get us out again."

But she didn't believe me. She jerked free and ran to Jessie. Throwing open the door, she jumped into the driver's seat and turned the key. When Jessie wouldn't start, she pounded the dash in frustration.

"That won't help," I said. "I've tried it before."

"How can you be so goddamned calm!" she shouted at me. "We're going to die here!"

I wasn't calm. I was shaking in my shoes. But I didn't tell her that. "Because our lives depend on it, and I want to go on living. Now get hold of yourself. And while you're at it, go inside the barn and see if you can find some baling wire. Do you know what that is?"

She didn't answer.

"Do you know what that is?" I repeated.

She glared at me. She hated me at the moment, but she also needed me. "No. But I'll look anyway."

I took my tools from Jessie's glove compartment and used them to loosen the battery cables. Maybe the Plott wasn't afraid of anything animal, vegetable, or mineral, but there was one thing that nearly everything was afraid of, including me. That was electricity. I just hoped Joe Turner was right when he said the battery was okay.

I carried the battery to the barn. Karen met me at the door. "I didn't find any baling wire," she said.

"That's okay. I decided I don't need it."

"But I did find this." She showed me a pitchfork. It appeared to be in pitching shape.

"Good. Hang on to it."

I returned to Jessie and took the bow and arrows from the back seat. Then I pushed her down a slight incline into a clump of bushes. There wasn't time to camouflage her properly, but I hoped Josh would be too intent on the barn to notice her sitting there.

The barn was built on three levels. The lower level was a long narrow area of mangers and stanchions where cows were once fed and milked. Opposite the milking area was a straw mow. A short steep wooden stairway led from there to the main floor where a rusty manure spreader still sat. On the third level above the milking area was a hay mow, constructed so that you could pitch hay down to the main floor and then into the mangers. On the west a large sliding door opened the main floor to the outside. On the south a small swinging door opened into the milking area. I guessed that's where the Plott would enter. It would have to be our first line of defense.

I left Karen guarding it with the pitchfork, climbed up into the mow, and pulled down a bale of moldy hay. I had a plan. The Plott should get here first, before Josh did, because I was sure that by now he was no longer on lead. I wished it were the other way around. That way we could ambush Josh and use his shotgun on the Plott. The way it was, we had to use the Plott to get to Josh to get to the shotgun. That made it harder.

That wasn't the only problem. The straw mow led under the main floor and then outside through an arch in the foundation—designed so the cattle could come under the barn and out of the weather. From inside the barn it was easy to see the arch. You could see daylight through it. From the outside it was hidden somewhat by weeds and brush, and unless you knew it was there, you wouldn't see it.

I didn't think Josh would notice it, especially now that it was late in the day. But I didn't know about the Plott. He'd grown in my eyes until he seemed almost mythical.

I strung the bow and handed it and the quiver to Karen. "You ever shot one of these?" I asked.

"I took archery one semester in college."

"What grade did you get?"

"An A."

"That's good enough for me."

"Please explain yourself." She didn't like where we were heading.

I pointed to the bale of hay I'd set on the main floor. "Hide behind there. When and if Josh shows in the doorway, I want you to shoot him. Aim for the gut. If you shoot high, you'll hit his chest or throat. If you shoot low, you'll hit his groin."

"Anything else?"

"No. That's about it."

"I can't do it."

"You have to. Our lives depend on it."

"What will you be doing in the meantime?"

"Trying very hard to stay alive. Take the pitchfork with you, too," I said, "in case the Plott gets by me. I'll let you know when I want it back again."

She looked at me. Resolution showed in her eyes and face. And a whole lot of courage. She even lifted my spirits. Then she looked in the quiver. "Which arrow, or does it matter?"

"The longest one. The one with the wide tip."

She pulled it out and examined it. "It looks lethal."

"It is. It's designed to kill."

"Hold me please."

I held her. She felt good in my arms, and much softer than I imagined she would. "Don't worry. We're going to make it out of this."

She gave me her best smile. "Who's worried?"

She shot the bow into the hay a couple of times, using the blunt-tipped arrows. She seemed a natural with it, much better than I ever was. I'd made the right decision by handing it to her.

Then she took her place behind the bale of hay. I took my place behind the wall of the first stall. Nothing to do now but wait.

Five minutes went by. The sun had gone behind some trees, and the barn was now draped with shadows. It was cool and musty and dim in here, not at all like the clearing outside, which still held a warm fragrant breath that wafted through the door into the barn.

Evening. A time for reflection, to let your mind wander where it would and gather what scraps of wisdom you learned that day. A healing time, a time to lick your wounds and mend your nets and patch your life with whatever comfort you could find. Never meant to be spent in the dark waiting for death.

Ten minutes went by. I was sorry now we hadn't kept on going. We'd done a better job of hiding our trail than I

215

thought we had. And maybe the Plott wasn't quite as good as everyone said he was. No—I'd seen him in action. I knew better.

I never heard him coming. There he was in the doorway, a hundred pounds of hard muscle and fury, his pale blue eyes staring at me. I hoped Karen didn't see him. Otherwise, she might flinch ever so slightly, and he'd go for her.

I picked up the battery, gathered my legs under me, and braced my back against the stall. "Psst!" I said.

The Plott whirled and came my way. His mouth was open. He made a low growl. He was so intent on death he didn't even recognize me.

He was incredibly quick and strong. I almost didn't get the battery up fast enough. But when I did, and jammed both posts into his chest, it knocked him backwards into the stone wall of the barn.

He got up and faced me. His eyes were glazed, his lower jaw hung wide open, spittle dripped down his chin onto the floor of the barn. He looked mad. I feared his rage.

He sprang again, knocking me back against the stall and banging my head. I lost my grip on the battery, but regained it again just as I fell under him. He went for my throat. He got the battery instead.

He leaped away, ricocheting off the stone wall again. When he recovered, he retreated a few steps and glared at me. Some of his fury was spent. He seemed more cerebral now and in some ways more dangerous. I didn't press him. I wanted to see what he would do. He did nothing for several seconds, just stood and stared at me as he had at our first meeting. Again he seemed to be measuring me, trying to pick my brain and find a weakness. Then he turned, trotted outside, and began baying at the barn.

"Garth, are you okay?" Karen asked.

"Okay," I answered. Some of the acid had spilled

from the battery and was now eating into my arm. Without any water handy, I'd just have to grin and bear it.

"You sure you're okay?"

"Yes. We won the first round. Hand me the pitchfork, will you?"

She did and I used it to cover myself as I sneaked to the door. I closed the door and latched it. When Josh got here, I wanted him to think that Karen had locked the Plott out of the barn. That would explain why he was still outside.

I returned to my post. Again nothing to do now but wait.

"He used cats," Karen said to me.

"To do what?"

"Reward the Plott for finding my sock. He used cats," she repeated. "Every time the Plott treed my sock, Josh gave it a cat to kill." She spoke without emotion, as if that were the only way she could deal with it.

"Josh told you this?"

"He told me everything, through the back window of his cab while I was sitting there in that damned dog box. God it was sickening! Sitting there smelling of dog, listening to him go on. Poor Josh! That's the way it came out. His mother abandoned him, his grandfather beat him, his own father wouldn't even claim him. Walter Lawrence was his father, but you probably already know that, don't you? But I bet there's something you don't know. . . . Josh killed Walter. He hit him over the head with a club when Walter was chasing me around the pond. Then let me take the blame for it."

"Josh told you that?"

"He did. He also said he killed his grandfather. He threw him into a ravine right on top of a tree stob. Josh said he hung there for several minutes, trying to get off. Josh sounded like he enjoyed watching it." I thought I heard her shudder. "He killed him because of the Plott. Josh wanted it. Buck wasn't going to let him have it."

"Then carried him home and took him to the hospital?"

"And cried afterwards, when they told him Buck was dead. He did!" she insisted. "He told me he did!"

"What else did he tell you?" I was trying to sort fact from fiction. I wasn't having much luck. I was missing something that might come to me later—if there was a later.

"He killed Betty Pierson and Frieda Whitlock. Betty was an experiment, he said. He thought the Plott was chasing a deer the first time he followed Betty's trail. The Plott only ran it a short way, then got off of it onto something else. But when Josh saw who it was the Plott had been following, it gave him an idea. So he stole one of Betty's shoes and trained the Plott to follow it."

"By using cats?"

"By using cats. He didn't intend for the Plott to kill Betty, or maybe in truth he did. But he said he didn't. He just wanted to see what the Plott would do."

"He knew what the Plott would do," I said. "The former owner had told him as much."

"Regardless, the Plott got to Betty long before Josh did. She was dead when Josh got there and the Plott was sitting beside her licking his chops. That was the start of it. There was no stopping him now."

"What about Frieda Whitlock?"

"He planned it down to the last detail. He sent Joe Turner on a wild goose chase out here to Mitchell's Woods, then left early from school and picked Frieda up on her way home. He stopped at Phillipee's Pond, bound and gagged her and forced her into the dog box in the back of the truck. He made her stay there for several hours, while he went back to school, then bought dog food at the elevator and had a drink with the boys at the Corner Bar and Grill. The hunt followed. But this time he made sure the Plott didn't get too far ahead of him. He got there in time to see it kill Frieda."

"That's good," I said. I was thinking of the straw I found in Frieda's hair, that it probably came from the dog box, not the love nest in the barn. But in the final analysis, what did it really matter?

"Garth? I don't like the sound of your voice."

"I'm okay," I lied.

"You don't sound okay."

"Don't worry. I'm still under control."

We were silent a moment, while I listened to the Plott bay.

"Where do you come in?" I asked. "What does Josh have against you? Just that you wouldn't date him?"

"It was more than that. Josh had a crush on me and I wouldn't give him the time of day. In his words, he couldn't understand why I would give it to his old man and not to him. Josh was just as good as he was. He said he used to dream he owned a hawk. And this hawk would do anything he told it. One day he told it to rip off my clothes and tear my breasts out, and it did. That made him glad, he said."

"Karen. I think that's enough." More than enough.

"Why? He can't hear us with that fool dog baying his head off outside. Don't you even want to know where my new Volvo is?"

"Where?"

"At the bottom of Phillipee's Pond."

"I'm sorry. But at least it's not you."

"So shut up and count my blessings?"

"Yes. Until we get out of here."

"What if we don't?"

"We will."

I felt my hand tighten on the pitchfork. The Plott's baying was starting to get to me. I was tempted to go outside after him. Only the desire to kill Josh Henry kept me from it. And all the time he called me Coach, knowing what he was.

219

I heard a rustle outside the door. I motioned to Karen for silence. She understood immediately.

"What's the matter, boy?" Josh said to the Plott. "She's in there, is she? You in there, Karen?" he called.

"Don't answer," I whispered.

I took a hard look at the pitchfork. It would do, but I'd rather have a hand grenade. Two of them. One for Josh, the other for Fido.

"Karen, can you hear me? I know you're in there. This hound is a world champion. He ain't ever blown a track yet."

Karen didn't answer. Though I thought I heard her spit.

"You might as well come out, or I'll send him in after you."

No answer from our side.

"Well, I gave you your chance." The door swung open. "Okay, boy, go get her!"

No Plott appeared in the doorway.

"What's the matter, boy?" Josh asked. "You unsure of yourself? That ain't like you. There ain't nothing to be afraid of in here, just a little old whore, that's all. Just like my mama. Just like yours, too, I bet. Huh, Boy? She was out whoring around? That's where you got those blue eyes?"

The Plott answered with a whine.

"Okay. This one time I'll go in first. Just to prove to you I can. How's that, boy? You can clean up after me."

Then Josh was in the doorway. I couldn't see him, but I could hear him breathe and smell his aftershave. Old Spice. What I used to wear in high school.

He didn't move. I kept waiting for him to move. I was afraid Karen would grow impatient and give herself away. Worse, she might get buck fever and shoot too quickly.

He took one step inside the barn and stopped. He was being cautious, giving his eyes time to adjust to the dim light. This was new to him. He wasn't used to being in the

220

front line, looking danger squarely in the eye. "Chicken-mean" was what his old coach called him, and it never showed more than right now.

I knew what was going to happen. He was going to talk himself out of it, turn tail, and leave the barn. Then what? I had a good idea. When he couldn't squall a coon out of its den, Buck Henry would smoke it out. I imagined Josh knew the technique.

"Shoot!" I hissed at Karen.

But she was a millisecond ahead of me. The arrow had already left the bow. It whizzed overhead and struck something soft. I heard Josh grunt. Boom! His shotgun roared, then twice more in rapid succession.

I rolled out from behind the stall and charged him with the pitchfork. Josh stood just inside the doorway. He held the shotgun in his right hand and with his left pawed at the arrow, which had pierced his gut. He was rubber-legged and wore a puzzled, glass-eyed look, as if trying to sort it all out. He reminded me of a lost child searching for his mother. He got me instead.

Then he looked at me and smiled. "Coach?" he asked.

I couldn't stop. I'd left the stall with blood in my eye. I intended to drive the pitchfork all the way through Josh Henry. But at the last instant, for a reason I don't yet know, I deflected my aim and drove the pitchfork into the wall of the barn instead.

Josh sank to his knees, then rolled to his side. He lay doubled up on the floor of the barn. His blood was a black pool in the dust.

I took his shotgun from his hand, being careful not to touch the trigger. It was an Ithaca, the semiautomatic he'd carried last night with me. Josh had fired three times. That meant there should be two shells left.

I glanced outside. The Plott was standing about twenty yards away. He saw me. He didn't wait to see what I'd do. He took off for the woods and safety.

I brought the shotgun to my shoulder, laid my cheek

against the stock, imagined he was a low-flying pheasant, and fired. I rolled him, but he got to his feet and continued toward the woods. He was too far away to risk another shot.

Then I had a new worry. I'd forgotten all about Karen. I set the shotgun down and ran up the short flight of stairs to the main floor. She lay face down behind the bale of hay with her arms cradled around her head.

I knelt beside her. "Karen?" I asked. "You okay?"

"No!" she wheezed. "I just killed a man!"

"We both did," I said, trying to share the blame.

"No! I saw you! You couldn't do it!"

I turned her over and made her look at me. "That's because there was no need," I said.

She wasn't ready to forgive me for what I made her do. "His blood is still on my hands!" She showed me her hands as if to prove it.

"You're wrong. His blood is on his own hands. You're a lawyer. You know what I mean."

"I'm also a woman. I know what that means. Sometimes the two of me aren't in agreement."

I left her sitting on the bale of hay and went downstairs to check on Josh. He was dead. The arrow must have cut a main artery. But then that's what it was designed to do.

I closed Josh's eyes and dragged him outside. Already he'd started to stink of urine and excretement. For that and other reasons, I didn't want to be in the same barn with him.

Once inside, I closed and latched the door behind me. Then I picked up the shotgun and went upstairs. With the Plott still on the prowl, we'd wait for daylight before getting out of there.

20

It took me a while, but I made a nest in the hay mow, settled in, and tried to get some sleep. No sleep came. A few feet away Karen sat in a dusty stream of moonlight, her face a silky contrast of shadows and light. She was crying softly to herself.

"It's lonely in here," I said. "I could use some company."

She shook her head.

"Suit yourself."

She turned to look at me. "You don't understand, do you?" she asked.

"What don't I understand?"

She looked away. "Never mind."

I sat up. I wasn't sleepy anyway. "Would you rather I'd nailed him to the wall?"

"Yes!"

"He was going down. There was no need."

She turned to me. "There was a need! My need! What about me!" Tears were streaming down her face. "I mean there you sit, head back, eyes closed, not a God damn care in the world! And rational! Like it happened to somebody else!"

I crawled over to her and took her by the shoulders, "What about you?" I asked. "Do you think I'd be here now if I didn't care?"

"Talk's cheap." She tried to twist away.

I kissed her hard, not caring if it hurt. Her response was an arched and stone-lipped silence. I kissed her again—gently and with care, not holding any of me back. She shuddered. So did I. Then the hay slid out from under us, as the dam between us burst.

A few minutes later we lay peacefully in each other's arms. A few minutes after that we were both asleep.

I awakened to the yip of the coyote pack. They were close, moving closer. I thought about Josh lying outside the barn. I didn't want them to find him.

I carefully untangled myself from Karen and laid her down in the hay. She didn't awaken. I put on my pants, crossed the mow, and climbed down the ladder to the main floor of the barn. I could hear the coyotes yip, yip, yipping their way toward me.

I stopped at the door and listened. The coyotes were closing fast. I opened the door, dragged Josh inside, and closed it again. I felt better. The coyotes wouldn't get through it.

I stood a moment and tried to pull the pitchfork from the side of the barn, but couldn't. A madman must have put it there.

I'd taken two steps up the short stairs that led to the main floor when I heard him growl. I'd heard a lot of sounds that raised goose bumps over the years, but none more terrifying than that. I didn't know where it'd come from, whether he was ahead of me or behind me. I just knew I was afraid to move.

I wanted to call to Karen and warn her, but I didn't trust my voice. Also, I didn't want to provoke him to action. I tried to wait him out. Maybe he'd get tired and go home.

Five minutes went by. I counted every heartbeat. I

knew I hadn't imagined the growl. I could smell him. He smelled like dog. And something else I couldn't recognize. A pungent smell. One that caught in my throat and made it hard to breathe.

Meanwhile the coyote pack had found the barn. They stood ten feet away from me, yipping at it. It was all I needed. If my nerves weren't shot before, they were spaghetti now. Besides that, Karen was awake. I could hear her calling to me.

"Stay where you are," I said as calmly as I could.

"Why? What's wrong?"

"I'll be there in a minute. Just stay where you are."

I still hadn't seen the Plott. I guessed he was behind the feed bin a few feet up and to my right. I took another step. He growled a warning. I was right. Behind the feed bin.

I wondered how many steps he'd let me have before he attacked. Probably not many. I took another step to test my theory. This growl was deeper, more menacing.

"What's going on down there?" Karen asked.

"Nothing. Stay where you are," I answered, trying to keep my voice flat and free of all emotion. One wrong note and the Plott would be on me.

Then I had an idea. It wouldn't work forever, but it might get me to the main floor. I held my arms out stiffly in front of me, as if I still carried the battery, and took another step. He growled and retreated a little way. I took another step. The same thing happened.

Two more steps to go. Part of me said to cut and run. This was as far as I was going to get. The other part said to keep going as planned. I'd climbed six steps. I only had two to go. The odds were three to one in my favor. I went with the odds.

I reached the main floor of the barn. I could see the Plott now. His eyes and his teeth. They glared dully at me, like a jack-o-iantern whose candle had just about burned out.

He was cornered, backed up against the feed bin as far as he could go. One more step his way, and he'd attack. I wasn't cornered. But one small step away, and I'd expose my flank.

The coyotes seemed to sense the drama inside. They'd suddenly gone silent, like they were listening in.

The Plott's growl rumbled from his throat, thickening and deepening. Time to do something, even if it was wrong. I suddenly wheeled and started for the ladder. I didn't look to see what the Plott would do. He could see for himself.

I didn't try to climb the ladder a rung at a time. That would be suicide. When I was about three feet away, I jumped for it. I nearly missed, catching it with my left foot, as I spun backward and slammed into the hay.

That probably saved my life. The Plott had aimed for where I should have been, hit only rung, and fallen backwards. That didn't stop him, though. He was trying to climb the ladder to get to me. Slowly but surely, he was scratching and clawing his way up it.

"The shotgun!" I yelled at Karen. "I need it!"

But she was already on her way. She leaned over a bale and handed it down to me. In my haste to shoot, I banged the barrel against the ladder and had to adjust my aim. That was all the time the Plott needed. He flung himself from the ladder, dived into the straw mow, and was gone.

I took a couple steps down the ladder to make sure. As I did, my hand felt something sticky. It was blood smeared on the rungs. I checked myself. No, I wasn't bleeding. It had to belong to the Plott.

Keeping the shotgun ready, I climbed on down to the main floor and walked to where the Plott had been standing next to the feed bin. There was blood here, too. Not a lot of it, but enough to tell me the Plott was wounded. That was both good and bad. It was good in that it would slow him down and eventually take its toll. It was bad in that a wounded animal was usually more dangerous, more likely to be hunting you, while you were hunting for it. But then the Plott didn't need any extra incentive.

What happened next took me by surprise. The coyotes had all started yipping at once when something erupted in their midst. It sounded like a dog fight, but one like I'd never heard before. This one was long and savage, without quarter. And when it ended, in an eerie silence that threatened to push in the walls of the barn, I knew the loser hadn't walked away.

Karen and I didn't sleep the rest of the night. We sat guarding the main floor and took turns telling each other the story of our lives. And when dawn finally came to the square of the window, I felt I knew her well. Better than I wanted to. Too bad she was married. Too bad I wasn't. It would have made things a lot easier.

I climbed stiffly down the ladder and took a look around the barn. The Plott wasn't in here. Karen climbed down the ladder and joined me on the main floor. It was time to go.

Outside, we'd gone about ten yards when I saw Sam, the Coy-Dog, lying on his side. He was a handsome dog with a shepherd's build, powerful neck and shoulders, and a beautiful buff-colored coat. He was dead. His muzzle had been crushed, his throat torn out.

We started southwest toward Fred Pierson's house, which also seemed to be the direction the Plott was traveling. Occasionally I'd see a splotch of blood, spotting the foliage like red paint dripped from a cheap brush. But they were old signs. The blood had already dried.

An hour later we stopped to rest, Karen sitting on a stump, I on a fallen limb a few feet away. Beside me was a tree marked with blood. It looked like the Plott had stood here for some time using the tree as a prop. The blood on the outside of the bark was dry. That deep in the grooves was still tacky.

We'd been walking for hours, in circles it seemed. The cool deep woods had given way to a jungle of small trees, bushes, and vines. Here the woods steamed in the sun, and deerflies buzzed us every step of the way.

This wasn't familiar territory to me. Somehow I'd gotten us too far east, and we were more in line for Josh's pickup than we were Fred Pierson's place. I glanced at the sun. No help there. It was directly overhead, the clouds thickening around it like curdled milk.

"You recognize any of this?" I asked Karen.

"Not really. But it was in a place like this that I lost my shoes."

"The same place?"

"I can't be sure. Why?"

"I think we're lost."

She shrugged. "What else is new?"

I gave her a smile. "You'll do."

She smiled back. "For what?"

"About anything."

We walked deeper into the thicket. Here briers and scrub brush had completely taken over, and we couldn't take a step without entangling ourselves. A turkey buzzard, then another began to encircle us.

"Go away!" Karen yelled at them. She waved her arms. "See! We're still moving!" She bent down to untangle a brier from her ankle. "Barely."

I looked at her feet. They were a mass of scratches and welts. I wondered how she stood it? "Not much farther," I said.

She looked up at me. Her bright hazel eyes spoke for her. "No problem," they said.

I stopped a moment to watch the buzzards glide, each concentric circle a little smaller than before, as they swirled their way down like a black whirlpool, then up again when they saw us. Amazing how such ugly creatures could attain such grace.

We moved on, weaving our way back and forth

228

through the maze of briers. Then we were immersed in sweetness, so thick it was almost overpowering. The rose smell of a mortuary, but compressed until we were drowning in it. It was multiflora rose—usually found in pastures and usually a sign of overgrazing. I knew now where we were. We had gone southeast, not southwest. The road was less than two hundred yards away.

I glanced down and saw a trail of dried blood leading into a small thicket. I put my finger to my lips for silence, showed Karen the blood, and walked with her around the thicket. There was no blood leading out.

I clicked the shotgun off safety and walked slowly into the thicket. The day had gone limp, and the sweet hot air, along with the deerflies, enveloped me. Then I saw the Plott. He lay facing me a few feet away. I took bead on his head and slowly began to squeeze the trigger. I stopped. He wasn't moving. He wasn't even looking at me.

Keeping the shotgun ready, I edged closer until I was only a yard away. If he'd blinked an eyelash, I'd have fired. But he didn't. The Plott was dead.

I ejected the last shell and watched it bounce beside him. Then I went back after Karen and gave her a ride on my shoulders out to the road. Just as I set her down, I saw a vehicle coming toward us. It looked like Fred Pierson's jeep.

"End of the line," I said.

"So soon," she answered. She looked up and saw Fred approaching. "There's still time to go back."

"I don't think so."

She sighed and put her hands on my shoulders. I leaned down and kissed her hand. "Not good enough," she said.

I put my hands to her face and kissed her just as Fred pulled alongside us. Then I pulled her to me and held her. We kept him waiting for quite some time.

Fred drove Karen back to Oakalla, while I stood in the road, shovel in hand, watching them go. I felt suddenly empty without her, knew it was something I would have to get used to. Maybe another time, another place we could have made a go of it, but then what else was new? Her arms had said I'm willing, but her eyes had said goodbye. I smiled to myself. It sounded like a line from a country song.

I fought my way through the briers and multiflora rose until I came to the thicket where the Plott lay. I planned to bury him, deep enough so the scavengers would never find him. He was, after all, a world champion. Except for a horseshoe pitcher named Ed Sharpy, the only one I'd ever known. And he'd killed the Coy-Dog and gotten this far on just three legs. The bottom half of his right rear leg had been shot away.

What had happened to the Plott in his puppyhood that made him a killer? Perhaps everything. Perhaps nothing. I wasn't perfect. Neither was nature. Neither was anything else that I knew of. It was part and parcel of what made life interesting—and beautiful and unpredictable, and sometimes violent.

I had no insight to offer. I knew the luck of the draw had a lot to do with it. If Josh and the Plott had never met, who knew where both might be now? But I was willing to bet that had their paths never crossed, Betty Pierson and Frieda Whitlock would still be alive. And Karen would still be guilty of a crime she didn't commit and Norma Rothenberger's hatred for Maynard Wilson would still be festering, waiting to erupt. And where would I be? Probably killing another Saturday alone.

It had started to rain, a soft steady rain that washed the rose scent from the air and made it clean again. I entered the thicket where the Plott lay and began to dig.

21

It was Sunday morning, the sun was again shining. Danny had gone after Jessie in his wrecker, and an ambulance had gone after Josh Henry. I'd helped Fred Pierson bury Sam, the Coy-Dog; then we'd stopped by his house for a beer before he'd driven me back to town. The only thing he wanted to know was if Sam had put up a good fight. I assured him that Sam had. The rest of the details I'd left up to Clarkie, who'd decided to wear his badge again.

Then I went home and told Ruth the whole story— most of it anyway. I left out the part about Karen and me, though from the squint in Ruth's eye, I needn't have bothered. But in the telling of it, something didn't ring quite true. For Ruth either. She sat back in her chair and looked thoughtful.

"What is it?" I asked.

"Nothing. It's not important."

"It is, or it wouldn't bother you."

She thought it over some more and decided to tell me. "Last Sunday, when we were talking, I said, 'That might explain a lot of things.' We were talking about Buck Henry's death at the time."

"I remember that. What was your point?"

"My point was, and is, that Wanda Collum volunteers as a pink lady at the hospital. She was there the night Josh brought Buck Henry in. Well, since they were practically neighbors, Wanda had an interest in the situation. Not that she was sorry to see Old Buck go, but he had become a landmark in that end of town, and had even borrowed a dime or two from Wanda. Never paid it back, though, which is one of the reasons she wasn't sorry to see him go. Be that as it may, Wanda nosed around the emergency room at the time they were supposedly working on Buck. They were just standing there, she said, drinking coffee, wondering how they were supposed to do anything with a stiff."

"A *stiff?*"

"You got it right. Buck Henry was *stiff* when Josh brought him in. He'd been dead for several hours."

"They were out in the woods when it happened. Josh *did* have to carry him back to the house."

"That was another thing they were wondering about. Buck had bled precious little for a man impaled on something. It seemed to them he was long dead before he ever landed on that stob."

"Why didn't they say something to somebody?"

"They were both young, the nurse and the intern. They didn't want to make any waves, have someone think they were crying wolf. Besides, they had good reason to think Buck Henry died of a heart attack. What happened to him afterward didn't really make too much difference."

"Thanks, Ruth. You just stuck an iron in my spokes."

"You asked. I told you."

"I was sure Josh killed Buck, and I knew exactly why. Now it looks like Buck died out in the woods, Josh found him, then threw him into the ravine."

"What if it does? Just remember, Garth, Buck Henry didn't swan dive on that stob. Just because Josh didn't kill him doesn't mean he didn't want to. He just lacked the courage to do it while Buck was still alive. Once Buck was dead, it got a lot easier."

232

And with that came my moment of truth.

I called Diana. "How would you like a visitor later on this morning?"

"I'd love one. What's the occasion?"

"No occasion. I just want to see you."

"Same here. How soon?"

"A couple hours. There's somewhere I have to go first."

"I guess I can wait that long." There was a pause. I could almost see her smile. I loved her smile. It was evil itself. "Bring your pajamas."

"I plan to."

I hung up. Ruth was sitting in her chair smiling at me. I didn't ask her what her smile meant. I was afraid she'd tell me.

"May I borrow your Volkswagen?" I asked.

"For how long?"

"Today, part of tomorrow."

"Just have it back by Tuesday. I've got a party to go to."

"What kind of party?"

"A birthday party. Cousin Ada's seventy-fifth."

"Sounds like a hot time."

She gave me a knowing look. "You might be surprised."

I probably would at that.

I got in the Volkswagen and drove east on Jackson Street, stopping in front of Maxine Lawrence's house. Maxine was outside, working in her flower bed. As usual, she looked content.

She looked up at me and smiled. "Morning, Garth. What's on your mind?"

"I've got some good news and I've got some bad news."

She decided to play along. "What's the good news?"

"I know who killed Walter."

"And the bad news?"

"You did."

She continued to work in her flower bed, weeding around her azaleas. "I tried to tell you that. But then you said I was too good a person. So I figured if you said it, it must be true."

"The day you followed him and Karen to Phillipee's Pond, you weren't visiting Opal Starcher when it happened. You were here. You saw him stop for Karen and decided to follow them. But you didn't go alone. You took your son's baseball bat with you."

She sighed and sat down in the flower bed, facing the house. She wouldn't look at me. "I never intended to kill him. I knew where they were going. I'd heard people talk. I just wanted to scare him, that's all. Smash the windows out of that fancy new car of his. But by the time I got there, here he was chasing her around the pond. Making a fool of himself. Making a fool out of both of us. I didn't think what I was doing. I just started up that hill after him. And when I caught up to him, I hit him. Only once. That's all it took. Then I threw the bat down and came home."

"And when your son missed his bat?"

"I said I didn't know where it was. Which in one sense, I didn't."

"Did anyone see you there at the pond?"

"Josh Henry did. I nearly ran over him on my way out of there. I kept waiting for him to come forward, but he never did. In time I knew he never would. I was in the clear. I'd gotten away with murder." Then she slowly turned to look at me. "Until now."

I shook my head. "You're still in the clear, Maxine. Josh Henry confessed to killing Walter yesterday. When the word gets out about Josh, no one in town will doubt his story."

"Why would Josh do that?"

"He wanted to kill Walter himself, just like he wanted to kill his grandfather Buck. But he lacked the courage. Since he thought the person he told would be dead, and

234

unable to tell anyone else, he took credit for Walter's death. Josh was a troubled boy. I can't rightfully call him a man, even though he was thirty-four years old. Maybe in time he came to believe he really did kill Walter, just as you in time convinced yourself you hadn't. Partly anyway. Enough to fool both of us."

"Except now you know different."

"My lips are sealed."

"Why? Don't you think I did wrong?"

"Very wrong. But I also think you had good reason and that you've served your time—a life sentence. If justice is satisfied, so am I."

"I'm not so sure I am."

"It's up to you."

I'd said what I'd come for. I got in Ruth's Volkswagen and pointed it toward Madison. In the rearview mirror I could see Maxine Lawrence still standing beside her flower bed. Then she knelt and began to weed.